REBIRTH OF THE UNDEAD KING

Book 1

Ink Bamboo

Rebirth of the Undead King by Ink Bamboo
© 2018 Kevin Butman

Cover by Judy Yao

https://www.deviantart.com/eikyrona

"Death is not the greatest loss in life. The greatest loss is what dies inside of us while we live."

NORMAN COUSINS.

CONTENTS

PROLOGUE

The death of the undying.

Sitting on top of a crystal dome, three figures faced against each other. A tower of decomposing corpses laid around them, evidencing how long they had struggled for. Fine golden threads seemed to rise from the bodies of the fallen before vanishing into the infinite nothingness. They were the remains of those who claimed authority over the world — the gods.

After gathering his breath, one of the figures shot forward. Hair strung out of infinitely thin ice swung from left to right as it followed his movements. It painted a beautiful scene where strands of blue embraced gold-tinged drops of blood in a delicate waltz.

Alas, the beauty of his sword dance wasn't reflected on his face. Influenced by anger, the man couldn't hold back from cursing the one responsible for the carnage around him.

"Die, Amro!"

The God of Ice, Ymir, lunged forward once again. Each of his moves drew sharp arcs in the air as his blade approached the Sovereign of Death. There was no hesitation in his attack, but even his best efforts weren't enough to get through his opponent's defenses.

Not far from him, the Goddess of Light wove endless shields of gold. Her prideful gaze followed after an unrelenting barrage of shadows coming her partner's way. Pushing her power to the limits, Alexandra tried to protect Ymir from each and every strike. Unfortunately, neither of them was a match for their opponent.

Seeing his attackers struggling, a smile surfaced on the Lord of Death. His dark robes fluttered as he extended his right hand, chains of darkness shooting towards these last remaining enemies. The facade of arrogance he displayed was the last thing holding his mind together. Deep inside, he couldn't help but constantly worry.

How? he wondered. *Just how were they able to invade my domain?*

Amro knew his opponents so far had been inherently weaker than him. The laws of death he controlled were absolute, part of the world ever since its conception. The gods he had faced shouldn't have been able to initiate an attack of this scale on their own. That brought fear upon him. Fear of the mastermind who remained hidden.

Still, fear wouldn't hold him back from doing what came natural to him. Being on the receiving side of this assault, there was only one reasonable thing for him to do.

"Die."

The chains of darkness shot by Amro coiled around Ymir and Alexandra, holding them down despite their efforts to break away. Amro knew the bindings wouldn't hold for long, but a moment was all he needed. With enough time, he would be able to summon his greatest strength, one he had been unable to bring to his side all along: his army of death.

Unfortunately for him, fate wasn't on his side. As the portal to his kingdom of undead soldiers opened, a criss-cross pattern of white energy sealed it away. The God of Space,

Zephyr, had joined the fray.

"Zephyr, even you dare to join their camp! Are you not afraid of the consequences?" Amro's eyes burned with rage, burying away the disappointment he felt for his fellow gods.

"You fail to understand our goal, Amro. The laws of death must cease to exist, their mere existence is a threat to all gods. Just think about it. Without the possibility of death, there would be no end to our rule."

Unrelenting desire and madness tinged Zephyr's voice. His wish for of immortality had blinded him to reason. "You know that's the way it should be, Amro. Gods should be far above all, even death."

"Have you gone mad, Zephyr? Immortality is not that simple. Everything will meet their end in death, even us," said Amro.

"Of that we're certain, my friend. Today, you will meet your end!"

The fight resumed and many more gods joined the fray against Amro. Each of their moves weaved destruction into existence, chaos into order. Unfortunately for them, that was their mistake.

Numbers didn't matter to someone like Amro. Every death he brought upon the world replenished his strength and intensified his drive. Even after fighting tens of lesser gods, the Sovereign of Death still brimmed with energy, ready to slay the trespassers entering his kingdom.

"Come! Exhaust your lives at my hands. I'll show you the meaning of true death!" roared Amro. Anger swirled in his voice along with disappointment. The gods had turned against the natural laws of life and death — their foolishness needed to be corrected.

He could have accepted it if they craved immortality

as a tool to ensure the integrity of their domains. After all, gods were duty-bound to guard the laws they controlled. But that wasn't the case. Zephyr's words had confirmed that fact.

The stubbornness in Amro's enemies was born from ignorance, arrogance, and most importantly, cowardice. They feared death, they feared him and his domain. It all combined to create a sense of entitlement. Perhaps, if he disappeared, so would their fear.

Did they seriously think they deserved their place as gods for eternity? Without death, there could only be stagnation.

Days went by and even with the difference in numbers, Amro was able to hold his ground. Despite the many sacrifices the gods had made, the tides of battle were still in Amro's favor. However, a dark premonition still gripped the Sovereign of Death's mind.

As if smelling his fear, Alexandra took a step forwards, making his omen a reality. "It's time."

When she spoke her command, a golden portal opened amidst the battle-field. Abundant life energy emanated from it as a woman covered in white came from within. Each of her steps carried boundless authority as she walked to the middle of the battlefield.

"Vita!" said Amro. His voice held pleasant surprise as well as traces of confusion.

"You've got to stop them, Vita! Their desire for immortality has blinded them," he said, burying the warning his war-borne instincts gave him at the sight of the Goddess of Life.

"You seem to misunderstand, Amro," mocked Alexandra. "She's not here to join you."

A cold and arrogant grin surfaced on her face; it was easy to understand what her words implied.

Amro's gaze turned towards Vita. He waited for her to

rebuke Alexandra, but only silence came in return. The words he wished to hear didn't leave her lips.

"Amro, my dear," she said, finally breaking the silence around her. "It's time for the law of death to reach an end. We need an age of life and prosperity amongst the gods. Please desist with your futile efforts. If you do so, I can guarantee your safety."

Even if eons of existence had made him indifferent to the world, Amro couldn't help but feel betrayed by her words. He had been fond of the goddess, for both of their laws originated and ended within the boundary of each other. This had led to an unspoken understanding between the two of them. Had it all been a lie? Just how long had this faction of gods harbored the desire to execute this plan?

Sensing an opening caused by Amro's uncertainty, Alexandra shot forward. It was her chance to break through the god's defenses. This wasn't part of her plan when she asked Vita to step onto the battlefield, but it was a pleasant surprise, nonetheless.

Her smile intensified as the spear of light in her hands successfully pierced through Amro's god-spark, a condensation of his connection as a god to the natural world.

Amro stared at Vita, disregarding Alexandra's attack in its entirety. His heart was filled with doubt. Why was it that she chose to break the order of nature? Life and death were supposed to be complementary, two sides to the same coin.

He did nothing but stand in complete confusion. There was no use in fighting anymore. Vita's fighting power rivaled his own. Going without his army of death against her while she joined forces with the other gods could only end in one way.

Embracing the moment, Amro ignored Alexandra and her spear. His eyes focused on Vita, trying to decipher the reasoning that had led her down this path.

"With no death in your way, you'll finally be able to become an Overgod," Zephyr said. The elation in his voice was "impossible" to miss.

Many gods approached Vita to congratulate her on her future ascension. They believed that once a god's laws reached a perfect state, they would experience a sudden rise in power; one enough to alter the nature of reality itself.

Meanwhile, Amro's eyes remained set on Vita, unmoving. *What had gone wrong? Did he make a mistake at some point?* The situation he was at forced Amro to remember the entirety of his past in order to make sense of it.

For eons, he had dominated both the mortal and immortal world. Death itself, a law woven into the fabric of existence, had been the only true certainty in nature. He had been born a mortal man, but his affinity towards death had ensured his rise as a god. Wherever he had gone, death soon followed after him.

His mother left him at birth and his father killed himself shortly after. Those were small details of his past that Amro learnt after he took control of the underworld. As a mortal, he caused the annihilation of many. Kingdoms rose at his will and nations fell at his whim. Fate had bound his path to incarnate death from the beginning.

However, that just made Amro appreciate life even more. Not out of fear for his own ending, but because he knew that the brighter a life, the more meaningful its end would become. Only by living life to its fullest potential would there be no regrets when it ended.

That being said, Amro realized something. If he fell here, there would be no one to take his place. The gods would block anyone who tried to rise to the throne of godhood by making use of the laws of death.

With him out of the way, they would try to change the course of nature, the fabric of reality itself. After being the God of Death for so long, he couldn't accept his end to have such consequences. It was his duty as a god. Not to himself, but to the world.

I'm such a fool, thought Amro. *I've grown far too complacent.*

He believed he had finally found someone who could understand him and his struggles to safeguard the course of nature. Death's existence brought constant change to the universe, never allowing it to fall stagnant. He believed Vita had understood this as a fellow god. Oh, how wrong had he been.

As his remaining life-force was extinguished by Alexandra's spear, a single thought sprouted from within Amro's mind.

The pantheon needs to change.

Seeing Amro vanishing into nothingness, the different deities celebrated their victory. Thinking about the rewards they would reap after this battle made it hard to contain their glee.

Yet much to their dismay, this blinded them from noticing the resolute look in Amro's eyes. Within them laid an unrelenting drive that didn't fade even during his last moments. Only Vita stared at him until he vanished, perplexed about what had gone through his mind during his last moments.

She respected her fellow god for his conviction and principles—both beyond her own. Despite that, her desire for power burned greater than any other feeling she might have held toward him. Nothing and no one would stop her from achieving the goals she had set for herself. Without the God of Death barring her way, it was only a matter of time for her to achieve further greatness.

Her choice, cruel as it may be, had opened up a new path for herself. The promises of immortality she had given the gods would eventually become a reality, further increasing her own power. With so many gods depending on her, her authority was set in stone.

All that was left was consolidating her rule amongst mortals, changing the course of the world's will. Once she brought a change to the realm of the gods, she would be virtually unstoppable. All she required now was time.

Unfortunately for her and the other gods, change could sometimes go unnoticed. Just like the changes happening in the mortal world of Gaia.

Inside a forest forgotten by civilization, a small stone beneath the earth glowed with an aura of death. It pulsed with greed every time a creature died, using the energy gathered to nurture the accursed object sealed within.

The one and only phylactery of Amro, the God of Death, still remained dormant within the mortal world. A small legacy from his time before ascending, a relic so old that even its creator had barely remembered it before dying. Within it, a small fragment of Amro's soul remained, one he had sealed inside the stone before his ascension as a god.

This old legacy of his time before ascension would be the key to his path of revenge. Even if he couldn't defeat the alliance formed by the Goddess of Life in straight-up combat, he could always find a way to bring her and the other gods down. All he had to do now was wait. Wait for destiny to send the right person to serve him as a vessel. Wait for the right set of circumstances to come.

Amro knew powers beyond his own lay dormant in the world. A direct challenge to the natural order set by the pantheon would never be allowed — such was the way of nature. Whether it would be through his hand or through someone else's, however, they needed to be stopped.

Compliant to his beliefs, Amro wouldn't have to wait for too long. Not far away from the forest where his soul laid dormant, a kingdom was having an emergency meeting.

Inside a throne room, the king sat and considered the proposals made by his subjects. They were trying to tackle the issue of lacking resources for the war they were waging. This was the Kingdom of Nyx, a small nation currently dealing with the tides of a civil war.

"My Lord," spoke a man with a waist as wide as a bear's. "Proceeding with the logging of the southern forest would be the best way to fulfill our immediate need for resources. We can use the wood to fix our siege weapons. Moreover, once the forest is cleared, we can have the southerners search for ore veins."

The King considered the proposal. After a few seconds, he turned towards his advisor.

"Tell me, if we do not fix our siege equipment, how long can our armies hold?"

The advisor thought for a moment before he answered. "My lord, we can hold the campaign in the north for another three years, but we would lose ground to the rebels. The best course of action would be to crush them soon, and in order to do that, we require more weapons to equip our troops."

The king sighed. Many small villages would have to be demolished in order to log the forest in the south. A move that would put yet another stain on his already ruined reputation. Should he decide to evict the commoners from their homes, an additional rebellion might rise in the southern region.

Noticing the hesitation in his father's eyes, the prince decided to take part of the conversation. "Father," he said. "We can send a pre-emptive squad to burn down the villages."

The king turned to his son, waiting for him to finish his proposal. He didn't think his son was stupid enough to suggest such a thing without thinking of the consequences.

"Once the villages are burnt, we can finish off the survivors. That way, we could log the zone without having to worry about any rebellions rising," explained the prince. "It's not like they contribute a significant amount in taxes. If anything, they're parasites, father."

The king frowned. That may stop the chances of a rebellion happening in the south, but if the news were to travel, trouble could arise in the eastern and western fronts of the kingdom.

Seemingly aware of his father's thoughts, the prince continued. "Don't worry, father. We'll have people pretend to be survivors from the southern villages. They'll convince others that the rebels from the north tried to incite a revolt in the south and attacked them when the villagers refused."

The king smiled, the remaining worries in his mind fading away. With such a vicious and creative mind, his son would make a fine king someday. In his mind, rulers didn't need mercy — they needed solutions. His son knew how to manipulate the masses to achieve his goals, he wasn't one to fixate on the details. That alone ensured his future success as a ruler.

"So be it," the king ordered. "Destroy the villages in the south and then proceed with the logging."

After listening to the king's command, his subordinates left the room. Such a big plan required equally big preparations.

CHAPTER 01

The fate of a town is to perish; the fate of a man is to live.

L ife in the kingdom of Nyx was not easy. The war of exhaustion carried against the rebel forces in the north had driven the prices of food and many other resources beyond what most citizens of the kingdom could afford to pay. To make things worse, able-bodied men who farmed the land were conscripted to join the army, leaving their wives and children on their own.

Several villages existed at the southern border of the kingdom. Amongst them, a humble group of settlements had their place in the forest. The people from these villages were not remarkable in any way, nor were they of much relevance to the kingdom's economy. They survived thanks to farming, hunting and the extraction of natural resources from the forest.

This forest, known as 'Halt', contained many things useful to the townsfolk. Strong trees with precious timber grew throughout the forest whilst animals fat with meat wandered through the thickets. With these resources at hand, the townsfolk managed to cover their daily needs.

Despite that, they remained humble, victims to their

own fear. Legends told by the village's elders warned them not to succumb to their greed. Those who ventured too deep into the forest would never again be seen alive. Only their corpses would be found from time to time.

Thus, children in these towns worked as soon as they reached the age of five, for every member of the village had to carry at least some of their own weight. Boys learned how to hunt, log, and mine, while girls learned how to farm, cook, and sew. The few needs that could not be supplied by the village were usually fulfilled by caravans of hunters and merchants carrying different products.

The merchants came from the northern towns and cities, which made them capable of providing a variety of products that complemented the southern settlements' own. This created a healthy system of trade. All in all, the village lived in harmony despite the various limitations they had to face.

However, exceptions are the norm even in paradise. Zaros was a young boy living in one of these villages, only 13 years old of age. His hair was as black as coal and his skin was slightly pale from his lack of proper nutrition. His mother had died giving birth to him, while his father had been conscripted by the army, yet to return if he was even still alive.

Before his father's departure, he had been entrusted under the care of the village. Sadly, that protection didn't last for very long. Given his circumstances, Zaros had to face a reality harder than the rest of the village's children. From a young age, he had to learn how to hunt, log, mine, sew and cook all on his own. His weight was his own to carry. Expecting help from others who had their own burdens was nothing short of foolishness.

As such, Zaros would usually wake up at three o'clock in the morning in order to prepare his hunting tools. Maintaining them was essential as replacing them would be too expensive for him to afford. Only after this morning ritual would he go out and hunt.

Hunting every morning was crucial as food was impossible to keep fresh for long. Ice magic was an option but their settlement was too humble to host someone like a magician. That would remain a luxury affordable only to those living in the capital. Because of this, Zaros prioritized hunting as a daily event on his itinerary. Otherwise, no amount of forest fruits would be able to cover his caloric intake.

That being said, given his young age and limited resources, Zaros chose to hunt only around the forest's border. It was common knowledge that the deeper he went inside the woods, the stronger the creatures he would meet.

Zaros's skill at hunting became more polished every day, even under the shadow of his humble background. Had someone actually taught him, he would have turned him into a skilled scout. Without that training, however, he lacked both the resources and instruction to achieve his true potential.

However, suffering hardships had earned him the villagers' approval. His work ethic was recognized even by the adults. Unfortunately for him, his way of life didn't garner the same appreciation from most of the town's youths. All they saw was someone stealing their parents' favor despite being nothing more than a stray in their eyes.

This morning, like many others, Zaros visited the village in order to trade. After his morning hunt, he had decided to exchange his leftover game for a resource with more liquidity. What could he do with the beasts' innards otherwise?

"Hello, young man," greeted a middle-aged woman. She was the village's butcher and the owner of the small establishment Zaros was visiting. Her shop specialized in processing all kind of resources; wild animals, meat, and leather alike.

"Hey, old lady," said Zaros, a mischievous smile on his

face.

The butcher's nose twitched at the boy's greetings before she quickly resumed her usual merchant-like demeanor. Zaros was known to be a bit of a troublemaker. His lack of interaction with other children made him behave like an adult — one without the reservations that came with age.

"I'm here to sell some pelts," said Zaros as he placed a bag of them over the counter. Blood dripped from the bag, evidencing just how 'fresh' they were.

"I've told you I can process the hide myself if you just bring me the animal," said the butcher. She was considerably irked by having to clean every time the boy visited. "The way you do it is still a bit too crude."

"You think I don't know you keep some meat from the animals you pelt?" Zaros swiftly rebuked.

The butcher's nose twitched once again. Dealing with the mischievous brat was too troublesome sometimes. She couldn't help but curse the wandering merchant responsible for teaching Zaros how to get the best of her.

"Come on, don't make things up; your lies could tank my business. I'll buy them for 10% above the normal price," she said in an attempt to buy his silence.

"20%, I'm aware of your margins," Zaros complained.

The butcher had to do her best to avoid her expression souring. She truly despised being seen through in such a way by a mere child. All she could think about was how to make him leave her store with haste.

"Fine, but you are to keep those rumors to yourself," she answered. She didn't want the other villagers trying to haggle with her in the future. Her eyes scanned each pelt carefully, calculating their full worth. A moment later, she pulled out five copper coins from her purse.

Zaros's face pinched with indignation. "Hey! It should at least be eight coins!"

"I'm sorry, we have way too many pelts in stock. No merchant caravans have come in the past couple of days so we have an excess of inventory," she clarified, a slight smirk pulling up the corners of her lips.

Zaros scowled at her, making the difficult choice to let this one go. To the butcher's chagrin, he took his coins and exited the shop without waving or saying goodbye. She could only smile wryly at that. It was a common interaction between her and the child.

Contrary to his behavior, Zaros felt full of joy. Thanks to these coins, he would be able to buy a dress for Alice. She was a cute, young girl he had fallen for. Such a gift could gain him at least some of Alice's attention. Perhaps even her affection.

Alice, daughter of the village chief and the village beauty, was the most admired girl among the village's younger generation. It was only normal for Zaros to be infatuated with her as well. However, Zaros knew his chances paled in comparison to the many youngsters who were not on their own.

The odds seemed insurmountable for a young man with no backing like him. Without a family, he had a hard time acquiring the most simple of luxuries. His only fortune was getting along with the adults in the village, giving him a chance to overcome his situation with hard work.

Zaros's chest perked up as he fantasized about the future. A future where he joined their hunting parties and traveled the northern towns on his own. A future where he turned around his status. At times like this, his childish and naïve imagination came into full display.

Part of Zaros always wanted to be a leader of sorts. His

goal from an early age had been to prove to the other youths that he didn't need a backing to become someone of importance.

He was aware of the hidden disdain of those who had it easier than him. Even then, he was confident in his ability to fulfill his goals. Of course, the prospect of having a future where he achieved those dreams was enough to cloud his mind from the difficulty it implied.

With those fantasies in mind, Zaros made his way to a small shack. Hidden away, it was a bit far from the outskirts of the small village. And although it looked simple, it was something he could call his own. He had built it from scratch two years ago using some leftover wood gathered from the villages and settlements in the forest.

His parents' old house had been given to another family as it was considered wasteful for a child to hog it as his own. In a certain way, things were bound to belong to the strong. Even then, he had no complaints. He understood that without enough strength to protect his house, he would have become the target of many people's hatred had he kept it.

As he made his way to collect the coins he had hidden, he heard the sound of galloping horses approaching his way. Overwhelmed by curiosity, he climbed a tree to get a better look at the incoming beasts. From his vantage point, he saw men in shabby armor riding their mounts.

No insignia decorated their gear, and no banners adorned their caravan. Many of them donned rusty swords at their sides while others carried rickety bows on their backs.

Excitement filled Zaros at the sight of the armed men. They resembled the hunter parties that often came from the northern towns.

People like them would usually carry wares for sale as they made their way to the forest. This meant he would be able to buy some interesting things that weren't usually available in his village. What's more, he would be able to hear tales of adventure and war — such experiences, even when embellished, were bound to be enriching for his own growth.

While Zaros was focused on the riders and their gear, the riders' scout observed him from a distance. The scout took his time, careful to confirm the young boy posed no threat to him nor his party before he and his steed approached the boy's tree.

"Hey, boy, to what direction is the village of Ruk?" he asked.

"I'm not a child!" rebuked Zaros from atop the tree. "It's just east of here. Follow the road and you'll see it in a few minutes."

"Thanks. Be sure to come to the village, you'll be surprised by what we have prepared," said the scout with a smile.

Zaros nodded. His interest was piqued by whatever the group of armed riders was carrying with them. He was sure he would find something interesting amongst their wares. Should they carry any clothes, Zaros might even be able to find something exceptional for Alice. Any dress from the capital was bound to be better than those crafted by their own village's tailor.

He rushed to his shack and dug through his few belongings, eager to find the bag of coins he had hidden in their midst.

Back in the caravan, the scout returned to inform his leader of the direction they should follow. "Hey Zac, why did you let the kid go?" asked a man geared in a slightly more elaborate armor. He was the man responsible for their group, the party's leader.

"It's too much of a hassle to chase after him right now, he could ruin our cover. I'm sure he'll make his way back to the village on his own anyway," replied the scout. "Even if he runs, how far can he make it?"

The burly man frowned, "You know our orders were to not let anyone slip by, right? If he just happens to get away, you will be court-martialed."

Zac shrugged. "You do not understand how these village kids think," he said. "They can't contain their curiosity when someone visits their village."

The burly man sighed. Expecting more from the band of misfits he'd been assigned would only lead him to disappointment. As the proud captain of the army's 22nd Division, he was used to having more disciplined men working under him. Unfortunately for him, this mission required the use of 'disposable' personnel. So, rather than risk his brave men, he employed a group of mercenaries along with one or two of the worst rungs from the King's army. Anyone who wouldn't be missed.

Eventually, the band of misfits made their way towards the village. Indifference and bloodlust filled the air the group breathed, their intentions slowly coming to the surface.

Initially, the commoners paid them little mind as they trotted into the village. Caravans with hunters and merchants were a common sight every now and then. Only the children, driven by their own curiosity, came near them without reservation.

"Sir," said one of the children, "what special treats does your group bring?"

"Do you bring knives and swords, sir? My father said he will teach me to hunt as soon as he could find a weapon suitable for me."

Question after question fell on the captain's shoulders, each of them increasing the burden his heart faced. Unfortunately for the children, he had already grown callous to such feelings. They weren't enough to stop him from following through with his duty.

He gave a last look at the pitiful people around him. Pushing his own emotions aside, he made way for the king's will.

"Execute them!" he commanded. "These commoners have refused to join our revolutionary army. Since they want to dedicate their lives to the kingdom, we'll give them that pleasure in death."

Empty words. They were nothing but a charade — one done in order to hide the commands he had been given. The captain was aware of how ridiculous they were but he had no choice in the matter. It was the excuse he was told to give the mercenaries, and as such, that which he would present as the 'truth' to others. Despite his own reservations, the captain believed the royal family's commands were absolute.

The few villagers who had gathered in curiosity gasped in horror. The man's words made no sense to them. As a village far from any town, they had contact with nothing aside from the forest. Their lives, despite being simple, held enough peace for them to remain happy. That's why they refused to join the complicated circle of politics that surrounded the kingdom.

However, their humble nature did not make mean they were dumb. The faces of many adults grew ashen as the implications of the declaration washed over them. Once someone fell suspect to working with the rebels, both them and their family would be executed without a chance to defend themselves.

"Die!"

The mercenaries took their weapons one after the other, swinging them in the screaming villagers' direction.

There was no mercy. In fact, the inner competition amongst them brought out the worst of their nature. To them, it wasn't a matter of life and death. It was a game.

Presented with the incoming assault, many of the villagers used whatever they could find to fend off the riders. Alas, their pitchforks and dull knives proved to be inadequate for the task. There was no way for them to successfully fend off the attack of bloodthirsty fiends.

"Dad!"

"Son!"

Screams of terror and pain merged into one unintelligible sound. The children close to the mercenaries were the first to fall. Young and vulnerable, they were the easiest prey the mercenaries could get.

"Please, no, we are not rebels!"

"Goddess, please save us."

Some prayed, and some tried to reason their way out, but logic and piety had no place in the mercenaries' ears. They only spoke the language of money. Once paid to do a job, they would finish it, gruesome as it may be.

Blood painted the ground and buildings. Men, women, and children ran with all they could, but none could escape the mercenaries. Slowly, a scene of carnage took place inside the village. No one was spared.

CHAPTER 02

Fated.

F ar away from the presence of death, excitement took over the mind of a young boy. His hand wrapped around his hidden treasure, a small bag of coins he had hidden for safe keeping. Months of saving his hard earned money made him appreciate the small pouch in his hands.

"Found it!" he exclaimed, tying the small bag to his waist. "I better make my way back."

Zaros exited his small shack, taking a moment to make sure it was covered once again with leaves and stones. Simple as it was, it belonged to him. He didn't wish for the village's youths to find it and play a prank on him. God knows they had done it a couple times already.

Regardless, it wasn't time for him to think about the past. He needed to make his way to the caravan and seize the chance to purchase something nice for the girl in his dreams. Merchants often sold their more valuable goods in the first few minutes after their arrival. Supply and demand meant the forest settlements had very few opportunities to buy luxury goods like textile goods.

As he ran back to the village, a premonition surfaced in Zaros's heart. "It is quiet, too quiet in fact." Silence meant a single thing in the forest — danger.

Did that convoy bring an exemplary with them?

It was the only explanation Zaros could come up with. He had once seen a hunter who had broken through the limits of 'rank one', a level of strength rarely seen in people outside the military. Like the name implied, it was the first step into reaching a new height of power.

Zaros could still remember when that man had visited the village. Back then, everyone felt a strange sense of pressure wash over them. Even the animals in the outskirts had grown quiet. Zaros still remembered the vivid image of the man's back, it had become the goal of every youth inside their settlement.

Putting his memories aside, Zaros saw the village in the distance. It looked empty, almost desolate. It was a scene different from the one he remembered from an hour ago.

After Zaros walked inside the village, he discovered the reason for his premonition. A feeling of fear clogged his throat at the sight of a situation he had never expected.

Blood.

Corpses.

A tower of bodies now laid at the village's center, stacked taller than the buildings themselves. It was a monument born from bloodlust and massacre. A testament to the insignificance of life.

Following the shocking sight, the stench of death attacked Zaros's nose. He choked and gagged before he managed to cover his mouth and stumble back. The old man who had taught him to hunt, the merchant who had taught him how to read, write, and barter, and the butcher he had loved to tease — everyone he knew and cared for had become no more than a blood-soaked corpse.

Zaros's hands trembled as he moved towards the monument of death, hesitant to touch the bodies that had once been his friends. The only family he'd ever known in the stead of a dead mother and a missing father. People who weren't obligated to teach nor raise him into who he was, but had still spared some effort in doing so.

Yes, his life had been far from perfect, but this people were all he had. Zaros tried hard not to be a burden to them, for he had seen the struggles they tried to hide away from others. They were just like him, striving to survive in a land that didn't have much to offer.

Slowly, Zaros closed their eyes, desperate to hide away from their terrorized gazes. However, his hands halted once they reached the face of the butcher. He had spoken to her just a few hours ago, teasing her as he always did. Now, here she laid, her body now lifeless in front of him. He couldn't help but feel a mix of anger, sadness and fear.

The feelings were so overwhelming he nearly failed to hear the small group moving towards his position. Instinctively, he took cover, hiding beneath a broken cart.

He could see them. Their gear resembled that of the group he had met earlier, causing a horrible epiphany to slam into his mind. Was this his fault? That group he had seen... they were not merchants, nor were they hunters. They were murderers.

He needed to hide. Lest he ended up as another victim.

Ignoring Zaros's presence, most of the mercenaries drank and laughed, joking around as they celebrated the success of another mission. Their attention wasn't on their surroundings but on their drinks. The alcohol stored by the villagers had become a secondary reward to their slaughter.

Zaros's chest tightened after he saw them walk in his direction. One of them in particular caused chills to climb down his spine. Zaros recognized him. It was the man who had asked him for directions.

Unlike the rest of his party, he didn't seem to be enjoying the alcohol. Instead, he looked vaguely dismayed, seemingly ignoring the words of encouragement his party sent his way.

"Hey Zac, don't be so upset. Look at all the booze we pillaged. Come on, you should enjoy some with us," insisted one of the party members.

Zac couldn't help but shake his head in refusal. His mind still lingered on the boy he had let go earlier that day. The fact that he hadn't been taken care of meant punishment would come his way. He had been too confident in the boy's return. *Perhaps he heard the screams and escaped*, he thought.

Even if the kid was to die later on his own, Zac knew he was doomed. As long as he couldn't provide proof of the boy's death, punishment would still fall on his shoulders for disregarding his duty. After all, his captain did warn him about being careless.

"I need to stay sober until we find that kid," Zac said, pushing the bottles his friends offered out of his way. "You know I will be skinned alive if he doesn't show up."

Zaros knew that they were talking about him. They knew he was still alive. Aware of their intentions, Zaros hunkered back into his hiding spot. If he wanted to live, he needed to find a way to slip away unnoticed.

Much to Zaros's luck, the mercenaries failed to notice his presence. After throwing a pair of bodies into the pile of corpses, they seemed ready to leave. However, one of the bodies twitched, showing signs of still being alive.

"You dare?"

Infuriated by his victim's resilience, Zac took a dagger tied to his waist. In an attempt to vent his emotions, he stabbed the body over and over again, leaving no doubt about his death. It took him nearly a minute of unhindered violence to feel at ease after which he naturally left. He still needed to find the one who got away.

Seeing his pursuers leave, Zaros took the chance to inspect the faces of the two additional bodies. They were two people he was also fond of: Alice and her father. Regret, pain, and fear — a myriad of emotions flooded Zaros as he felt himself being stripped away from his innocence.

How long, he wondered. *How long do I have before I share a spot next to them?*

His instincts screamed at him to run away, to hide, to ensure his survival. But he couldn't. He needed to do one thing before that.

Zaros waited until the patrol moved completely out of his sight before moving towards the pile of bodies once again.

Alice's corpse laid still, her once delicate face tarnished by bruises and cuts. The look of grief on her lifeless eyes drew an unsteady breath from Zaros's lungs. Even her dress had been torn in several places, evidencing a cruel reality Zaros was still too naïve to understand.

Resolve filled Zaros's eyes. He had to survive. It was his job to take revenge for what had happened here.

Perhaps he would be able to find help in another village. Once he got in touch with them, he would be able to send an envoy to the nobles living in the north. They would surely look into this event.

Having formed a plan, Zaros scrambled away from the bodies, sprinting toward the edge of town. He needed to get away, quickly. His utmost priority was to make it out alive. However, his haste was the cause of his downfall.

From a distance, one of the many outlaws spotted a rushing figure. He turned his gaze upon the small boy running away from the village.

"Zac! Isn't that the kid you were searching for?" asked a mercenary as he tugged on the scout's jacket.

Zac stood there, dumbfounded for a second. *It seems the heavens have decided to smile upon me,* he thought. It didn't take long before he darted away, chasing after the boy. The rest of the group exchanged a brief look. Confusion and excitement raced through them as the thrill of the hunt pumped adrenaline through their veins. Without another word, they rushed after Zac and the boy.

A quick glance over Zaros's shoulders revealed his pursuers. It would be hard to outrun them, so he had to come up with another way to leave them behind. Perhaps his knowledge of the surrounding area would help him far more than his lacking speed could.

Betting on his familiarity with the forest, Zaros moved away from the main trails. His goal was to move deeper into the woods, into those areas so dense with trees that even wild beasts could get lost. His best chance for survival laid there. After all, he knew most of the area like the back of his hand.

He kept running, his focus completely on the act of escaping. Even his body did its best instinctively, straining every fiber of his muscles to run at his maximum speed. Yet despite his efforts, the distance between him and his pursuers shortened with every step. His options began to dwindle, leaving him with only one choice: running into those places he had always avoided.

Perhaps the beasts that inhabited those areas would be deterrent enough to his pursuers, disregarding how much of a risk they would pose to himself.

As he approached the deeper parts of the forest, silence

overtook his surroundings. Some might believe it to be a sign of peace, but an experienced hunter would know otherwise. Silence in the woods meant only one thing — danger.

Ignorant of Zaros's plan, the mercenaries continued their chase. None of them paid attention to how far away from the village they were going. While some of them were ignorant about this area, the others just didn't care about the risks that lay inside. If a kid could go into the forest despite the risks, why would they need to be afraid of danger?

Moments later, the mercenaries got into a shooting distance. Seeing Zaros was within their range, one of them knocked an arrow on his bow and took aim at the boy.

Zac grinned and glanced over his shoulder. "Whoever catches him will get a night of drinks on me!"

The archer immediately let go of his arrow. He could already taste the wonders of falling drunk on the scout's pocket. His arrow whistled through the wind as it approached his target, ready to pierce Zaros through his back.

However, be it by fate or by chance, Zaros's exhaustion made his steps falter, causing the arrow to miss its intended target. All it had been able to do was leave a scrape to the side of his leg, nearly causing him to fall.

The archer was infuriated. Even though his arrow was coated in poison, if someone else took the finishing blow, his reward would be forfeit under a barrage of excuses from both the scout and his competitors. That being said, this excited the other mercenaries further as they still had a chance to claim the prize. They sped up, intent on catching the boy.

Zaros's leg rapidly grew numb. However, he had no time to stop and check his wound. His opponents were coming closer, each of their footsteps becoming louder than the one before it.

Fortunately for Zaros, the sound of their rush was his salvation. Not far from them, a beast had taken notice of their intrusion into his territory. His sense of hearing had revealed the presence of the humans near him.

A smirk surfaced on the beast's visage. Who was he, but the proud ruler of this side of the forest? How dare mere humans step into his territory?

The beast stood up from his resting position, stretching his paws as he readied to meet the invaders. With a small nibble, the creature took a moment to bite an itch out of his silver fur before he began chasing after the trespassers at a great speed.

Hearing a howl in the distance, the mercenaries soon took notice of the beast. They directed their contempt towards the ignorant creature. How dare a simple forest fiend challenge them? Even if their party had neither ranked knights nor magicians, they still had the strength to deal with a beast like this.

The archer's gaze flitted away from the kid to his group before he offered a suggestion. "Let's deal with this creature first. The tip of my arrow was covered in poison, the kid won't make it far."

The others grumbled at the suggestion, knowing it gave the archer a better chance at claiming the kill. A night of drinks paid by the scout was a hard offer to part from. However, the threat before them left them with no other choice.

Zac shared their frustrations. Every second they wasted here allowed the boy to gain more ground. The situation, however, demanded their full attention. Killing the boy would mean nothing if one of them died along the way.

Meanwhile, Zaros ran as fast as he could. Each step of his became heavier than the last as he felt his strength being sapped away. He felt too tired, his breathing was becoming ragged and his gaze was growing blurry.

Is this it? Will I die here? Will I be unable to find justice?

A flurry of questions assaulted Zaros's mind as his legs slowed, heavy from exhaustion. Eventually, he could no longer move. Not even his resolve could replenish the lack of energy. He could do nothing but lay beside a bone-white rock, resigned to unwillingly face his death.

Darkness took over Zaros's sight, his consciousness beginning to fade away. *If only I had a chance to change things*, he thought. Unfortunately for him, living beings were given only one opportunity. All were equal upon death.

That is if fate didn't have a need for them.

"Mortal, what is it that you regret the most?" An arrogant and mechanical voice stopped Zaros from joining the ranks of the fallen, his last bits of consciousness held tight by the unspoken authority in the statement.

Being powerless, Zaros thought. If only he had power, he would have been able to stop the men chasing him. Had he held some strength, he would have been able to live a better life before all of this. If he had the opportunities at his disposal, he would be able to go look for his father, ensure protection for his friends and free himself from the shackles of his lacking background.

"What a noble, yet naive goal," criticized the voice. "Power without guidance brings corruption, so I'll offer you both. In exchange, you must offer yourself, your future, and your everything to my cause. The price you will pay will not be fair, but I won't force it upon you. Are you willing to take this deal?"

Zaros didn't need to think about it, the answer came from the deepest depths in his soul.

Yes, I'll accept your deal. Take whatever you want from me, but grant me my wish.

Zaros's inner-most desires had spoken for him. Every remaining ounce of logic and reasoning had been destroyed by his exhaustion. Only the purest form of his desires remained.

As he spoke those words within his mind, Zaros's consciousness vanished into the dark. The breath of life left his body in an attempt to separate him from the world.

However, time suddenly came to a stop.

The consciousness who had spoken to him sighed. "Very well, I'll agree to this deal. I'll help you accomplish your goal, and in exchange, you will have to help me achieve mine. I hope you don't come to regret this moment."

The voice faded away. From that moment onwards, there was no longer Zaros, the village boy, nor Amro, the God of Death. Now, their lives were bound to each other.

Horrible premonitions plagued seers and sages throughout the world at that moment. Many collapsed trying to make sense of the horrible scenes in their visions. However, everything they saw was beyond their understanding. It was too late to stop it from happening.

Before time resumed itself, Zaros's wounds crept close. Unconsciousness held him tight as a new aura raced throughout his body. Now, death's doors closed before the boy — the gatekeeper awaited the name of his new targets.

CHAPTER 03

A wolf's last wish.

In the distance, the mercenaries took defensive positions as they encircled the wolf-like creature. Most of them readied their blades as the party's archer distanced himself from the encirclement. He pulled his bow taut, waiting for a chance to shoot the silver-coated beast.

The wolf's visage seemed to carry a sneer. Since when did puny humans find the courage to threaten him? As far as he was concerned, they should just lie down and offer themselves as tribute for having the mere audacity of treading onto his land. Of course, the hunters in the small settlements had never posed a threat to him. He had a reason to be arrogant.

Thus, the beast found himself livid when he smelled the scent of bloodlust coming from Zac and his group. Seemingly accepting their challenge, the wolf positioned himself forward, preparing to pounce at his enemies.

Tension filled the air, until finally, the whistling sound of the wind shattered the standoff.

The archer behind the mercenaries' party took the initiative to release his arrow towards the wolf, trusting his companions would take the opportunity to strike. Danger. The beast felt the change in the flow of the wind as he pounced towards Zac's direction and thus managed to avoid the arrow. However, Zac didn't miss the chance and used his sword to block the wolf's jaws.

Seeing the wolf unable to use his powerful bite, the rest of the party charged forward. Yet unfortunately for them, they were underestimating the beast's strength. Before they could land their strikes, Zac's sword began to crack under the pressure of the creature's teeth.

Zac let go of his broken blade as he took a step backward. Then, he launched a kick in the wolf's direction. It didn't take him long to realize that fighting the beast in close quarters without a weapon was suicidal. He needed to create some distance.

The kick connected and sent the wolf back giving Zac a chance to move backwards. Taking this opportunity, the other mercenaries approached the wolf, using the chance to thrust their weapons in the beast's general direction.

Sensing their approach, the wolf twisted his body and evaded one of the mercenaries' strikes. Unfortunately for him, he was grazed by the strike of a second mercenary. But it wasn't over. As the creature fell to the ground, an arrow tinged with a green paste sunk into its paw. Far behind the party, the archer hadn't missed his chance to strike.

A smile crossed Zac's lips. His team had coordinated this fight perfectly. At this rate, they would be back on the boy's trail without losing too much ground. After a couple of breaths, Zac took the backup dagger he carried on his thigh, ready to re-engage the beast.

The wolf grew angry as he bit off the arrow from his paw, blood dripping slowly out of the wound. His snout frowned as a slight stench coming from his paw assaulted his nose. It made him realize that these sly humans were using despicable means against him.

The archer smirked when he saw the beast's human-like reaction. His last arrow had been imbued with the same poison he had struck the boy with only minutes prior to this. It wouldn't be long before the wolf fell down on his own, gaining him credit for another kill. The archer readied another arrow, preparing to shoot the beast when the next opportunity presented itself.

Zac moved with more caution, giving a chance for the other mercenaries to engage the beast before he did. Engaging the beast with a short dagger was inherently more dangerous than doing so with a long sword. Even more so when his was already broken.

Eventually, one of the mercenaries charged forward, striking the side where the wolf had been previously injured. His opportunistic choice proved to be the right one as the wolf failed to dodge the attack.

The beast growled, infuriated at the cunning humans' approach. Instead of moving sideways, the beast decided to pounce forwards. However, his attack lacked the ferociousness it did at the beginning, showing both the effect of the poison and the damage he had received so far.

Seeing the sluggishness in the beast's movements, a mercenary stepped forward. This time, he used his sword to block the beast's paw, gaining time for his comrades to take action.

"Go!"

Zac grinned as he sprinted from his companion's side, ready to stab the wolf's ribs while the beast's attention lingered somewhere else. Despite sensing Zac's approach, the beast's pride bound him to keep attacking relentlessly.

Even if he was to take fatal damage, the wolf had an instinctual desire to take at least one of his opponents down with him. How could he, a noble creature of this forest, be killed without taking one of them with him?

However, just before the creature could deal a lethal strike to his opponents, another arrow pierced through his maw. Zac didn't miss this opportunity. With haste and maliciousness, his dagger plunged deep into the beast's ribs.

Assaulted by the two successive strikes, the wolf had no choice but to endure a third. He was slightly stunned, opening him up to Zac's incoming kick.

Seeing the beast whimpering on the ground, the mercenaries started moving to surround it. One of them followed Zac's example and switched his weapon with a secondary dagger. His blade now had several cracks spread from the tip to the hilt after blocking the wolf's strike. A little more and he might have lost his hand to the beast.

Strike after strike was delivered to the beast in succession, taking away the last of his strength. However, they didn't deliver the finishing blow. The beast had dared to attack them so now it would have to endure the pain of being at death's door.

The party of mercenaries took a moment to regain their breath before they got ready to depart and continue the search for the boy's corpse. As far as they were concerned, the poison should have finished its job by now. They were about to leave the spasming wolf to his own fate when they saw a silhouette approach them from within the forest thickets.

The figure seemed oddly familiar. *Wasn't that the boy they had chased for the last hour or so?*

Zac raised his brows in doubt. *Did he decide to come back and surrender himself?* Perhaps he had sensed the poison's effect and decided to beg for mercy. If that was the case, Zac was more than happy by the situation's development.

The archer at his side, on the other hand, thought

differently. He was more familiar with his own poisons than anyone else. *Just how can he still be alive?* he thought. *That poison was more than enough to take down a beast, much less a regular village boy.*

Before they could think anything else, the mercenaries felt an instinctive fear crawl through their spines. It suppressed any idle thought they were having the moment the boy's appearance was fully revealed. The cause wasn't his appearance, for he looked exactly the same as he had some minutes ago. It was something else. Something darker, harder to understand.

The air around the boy seemed to have changed. No longer were his legs trembling with fear and exhaustion. Now, only arrogance and confidence remained in each of his steps. Something about him was fundamentally different.

The mercenaries' instincts screamed at them to run, to hide, to do as much as they could to get away from the boy. However, their opportunity to do so was gone once the boy spoke.

"So are you the ones responsible for harming my vessel?" asked the boy, his voice filled with unquestionable authority.

Silence, however, was the only answer he received. None of the mercenaries could find the strength to answer. They were bound to remain silent by the aura of oppression exuding from their previous target. His presence alone reminded them of the fear of death ingrained in every living being.

"I guess it will take some time before I can control that," said the boy. Seeing that the mercenaries were unable to answer, he had quickly lost his interest. These men were not worthy of him uttering another word.

Bored by their cowardice, his eyes moved onto another

target, instead: the dying wolf right next to them.

The beast whimpered in fear. His instincts were far sharper than a human's. Unlike the mercenaries, he could understand the meaning of the existence before him. However, he had no choice but to lay on the ground, unable to escape the being approaching his side.

"Don't fight it, embrace it, let it take you whole," said the boy, a solemn look on his face as he knelt next to the wolf. His expression carried the vicissitudes of time. It felt lonely, yet reliable.

The wolf whimpered, carrying all sort of regrets within his cry. All living beings instinctually rejected death.

The youth smiled and nodded as he stroked the wolf's fur, placing his face on top of the beast's. "If it makes it easier for you, I'll let you have your revenge," he said. "Embrace it, forget about everything else. I am one to keep my promises."

The wolf closed his eyes after sensing the truthfulness behind the boy's words. The remaining threads of life inside him snapped and the fire of his life-force was extinguished. Following what the boy had instructed, the beast let go of his fears, entrusting his regrets into the boy's hands.

The boy smiled as his hands kept petting the wolf's fur gently. His touch was as tender as a mother's, and each stroke of his hands vanished a regret from the beast's mind. The movement of his hands slowed over time, stopping only when the beast breathed its last.

"Welcome, to the next stage of nature, young one. As promised, it's time for your revenge."

The eyes of the mercenaries opened wide at the phenomena happening in front of them. Decades worth of decay assaulted the body of the wolf as a now skeletal body rose from the ground. The group of men felt their sense of reality snapping at the sight.

What they saw defied their understanding of the world. It challenged everything they believed as common sense. As mercenaries from the outskirts of the kingdom, they had never heard of something like an undead beast, much less seen the birth of one.

As if he was unaware of their plight, the boy rose up and patted the undead wolf's head. His treatment towards the wolf remained as gentle as it had been during the creature's life. Strangely enough, his actions seemed more natural now that the beast was made out of bone.

The boy's fluid movements just intensified the fear inside the men's hearts. What kind of mentality did it take for someone to pet such a transgression of nature?

"Go, have your fun," said the young boy, a smile covering his face. With those words left behind, he turned his back to the mercenaries, leaving the wolf to its own mission.

The idea to follow after the boy didn't cross Zac's thoughts this time. The thought of being punished by his captain was pushed even farther back as he faced the imminent threat in front of him. An insult to life stood in his path.

The wolf stood there, completely motionless. Its eye sockets were devoid of life, but the mercenaries could feel its gaze over them. It felt unnatural and repulsive. If it was not for the pressure, the boy had been exerting moments ago, they would have already acted on their instinct to run.

The moment the boy vanished over the horizon, Zac and his comrades separated in fear, running towards the forest in an attempt to save themselves from the unknown creature. Their movements, however, served as a trigger to the beast's own.

Seeing them move, the wolf pounced at them. Thanks

to the boy's intervention, his wish for revenge would finally be granted.

If only our revenge was that easy, thought Amro, watching from a distance. He was now a fragment of his former self, no longer a god, but a mere shadow. Despite that, the certainty of achieving his goals remained as absolute as it had been before his fall. It wasn't arrogance, but confidence.

However, those goals would have to wait. For now, Amro had decided to focus on a much simpler task. He would get revenge for his host and finish his side of their deal.

He looked towards the sky, enjoying the sight of the blanket of night covering the firmament. It was a sight he had long forgotten. A beautiful one at that. Being back in the mortal world had its benefits.

Amro's steps grew steady as he moved northwards, back to his host's village. That place was now home to his next targets. As he did, he confirmed Zaros's consciousness remained asleep. The shock of a near-death experience was not an easy task for a mortal to overcome.

The boy still needed time to rest.

For now, the forest remained silent as night finished claiming the sky. Its inhabitants refused to make any noises as if calling attention to themselves carried unimaginable danger. Enjoying this peace, Amro made his way swiftly towards the village. There was still a death quota to fulfill.

CHAPTER 04

Revenge's first steps.

Amro made his way to the village in his new host's body. There were many things he had to do before he could achieve his own revenge. Upholding his end of the deal with Zaros was only one of them. The young man had given him a chance to erase his regrets. In exchange, it was only fair for him to put in some effort as well.

His steps were light and graceful, helping him reach the entrance to the village within minutes. Fortunately for him, the rest of the mercenaries were waiting inside, mumbling among themselves. It saved him the time hunting them down would have taken.

"Where's Zac? He and his party are taking too long to return," a man complained. He was the captain of the group, the one responsible for the entire operation. After waiting for couple hours, his patience towards his missing subordinate had started to get thin.

"I bet he is just searching for stragglers, sir," said someone else who was trying to appease him.

"And I bet he is just avoiding work. Isn't it weird that he left when we were just about to burn everything down?" complained another mercenary.

"If he is not here by night, I'll have him strung up by his legs and dragged by our horses once we find him," added the captain in anger. Zac's constant slip-ups had led him to lose his temper, especially so since he let a young man escape.

After killing everyone in town and taking all their valuables, the mercenaries were getting ready to burn the corpses in order to get rid of the evidence of foul play. The absence of Zac and his party was the only thing keeping the captain from setting everything on fire.

As the group complained amongst themselves, Amro's figure finally approached. He strode inside the village without much care for their presence, spending no effort to hide himself.

One of the mercenaries spotted him immediately and reported it to the rest of the group. "Sir, someone is approaching!"

The captain turned to the incoming figure. It was only a youth still early in his teens. Aside from the amber eyes boring into his own, nothing special could be said about the boy.

The captain frowned as he seemed to recall something. Wasn't this the youth his party had met earlier that day? It made sense if it was him who Zac was looking for. Perhaps the kid played a fast one on his scout, causing him to lose his tracks on the forest.

With his aura suppressed, the mercenaries had no clue of the power coursing through Amro's borrowed body. Years of waiting inside his phylactery had made him impatient to have some fun. Seeing the eventual desperation on the faces of humans as they realized the impossibility of their survival was one way to achieve that goal, despite how twisted it may seem.

For Amro, containing his aura wasn't a hard task. It was only a matter of growing used to his body. Moments ago, when he met the mercenaries in the forest, he had just taken control of Zaros's physique. During that time, he had been unable to contain his aura. Now, however, he had managed to hide it from prying eyes, looking no different from a regular boy.

"Someone bring him to me for questioning," ordered the captain.

A young and lanky mercenary approached Amro. He believed himself to be smarter than the rest of mercenaries who had attacked the town with him. Taking this chance to please their contractor was an opportunity to enter the army. Even though being a mercenary had its advantages, freedom being one of them, the pay received by a soldier was worth the compromise.

Amro watched the lanky youth's approach with a sneer on his face. He found it specially fun to crush the spirit of arrogant youngsters. Seeing the despair surface on their faces when they realized their own weakness was a guilty pleasure of his.

"Kneel," ordered Amro. His voice carried hints of boredom as if just dealing with the young man was something beneath him.

An invisible pressure assaulted the young mercenary as an unquestionable urge to kneel filled his body, leaving him with no choice but to obey. All of his instincts urged him not to move without his target's permission, lest his life be forfeit.

The captain stared at the lanky mercenary with confusion in his eyes. He couldn't help but ignore the other mercenaries' mocking laughter. Why had he kneeled? Was he somehow afraid of the kid? His instincts told him there was something more than what appeared to be on the surface.

Amro approached the kneeling mercenary, using the height advantage to place his hand on the young man's forehead. A displeased expression appeared on his face as he voiced his next command. Had Amro been at his full strength, the youth wouldn't even have been able to approach him without fainting on his own.

"Die," Amro ordered. His voice carried unrefusable authority, giving the target of his command to option but to obey.

Just like that, without any fanfare, the young mercenary's body collapsed to the ground — lifeless.

Amro stretched his hand, grabbing something escaping the body of the dead man. Earlier that day, he had promised Zaros to help him achieve his revenge. It made him question whether letting the mercenaries reincarnate would count as a slight to his promise. Thus, in order to avoid any troubles, he decided to take care of their souls as well.

A small speck of grey light squirmed inside Amro's hand, refusing to be contained. Unfortunately, it lacked the strength to escape, and could only struggle in vain. Seeing the useless strife of the soul in his hands, Amro used his power to ignite it ablaze. After that, he waited for the soul to start burning on its own before tossing it toward the rest of the mercenaries, allowing them to see the price of blocking his path.

From the mercenaries' point of view, their comrade had collapsed on his own, making a joke out of himself. The uncommon reaction unleashed laughter amongst the battle-hardened mercenaries, words of ridicule streaming constantly out of their mouths.

However, the captain and those with cautiousness in their nature could sense that there was something strange going on. They knew that there was no way for someone to react so dramatically unless they were legitimately scared. However, once they saw Amro throw something their way, their suspicions became a reality.

Initially, the boy's toss seemed like an empty gesture,

something done just to mock them. That, however, wasn't surprising. Most mortals held no magical talent, and definitely not the amount needed to perceive a soul's very essence. Amongst the mercenaries, only the captain was fortunate enough to sense a disturbance in the surroundings. He instinctively rolled away, not even taking the time to warn his subordinates.

As he did, the burning soul landing onto the group of mercenaries, killing everyone caught in the blast radius with soul fire. The captain alone managed to escape the explosion. Sweat rolled down his back as his mind filled with shock.

The waves of pressure assaulting his senses reminded the captain of the old master who had built the neighboring kingdom's mage division. Had he not seen the young boy throw something their way, he wouldn't have believed him to be responsible for the deaths of his comrades. How was it possible for a child to muster such an absurd amount of magical power?

Amro smiled, entranced by the chaotic feeling of wailing souls. It was common knowledge amongst gods that when a mortal died, their soul would leave for the reincarnation cycle. However, even to this day, he was ignorant about what happened when a soul was destroyed.

This uncharted territory provided endless amount of entertainment to someone who had seen it all. A soul's death, to his eyes, was a spectacle worth treasuring, no matter how many times he witnessed it. Such deaths were pure, unadulterated, blessed by an eternal nothingness. Ah, the beauty of the unknown. This was a realm of knowledge even he, a former god, was unable to comprehend. He would be willing to sacrifice all living things just for a chance to peer into it further.

Seeing the youth in contemplation, the captain stood still on the ground. His mind operated at its fastest speed, trying to decipher how he could appease the youth in front of him. Could this boy be a legendary being, hidden amongst common folk? He had no way to know, but every second the youth spent in silence would be an extra second for him to re-arrange his thoughts and fix his composure.

Amro enjoyed the spectacle from the burning souls until the very last one of them eternally departed from exist-ence. Only when the last languishing soul had its last moment did he turned to look at the pale-faced captain. A sadistic smile crept up his face. This particular specimen might be of some use to him.

"Kneel," ordered Amro.

The captain did not dare to disobey. Ignorant as he was, he recognized the difference in power between him and the young man. He knelt obediently as he cursed the day he was given an order to attack the villages from this forest.

"Speak, who is behind this?" said Amro, going straight to the point.

The captain felt troubled after hearing this question. Even if the answer pleased the mage in front of him, he would still lose his life at the hands of his king once his betrayal came to light. On the other hand, if he was to displease the mage right now, his life would probably be forfeit all the same.

"Honorable mage, I was foolishly blinded by greed and followed my king's orders. Please appease your anger. I'm sure my king would reward you handsomely if you were to over-look this situation and pledge your services to him."

Amro frowned. Him? Bow to a mortal man? It had been eons since such a notion was even considered. Oh, how the mighty have fallen, for him to be looked down upon this much.

"Such a stupid notion is not worthy of my answer," he

said. "Speak. What kingdom do you serve?"

The captain was not surprised. High ranking mages were always arrogant and aloof, often looking down on the rest of the world. Having one of them accept an offer would never be an easy task. The best he could do right now was to attempt to entice him with as many different resources as he could think of.

This part of the continent lacked those talented in the arcane, if he could get one to serve his kingdom, he would be handsomely rewarded.

As such, his answer followed the highest of etiquette. Bowing down, he continued, "I serve the kingdom of Nyx, honorable mage. I'm sure my king would be happy to grant you a fiefdom of your own if you joined his side. You don't have to care about the loss of this small village."

Amro frowned. Even if he placed little value on the lives of the peasants who died in this town, he had made a deal with Zaros. One which he planned to keep. Not doing so would bring dissonance between him and his new partner, something which could spell trouble for their future.

"Thank you," said Amro, bringing an expression of surprise in the bowing captain. "You've saved me the trouble of interrogating you any further."

The captain went pale. Was this mage already working for another group? If so, just how far had the kingdom of Nyx been infiltrated by other kingdoms? If this sorcerer was to use the information from his troops as political leverage, he would be forever remembered as a traitor to his nation.

Worrying about his own future, the captain carefully selected his next words. "Honorable mage, forgive me for overstepping my boundaries, but I have something to ask."

"Speak."

"Are you planning to let me live?" The captain's voice shook as he remembered the mage's previous display of power. If he decided to silence him, there was no way he would be leaving with his live.

"No," said Amro. His answer left no room for negotiation.

The captain could only smile in resignation. He understood the other party had no use in keeping him alive. His only remaining chance of living laid in appealing to the other party's sense of honor.

"May I then dare to request a formal duel with you?"

Amro pondered for a second before nodding in agreement. It would be a good chance to experience his current body's shortcomings. After all, his previous opponents had been dealt with by using the remaining power he had sealed inside his phylactery. This man might have thought of him as just a mage, but as the fallen God of Death, how could he not know of swordsmanship, poisons, and many other ways to achieve the end of a life?

Amro walked back to the bodies of the dead mercenaries and grabbed a dagger, gauging its weight on his hands. The captain was pleasantly surprised. He had initially expected the other party to use magic during the course of their duel. It looked like his opponent carried a strong sense of honor, choosing a method of combat that would give him a chance at survival.

Oh, how wrong he was.

"Begin," commanded Amro.

The captain stood up and assumed a combat-ready pose. He knew mages were both crafty and cunning. As such, he decided to not display even the least bit of arrogance. Channeling all of his strength, he prepared himself to evade at the least sign of trouble. He trusted his strength gave him at least the qualifications to defend.

Amro smiled. It seemed like the man before him had pretty good instincts. He had not hesitated to opt for the safest option during such an uncertain battle. If it was not for the promise he had made Zaros, he would probably entice the captain to join as a servant to his church once he was able to reclaim it.

Amro knew the captain had opted for a defense-oriented approach. As such, he decided to make the first move. He took a step forward, shortening the distance between him and his opponent in less than a second.

However, Amro miscalculated. He had used far too much strength. Before he could restrain himself, Amro could already feel groups of muscle fibers snapping on the lower part of his legs. This kind of speed was too much for his host's current body to handle.

The captain's eyes squinted. He hadn't sensed any energy fluctuations at all. How was it possible for the mage in front of him to run at such speeds then? Was the difference in their power this vast?

Unaware to him, this wasn't a speed born of energy enhancing the boy's body. It was the effect of using a body without any of the instinctual limitations human nature had imposed over itself.

Clash!

Seeing the boy right next to his face, the captain discarded all of his needless thoughts. He had used his sword to parry the incoming dagger, causing a deep fissure to appear on the blade just before both of them stepped back to gain some distance. The clash had been momentary, but it had been just enough to leave an unforgettable impression on him.

On the other hand, Amro frowned after he saw the conclusion of his attack. He was severely disappointed over his own results.

This body is immature for its age, reasoned Amro. *It seems to have lacked proper nutrition as it developed. I'll need to fix it into an acceptable state before taking the path of power once again.*

Even as he was immersed in battle, Amro thought of ways to fix his host's current weaknesses. The only reason he had been capable of cracking his opponent's weapon was because the flaws a mortal's weapon possessed could not escape his eyes. His physical strength and stamina were much too lacking to achieve this results otherwise.

Clash!

Amro sighed after seeing the mercenary's captain block a second blow. It confirmed his suspicions about Zaros's physique. However, this experiment needed to come to an end. His host's body would be severely injured if he kept fighting in such a forceful manner.

Coming to this realization, Amro channeled the environment's mana into his body, releasing part of his aura as he prepared his next move. Using both powers like this wasn't ideal, but it was more than enough to finish his opponent.

Aura and mana were inherently different from each other. Mana was the lifeblood of nature. It was a form of energy with different properties according to the environment where it originated. Aura, on the other hand, was a power born from the soul.

The captain sensed the change in Amro's demeanor. Instinctively, he decided to strengthen himself with everything he had by channeling what little environmental mana he could use into his own body. Knowing it wasn't enough, he even used his life-force to ignite whatever amount of aura he could muster.

He had only trained his body to rank one, the first step in the long road to power. Normally, he would only rely on external mana to strengthen himself. However, in a time of crisis like this, he was willing to sacrifice anything in exchange for a chance at survival.

Taking a defensive stance, the captain prepared himself for the worse. Perhaps, if the gods smiled upon his existence, he would make it back alive. Muttering prayers under his breath, the captain felt his senses sharpening to new heights, almost like he was on the verge of a breakthrough.

Slash!

Alas, it was all in vain. The captain's head rolled down onto the ground the very next second without a warning. Once Amro had grown bored with their fight, all his hopes of surviving had become forfeit. In his last moments, all the captain had left was the realization of his own weakness. Because of this unfortunate encounter, his name would be stricken from the records of the living.

As the body collapsed onto the ground, Amro extended his hand and caught the fleeing soul. This time, however, he didn't burn it. Instead, he proceeded to extract energy from it to recover the damage and over-exhaustion he had caused to his host's body.

Despite his skills and extensive knowledge, the passage of time had made him oblivious to how much strength a normal mortal could handle before sustaining injury. It was only normal for him to ease the healing process before the boy regained consciousness given how the boy hosting his soul was unable to muster mana or aura on his own.

Helping the kid attain his revenge might prove to be just a little more annoying than I thought.

CHAPTER 05

Awakening.

Amro sat down as he drained the soul of the mercenaries' captain in order to heal Zaros's body. Such a technique would be considered a taboo by many, but to Amro, it was a feat doable without hardship nor any moral concerns. The wails of the soul echoing in his ears posed nothing but a small inconvenience, one he had grown used to ages ago.

As he turned the agonizing soul into fuel for his host's body, Amro pondered over his own situation. The gods probably thought of him as dead, still unaware of his revival. He could make use of this to execute plans of his own. They were sure to have grown complacent with his disappearance.

That being said, it would take time to build up his strength once more. His revival hadn't taken long, but the price he had paid was enormous. Fortunately for him, his fated encounter with his new host had come at a perfect time, giving him a window of opportunity.

Amro was sure that once he regained his strength, he could battle most of the gods and come out victorious. Unfortunately for him, a small problem still remained: Vita. A battle against the goddess of life would be difficult, even more so if the other gods interfered. Preparations needed to be held before confronting her. Perhaps the mortal world was the answer to his problems. He just needed some time to figure it out.

Amro had sacrificed much of himself in order to have another chance at life. Even as the former God of Death, avoiding his own mortality came at a great price. Using a phylactery as a catalyst for rebirth allowed him to keep most of his memories, knowledge and the essence he had sealed inside when he created it, but it restrained how much of his power he was able to use upon taking a new body. That meant he would now have to share this body with his host, at least until he could come up with a better solution.

The only advantage he could count on now was time. With the gods' complacency on his side, he would have an ample amount of time to make his preparations for revenge. That meant he could spare some time to help his host with his revenge. After all, small actions like this would help strengthen the relationship between the two of them.

Seeing the wake of destruction around him, Amro decided to take some time to dig graves for the villagers. Even if they were not related to him, they were still important to his host. As the former God of Death, what good would he be if he didn't lay his host's acquaintances to rest?

"Humans will never change, will they?"

Amro could still smell the regrets lingering in the bodies of the dead as he buried them, a stench he was much too familiar with. Massacres like this were far too common in the mortal world. Those without power would often get involved in the plans of stronger forces. He could only hope for them to find peace in their next life.

When Amro finished placing the bodies into their graves, a feeling of exhaustion overcame him. It seemed like training his host's body would have to be the first priority on his to-do list. Even with his extensive knowledge, he could not overcome these basic, biological needs without consequences. At least not with the lack of alchemical reagents currently available to him.

Speaking of biological limitations, the damage he had done to his host's body could not be overlooked. Once the boy woke up, he would fall victim to the consequences of Amro's reckless behavior. This, however, was a small price to pay from Amro's point of view.

Unfortunately, it was still imperative of him to rest. Thus, Amro strolled through the destroyed town in an attempt to find a suitable place to rest.

Eventually, he ducked into a nearby cabin that didn't look too beaten up despite the mercenaries' destruction. Inside, he settled into the closest bed, before he allowed himself to comply with his mortal body's needs.

I grew arrogant with time, thought Amro. *I was wrong to believe a perfect balance could be achieved with Vita. I can only blame myself for not realizing her hunger for power.*

Before his death, Amro believed peaceful coexistence with the other gods was possible. Sure, they had struggles. They would declare war upon each other every other millennia. However, they had never before turned hostile toward a god's laws. The way Amro saw it, it was a declaration of war upon the world itself.

Unfortunately for Amro, despite being complementary, his path and Vita's ultimately led to separate goals. His major mistake came from believing his position wouldn't be challenged. A mistake fate had no qualms about throwing into his face.

Amro knew he was to blame for growing complacent. Even his juniors had shown more ambition than him. He had forgotten that only by aiming for new heights would he be able to keep his hegemony. Growing conceited was no different from chaining oneself. Ironically, his close brush with death had served as a reminder of this.

Sadly, it's too late to change the past, thought Amro. After a few seconds, as the energy from the dead captain's soul seeped through his borrowed body, Amro's senses came back to reality. The moonlight shone through the cabin's make-shift window, providing him light to see the wounds healing on his arms.

His host had many limitations. Low physical resilience was only one of them. He would need to find suitable methods to train him into a vessel worthy of carrying his spirit. Otherwise, it would be nearly impossible to accomplish both of their revenges. That, however, would have to wait until another day. Right now, his body needed some rest.

As his senses darkened, Amro's consciousness entered inside his own soul. This was his soul's domain, a physical representation of his life experiences, his state of mind, his everything. In Amro's case, a vast expanse of darkness extended across the horizon. The only contrasting object in view was the figure of a young boy. He floated along with the darkness, seemingly embraced by it.

Despite that, Amro didn't approach him. Instead, he looked at himself, finding ever-changing appearances overlapping against each other. Amro knew that inside this realm he could hold any aspect at will, he only needed to think about it. The damage he had received upon death, however, had blurred the lines of his own identity.

Sigh.

He knew it wasn't the time for him to think about that. In order to ease his relationship with his host, he opted to change into something the boy would find more familiar: a human figure clad in black robes. Once he did, he approached the floating representation of his host's consciousness.

Zaros's appearance inside Amro's soul domain remained the same, although he seemed weaker than usual. His skin was deathly pale, and even his hair had gone from its usual black luster to a dark shade of grey. His current condition reflected his soul's weakness; a small reminder of how near he had been to death not too long ago.

Amro frowned as he examined the boy's soul. "It requires just as much tempering as his body," he muttered. "His current self is far from what I would call ideal."

Unfortunately, Amro knew such a thing was easier said than done. For the time being, he had no option but to nourish the boy within his own soul domain instead. Fortunately, this meant Zaros's recovery process proceeded smoothly.

After a while, Zaros opened his eyes, finally capable of seeing his surroundings. What greeted him, however, looked no different from a drop of ink. The only visible thing in his view right now was the silhouette of a man covered by dark robes. Despite that, he didn't felt any discomfort. In fact, a strong sense of familiarity filled him when he looked at the man.

"Where am I?" he asked.

"Within me, as I am within you," answered Amro. "This is a space held inside our souls, somewhere your consciousness can reside."

"Your voice sounds familiar, didn't I hear it just before—" Zaros stopped himself before continuing further. Entertaining the notion of his own death was not a pleasant thought. Instead, he moved onto another pressing matter.

"Who are you? No, what are you?"

"Answers about myself will come in time, child. In regards to your first question, my name is Amro. You will find that we are now bound by fate." Amro's voice was clear and melodious, yet somehow authoritative and firm. "The moment you speak of was when we struck a deal."

Zaros nodded as he recalled parts of his previous encounter. A vague connection to the man before him lingered in his mind. He recalled entrusting himself to him shortly before falling unconscious in the forest. Desperate and scared, he had entrusted his everything before surrendering himself to fate.

Did I sell my soul to an evil spirit before falling unconscious? thought Zaros. *Perhaps this is something like the merchants' tales about demons.*

"The answer to that would depend on how you view me," joked Amro, seemingly able to read his host's mind. "It isn't the time for that, however. You should now have enough strength to wake up."

"Wake up? Am I asleep? Is this a dream?" Zaros asked. His gaze wandered around the black void that surrounded both him and Amro, trying to make sense of everything he was told.

"Something very similar," answered Amro. Without more delay, he approached Zaros's spiritual form and tapped on his head.

Zaros woke up with his body drenched in sweat. An intense discomfort poured from each and every one of his muscles.

While Amro could use power beyond Zaros's normal capability at the cost of straining his host beyond his physical limits, the consequence was none other than the boy's current state. Even with Amro's healing, it would take Zaros some time before the pain spreading throughout his entire body disappeared.

Everything hurts, thought Zaros.

"This small amount of pain should be a small price to pay for everything that happened," said Amro, clearly disregarding his own responsibility in the matter. "You are still way too weak for me to use the full extent of my powers with your body."

Zaros was taken by surprise. Not only did Amro's voice echo from within his head, he had also been able to read his thoughts.

"What do you mean by that?" asked Zaros as he made use of this new form of communication.

"You had wished for power. It just means you're quite far away from achieving your goal," said Amro. "I might have taken care of the men who destroyed your village, but the ones behind it are still out of your reach."

Zaros's hands clenched in anger. His mind wandered back to the corpses he had seen strewn around his village. In a display of madness, his friends and acquaintances were stacked in a tower of lifeless bodies. The mere memory of this caused his nails to dig into his palms.

"Who was behind it?" asked Zaros. He found himself eager to hear the answer. In spite of his weaknesses, his goal hung clear in his mind.

Amro sighed. He could sense that the young man he was bound to was too reckless for his own good.

"The man leading them referred to himself as a vassal of this fief's king. I don't know of their intentions, but it's clear they didn't want to leave anyone in this village alive," he explained.

Zaros's mind froze momentarily. What would the king want with his simple village? They had no riches. No hidden warriors. Nothing in his village could explain the king's actions. Not rationally, anyhow.

"Politics are much more complicated than that," explained Amro. "Regardless, his intentions are not important. The only thing you need to care about is getting stronger and eventually paying him a visit when you are capable enough."

Zaros nodded. There was a compelling logic in his partner's reasoning. He exited the cabin, only to find rows of bodies belonging to the mercenaries, lying around lifelessly.

"Did you deal with them?" Zaros asked. Mixed feelings made their way to his heart as he took in the new scene in front of him.

"Of course, it was part of our arrangement."

I wished for power, thought Zaros. *Power to claim revenge with my own hands.*

"Yet power without survival is meaningless. That is something I was also reminded of after a recent experience of mine," Amro rebuked. "You will have plenty of chances for revenge with your own hands once you have gained enough strength. In the end, these mercenaries were nothing but disposable tools. The real culprit is still safe and sound, far away from here."

Unable to argue with Amro's sound reasoning, Zaros made his way back to the small shack he had once called home. On his way back to it, he saw a series of crudely made graves with stones as their markers.

His feet froze. Again, Zaros turned to look back at the village. The corpses that littered the ground belonged only to the mercenaries. None of the deceased villagers remained.

"Thank you," he said. His voice sounded hoarse, like his clogged up feelings were just about to spill from it.

Amro didn't answer. It was only fair for the innocent to receive a proper burial when possible. In fact, that was something that could aid their souls in dealing with their grudges.

"What must I do to grow stronger?" Zaros asked. There was a strong sense of relief behind his voice.

"For now, how about getting some food? You might be ignoring it, but the grumbling of your stomach is getting annoying," Amro advised.

Zaros froze in place, slightly surprised at the unexpected answer. He had been far too concerned about other issues to realize just how much his body had been complaining about the lack of food. It was almost like he instinctively believed he had no need for food. Just where had such a thought stemmed from?

CHAPTER 06

Goodbye.

Zaros enjoyed an enormous and scrumptious meal for the first time in his life. The mercenaries had gathered all the food in the town to refill their provisions. Combined with the hefty amount of food the group already had, the meal served before Zaros was enough to feed an army. Of course, having no previous opportunity to enjoy such a feast, Zaros let none of it go to waste.

Meanwhile, Amro used the time Zaros spent filling his stomach to explain their situation. Much to his frustration, however, his lecture fell upon deaf ears.

"You're currently an unranked human, someone who hasn't taken even one step in the path to power. As you are now, you're useless in the grand scheme of things," said Amro. "Both your soul and body lack tempering. As such, we need to start your training as soon as possible."

"It's not like I was unaware of that, thanks for the encouragement," Zaros said sarcastically, unbothered by Amro's statement.

Ignoring the boy's retort, Amro continued. "Fortunately for you, your body's ability to assimilate mana was stimulated after I controlled it. At the very least, we've proven you are capable of using it. With some work, we might be able to bring out your full potential. It's only a matter of time before you step into rank one, the body's refinement stage."

Zaros nodded as he continued to eat. The issue about his body falling under his partner's control during his time of rest was surprising at first, but he had gotten over it after Amro's initial explanation. The former Sovereign of Death had an incredible talent to gloss over matters that concerned the boy's interests.

"Nonetheless, the path of mana is only one of the things I have in mind for us," said Amro. "Relying on nature is restrictive in comparison to relying on oneself. There are many other power systems you will have to learn in due time to make up for this."

Zaros wolfed down a handful of potatoes while listening to Amro. *I never expected to become an exemplary in this way,* he thought. The ability to communicate with Amro using his thoughts proved to be especially useful at times like this. Otherwise, not even Amro would have managed to understand the small glutton.

"Regardless, I have no shortage of methods to help you build your strength. I do think, however, that battling others for first-hand experience will be the easiest and fastest way for you to do so," added Amro.

"Will it be possible for me to become strong enough to go against the king on my own?" asked Zaros. A hint of worry crept into his voice as he explained his hesitation.

"That man whom you call a king is nothing more than another mortal in my eyes. It will be easy to dispose of him quickly," Amro said, slightly offended.

He had to force himself to remember that a boy from a backwater village had probably never heard of the God of

Death's name. He couldn't blame the boy for this. He could only blame his own church and his priests for not spreading his name far enough around the world.

"You make it sound like it's already a done deal," said Zaros.

"I dealt with the men outside, didn't I?" rebuked Amro.

Zaros rolled his eyes as he shoved another handful of dry jerky into his mouth. The flavor reminded him of the small boars he often hunted around the forest. The difference lain by the fact that these pieces had some salt applied into them.

Even Amro's arrogance couldn't decrease Zaros's appetite. After hunting to survive for years, the miracle of having so much food for himself could not be ignored. In exchange for that, Zaros was willing to happily ignore the nagging of an overconfident spirit.

Amro, on the other hand, began to grow increasingly annoyed. As a god, he had grown used to people begging for his attention all day long. How could this boy opt to ignore his wisdom?

"Are you even listening to me?" Amro demanded. Indignation clouded his thoughts until he remembered he was, to a certain extent, indebted to the young boy.

"I am. It's just that you talk about too many things," complained the boy. "How about giving me a moment to enjoy my food?"

"You don't understand, do you? We have to leave the village soon. Eventually, the ones behind this will send a search party when those men we killed don't come return," Amro said, his tone softening a bit.

"Can't you just deal with them like the last batch?" Zaros asked. After being enlightened by Amro's lecture, he wasn't interested in dealing with the henchmen when the true culprit sat on the safety of his throne.

"I already told you, the amount of times I can use my powers is limited. I no longer have a body, and yours is still far away from being able to extensively support mana or aura, much less refine it yourself."

"I'm pretty sure you buried that amongst everything else you said," complained Zaros. "Why not start there?"

Ignoring Amro's incessant nagging, Zaros packed the few personal items he had to his name. A worn down, crude knife with only a dull edge remaining, a set of poorly made clothes, and that bag of coins he had intended to use for a gift before this whole ordeal.

"The settlement closest to this should be a day or two away on foot. On the other hand, the closest town should be around a week from here," explained Zaros. "We could use one of the horses left behind by the mercenaries, however. I've never had the opportunity to ride one, but it could greatly decrease the time we need to get there."

"No," Amro replied. "You have to temper your body; basic physical activity is just the beginning of it."

Zaros sighed, it seemed like this new resident in his mind would only become bossier every day. He appreciated the help, but he could only hope Amro would lead him down the right path.

Before leaving, Zaros returned to the graves of his villagers, the ones dug by Amro. He bowed towards the grave of the butcher whom he had loved to tease, the merchant who had taught him how read, write, and barter, the old man who had provided him with his first hunting knife, and even to the other children whom he had never quite gotten along with. Alice's grave sat at the very end of the row of gravestones. Zaros resisted the urge to cry as he knelt before her makeshift resting place and laid the bag of coins onto the mount of dirt.

"I meant to buy you a gift before all of this," he said, digging a small hole before placing the coins beneath the grave marker. "I'm sorry I wasn't able to."

Interesting, thought Amro. A few rituals amongst the church of death involved gifting the dead some money. He knew Zaros was unaware of them, which made the coincidence all the more pleasant.

Zaros turned around to face all the graves again before he spoke his last words to them. "Don't worry, I'll exact retribution for all of you. I'll visit everyone again, once it's done."

"You have a way with words, kid," said Amro. He was able to see the souls of those resting in the graves calming down. The souls of those involved in tragedy would often be distorted by grudges and hatred, tying them down to the mortal world. After Zaros's promise to avenge them, however, they appeared to be willing to let go. With enough time, they would naturally enter the reincarnation cycle.

"We still have one more place left to visit," said Zaros, walking past the gravestones and deeper into the forest.

As he did, he couldn't help but think about the prowess Amro must have possessed in order to deal with all of the mercenaries. What kind of background did he have in order to pull off such a stunt? Had his guesses from before been correct? Was Amro some kind of demon or evil spirit?

Sensing his thoughts, Amro felt slightly irritated. Being compared to an evil spirit made his pride suffer a long-forgotten humiliation. Oh, how entertaining would it be when he revealed his origins to the child. The taste of his shock would provide him some valuable payback.

It didn't take long for them to arrive at an open field. The view of green grass extended on for a while, interrupted only by a few large stones sitting in the middle. One stone in particular seemed tidy in comparison to the rest of the stones lying around. Zaros placed his right hand on top of it, a sad smile appearing on his face before he knelt down in front of it.

"Mom, I'm leaving. I don't know if I'll be able to come back," he said. "I promise that if I find Dad, I'll let him see how his son has grown into a good man. I'll become strong, able to walk with my head up in pride, and I'll never be trampled on by others again. Your son won't disappoint you."

Zaros bowed thrice towards the stone, a last display of respect towards his dead mother's resting place. This was their settlement's graveyard. It was mostly inhabited by those who had perished hunting, Zaros's mother being a rare exception. From what the villagers had told him, Zaros knew she had been a humble woman overflowing with kindness.

After a minute of silence, Zaros raised his head and rose to his feet once again. His eyes filled with unspoken resolve. He had a new goal. To become renowned, respected, and feared. He would gain enough strength to protect those he cared for, to live the life he wanted, to never feel the pain of a loss.

Amro could only laugh. This small human's ambitions continued to surprise him. In fact, the intensity of the training he had in mind for him kept multiplying for every ambition Zaros decided to add to his list.

After some time, Zaros finally departed. No second look was given to his former home, and every step he took toward the next settlement carried growing confidence.

* * *

Back inside the forest, far from the village, an eerie silence permeated the surroundings. Two cloaked figures riding their horses investigated every inch of the woodland.

"I feel it should be close to here," one of them said. A black, linen robe covered most of his visible traits, leaving only the outline of his muscular body in sight.

"Indeed, there are traces of it around this place," his companion answered. Her delicate figure was hidden by robes matching his, which had left only a few strands of both black and silver hair visible to outsiders.

"Could we have arrived too late?" asked the robed man.

"Perhaps, but not many could have been able to get their hands on a prophecy like this. One of our few remaining seers died to get this information, so I refuse to believe others could have gotten here before us," answered the silver-haired girl.

"At least entering this backwater country was easy," said the man. "I don't understand why these barbarians would decide to live away from the mainland. The mana in here is stagnant. The gods clearly don't care about this place."

"Watch your mouth," advised the silver-haired woman. "Remember what teacher often says: 'Gods are able to sense when others speak their names.' Besides, we should be looking for the legacy. If master finds out we dared to play around during this mission, no amount of penance will save us."

Both of the black-robed figures separated, scouring the area on their own. Eventually, one of them came to a halt. Five bodies laid before him, all of them mangled to shreds. The rot of death filled the area, and the bodies that should have only been dead for a day or so looked as if they had been rotting for weeks.

"Over here, I found something!" he yelled, calling for his partner.

His partner rushed over as soon as she heard him. When she saw the bodies lying on the ground, she dismounted from her horse, intent on carefully examining them. Her hand swept over the bodies without any traces of disgust. On the contrary, her face held traces of extreme ecstasy, the reflection of a zealot in the presence of her god's work.

A sheen of black covered her hand as she performed the examination. Slowly, gray miasma started forming on the surface of the bodies she examined, further evoking her excitement.

"It's here! The legacy of our lord has finally appeared!" she exclaimed. "The death of these men must have been influenced by its aura. How fortunate of them."

"Then it should be near here," her companion added. "We should resume our search."

The cloaked woman nodded. She mounted her horse and resumed their mission. According to the last instructions she and her partner had received from their master, the legacy they were looking for would appear in the southern forest they were currently in.

Having found a clue of its whereabouts, both became ecstatic. The legacy of their lord was of utmost importance to their teacher. For reasons unknown to them, he was currently unwilling to leave their home. In turn, he had placed this responsibility on their shoulders.

Their power far surpassed the norm in this side of the continent, making his expectations high. Should they be successful, they would be blessed with countless rewards. Perhaps, they would overcome the shadow of their senior disciples. However, were they to fail, their souls would never know rest.

CHAPTER 07

A talented actor.

The journey to reach the next village should have taken two days of travel. However, Amro decided to make use of the trip as a small opportunity to temper Zaros's body and character, and therefore had him take detours and face hardships that were otherwise unnecessary. This kept going on for three days until they finally reached the nearest village. What had been left of it, anyway.

"As expected, your home was just one of many," voiced the fallen death god. "Their goal lay not in your village, but in this forest."

The village they had arrived at was in the same desolate state as Zaros's. The only difference to be found was that this one had been burned to the ground. Buildings and people alike. Despite searching around it, they weren't able to find traces of anyone making it out alive.

"Just what are they aiming for?" asked Zaros. He was feeling increasingly desensitized to the scenes of carnage.

"You can ask them yourself in the future. For now, I'm going to take a guess and assume every other village in the forest will be in the exact same conditions."

"I can't understand," said Zaros. "What could be so important to warrant this massacre? Is there no god who watches over justice?"

If anyone embodies hypocrisy in the world, it is that fellow, thought Amro, recalling the constant policy changes the Church of Justice often implemented. Justice was always subjective to that which posed the most benefits for that hypocrite. In hindsight, Amro realized that was the case for most gods.

"Remember this, boy. Justice, values, and fairness are nothing but excuses made by the weak when they can't face the strong. If you don't have enough strength, no one will care about your beliefs. Without power, you won't be able to do anything when faced with what you call 'injustice.'"

Zaros nodded in understanding. His father had been conscripted because he had no power to confront the military. His village had been ravaged because they had no strength to ensure their own safety. He found it hard to accept, but he knew reality wouldn't change because of his personal beliefs.

Seeing nothing would change by idling around, Zaros extended an offer. "I think we should go north now. If you're right, all the other settlements will be in the same state as this one. Instead, it will be better to try our luck in the border town to the north. I've never been there before, but I've heard wandering merchants speak about it. It's just outside the forest. We should be able to reach it in a matter of days."

"I agree," spoke Amro. "We could use a place to gather some information and supplies."

Having settled upon a course of action, Amro and Zaros continued their journey across the forest. During this time, Amro didn't ease Zaros's training but made it increasingly harder instead. Every day, Zaros would be forced to fight stronger beasts, entering parts of the forest he would have never dared to enter on his own.

If that wasn't enough, Zaros's nights proved to be no more enjoyable than his days. Instead of rest, they were filled with more grueling training inside Amro's soul domain. The fallen god had the ability to control the environment presented inside of it, recreating any scenario he was able to think of. As such, Zaros was forced to live through countless scenarios, relying on nothing but Amro's advice.

With time, each kill took less effort than the one before it. The boy's expertise at dealing with beasts grew alongside Amro's criticism of his flaws. The boy was rather pathetic at understanding the theory and underlying concepts Amro touched upon. However, his body betrayed his mind's standards, as the moves taught by Amro were ingrained into it by sheer repetition.

The improvement Zaros's skills achieved over a week could be said to exceed all of his expectations. Even if Zaros had received guidance from a couple hunters in his village, how could their skills compare to someone who had risen to the ranks of a god? Each one of Amro's pointers struck the essence behind the issue, leaving no flaws in his advice.

Even then, Amro couldn't help but feel disappointed. It was easy to teach a child how to grab a tool and use it, but to train them into masters of their craft required something else. It required talent — one the boy had not been given by the heavens.

With that in mind, Amro came up with a plan. Who better to go against the heaven's will than him? He had fought a big part of the pantheon after all.

If the heavens didn't give Zaros talent, then Amro would do it himself. The plan to slowly reform the boy's body using his own knowledge as the base slowly took shape.

Amro's plan aside, the journey eventually came to an end. The border town they had aimed to reach was now visible on the horizon. Through Zaros's eyes, Amro faced what would be the starting point of his new adventure.

Zaros, on the other hand, faced the town with complex feelings. He had always wished to travel outside the forest, albeit not in these conditions. Now, he was here on his own. No longer a child with a dream, but a boy with a grudge.

Should I report the mercenaries' attack to one of the guilds? he wondered. *No, Amro is probably right. There is a chance the people here were involved as well. I better focus on sneaking my way in the town.*

From atop a tree, Zaros could see everything beyond the town's walls. Buildings made out of brick, stone or wood intermingled along the streets. The simple notion of having paved streets displayed just how much more structured and civilized the life inside this town was compared to the life inside the small village he had come from.

"You should be careful when entering the town," said Amro. "We don't know if those mercenaries had people here waiting to catch any stragglers. I could probably deal with them, but it is better not to get yourself in such a situation."

As he listened to Amro, Zaros's eyes traced the town's walls. After a few minutes of looking around, his gaze finally landed on the western side. The buildings near that area were much more simple and shabby than those in the rest of the town. It reminded him of his own humble shack.

"That seems like a good spot to enter from," advised Amro. People were less likely to pay attention to those from the slums. More often than not, their low social standing provided them with a sort of protection.

"Very well," said Zaros, climbing down from the tree. It didn't take long for him to merge back into the forest. Using the trees and greenery as his cover, he managed to move further towards the western side of town undetected.

He thought about changing his appearance, realizing it wasn't worth it to do so after a moment. Days of wandering inside the woods guaranteed that he could look like someone coming from the slums without much effort. Now, he only had to wait.

Once the sun disappeared below the horizon, Zaros exited the forest with a struggling rabbit in his hands. The small critter whined, trying to free itself from the boy's grasp. Surprisingly, it wasn't enough to call attention upon himself. The lazy guards standing at the gates didn't see him until he was already dangerously close to them.

A barrel-chested man was the first to react to Zaros's arrival. His appearance was as polished as his discipline, making him look no different from Zaros in his current messy state. With an annoyed expression on his face, the guard moved to block Zaros's path.

"Hey, you!" he said, clear despise for Zaros in his eyes. "What are you doing outside? You know there are orders for no one to exit the town for the time being."

Zaros lowered his head in order to hide his expression. Anger mixed with annoyance were starting to surface. Never did he think he would still receive the same treatment even outside his village.

On his side, Amro shared Zaros's feelings regarding the guard's behavior. He decided to remember the guard's aura in order to pay him back for his manners later on. Moments like this made him reminiscence about his followers' fear and respect.

The guard felt a small shiver go down his back as a terrible premonition filled him. Nonetheless, he kept on nagging Zaros, using the pleasure derived from berating him to appease the fear in his heart.

"You punks from the slums are always making our lives harder! Can't you see how hard we have it already? How am I supposed to sleep when I have to stand up and deal with people like you every other hour?" The guard kept blabbering about his suffering so much that it appeared like it would never end.

"I am sorry sir, I was hungry," said Zaros in a mild tone. He knew that being confrontational now wouldn't bring him any benefits. Thus, he chose to act as meekly as possible.

Zaros had planned out his entrance during the last couple of hours. Everything was an act, one made to ensure as little attention as possible would fall upon him. Even the rabbit in his hands was part of it. As the weakest creature in the forest, it helped reinforce his current persona.

"Well, I am too," retorted the guard as he stared at the rabbit in Zaros's hands. "Perhaps we can strike up a deal. That small rabbit of yours isn't enough to fill up a growing child like yourself. Let me have it and I'll overlook your violation of the curfew."

Zaros was surprised at the man's display of greed. Did he really have the heart to take a meal away from someone younger than him? Zaros didn't need this food right now, but many others before him might have. It was no wonder the man was shaped like a water drop.

If he wasn't forced by the situation, Zaros would have broken away from his act. Unfortunately, he had no choice at the moment. It would've been unwise to act on his feelings. Thus, he put on a pained expression, pretending to be placed between a rock and a hard place.

"Sir, could you please reconsider?"

"No! You have two choices: you can give up the rabbit or

you can enjoy a night's sleep outside," said the guard. He knew no child from the slums would risk sleeping near the woods, not when there were dangerous beasts lurking in the forest.

Continuing his act, Zaros showed some hesitation before handing over the rabbit.

"I see you understand what the correct choice is," said the guard as he took the rabbit from Zaros's hands. "Go in. If I see you outside again, you won't be able to escape my anger."

With that situation handled, Zaros made his way inside the town. His plan was a complete success... almost. At the very least, he'd been able to enter at the 'low' cost of his afternoon snack.

"Congratulations, kid," commented Amro from within his host. "Your acting skills might be as good as your appetite. If your luck is as good as both those things, we might be able to find everything we need inside this town."

"That man was nothing like the hunters from our village," said Zaros, still unfamiliar with the outside world. "He lacks honor and integrity."

"Kid, your understanding of the world is still lacking," said Amro. "Situations like this are the norm. The weak will always be bullied by the strong. Just think about those men that came to decimate your village under the king's orders."

Zaros lowered his gaze and clenched his hands into fists. The life at his old settlement had been nothing but a bubble — one bound to explode when someone stronger than him willed it. As things were, he lacked the power to control his own fate.

As Zaros stepped into the town, several stares locked into him. The people of the slums knew each other very well, so a new and unfamiliar face like Zaros's had gathered the attention of many.

Unaware to the intentions of those around him, Zaros took in the view of his new surroundings. A simple gasp of admiration left his mouth. Even the slums of this town had an impressive atmosphere to someone like him.

Amro, on the other hand, decided to remain quiet. The greed contained within the gazes targeting his host would eventually drive their owners to do something stupid. When they did, he would be ready, waiting to reap some benefits.

CHAPTER 08

The Slums.

Zaros continued to take in his surroundings. The number of buildings around him was staggering. The level of deterioration they had, however, was just as impressive. The condition of this side of town evidenced exactly how much importance it had to the general populace: none.

As he walked further inside, Zaros noticed that the walls of the buildings were covered in all kinds of posters. Some of them were bounties for certain people, while others talked about the recruitment of workers for different jobs. Amongst them, a particular poster caught Zaros's attention.

It depicted a sketch of the forest, partially cut down by a burly lumberjack. On the man's hand, a small bag of gold was drawn as his apparent reward. The poster looked like an attempt to recruit able-bodied men to work in a large-scale logging project. Was this what they had intended to do to his home?

Zaros felt frustrated, it took great effort for him to hold back from tearing down the announcement. Eventually, he realized it did him no good to continue stewing in his anger. Thus, his gaze left the poster. He still had to look for a place to sleep.

His odd behavior, however, was enough to get a target placed on his back. The few possessions of his — a crude knife, a small bag containing his clothes, and some furs he'd gathered while hunting in the forest — were already considered a sizeable amount of wealth by the hoodlums. Thus, Zaros's 'small fortune' had gathered him an undesirable amount of attention.

Not that he was aware of it.

Zaros had seen this large town from a distance, helping him learn of its general layout. Seeing it up front, however, gave him a different impression of this place. The living conditions, the stench in the air, and the deterioration. All of it provided information he wasn't able to gather from far away.

Some people laid deathly still at the side of the streets, the thread holding their lives from departure unfortunately thin. Children fought for near-rotten food, and many with eyes void of hope just sat waiting for their end to come. The poor living conditions of this side of town pained Zaros's heart.

What shocked Zaros the most was an old man sitting against the wall of a deteriorated building. It was clear that he had lost a leg from the way his skin stuck to his bones. Just like the rest, he seemed to have been starving for a long time. A small piece of wood lay in front of him with a poorly written scribble.

"Lost my leg in the war, please help," it said.

The pain this sight brought upon Zaros's heart hit too close to home. Even his father had been conscripted to join the army, his whereabouts still unknown. Was this the fate of this nation's soldiers? What kind of country would ditch those who had sacrificed their lives against their own will?

Sensing Zaros's fluctuating heartbeat, Amro chimed in. "Child, this is the way of the world. If you truly wish to change it, rise to the challenge. Indignation without power amounts to nothing."

Amro's words did nothing to appease Zaros's feelings, however. Instead, they only managed to redirect his anger to himself — to his lack of strength, his uselessness, and his ignorance of the world.

Once he adjusted his mindset, Zaros approached the starving veteran. Carefully, he placed some of his dried rations onto the man's lap. Even if he was powerless to change the fate of this old man, he hoped his small act of kindness would serve to show his gratitude for the services the man had done for his country.

The old man's clouded gaze rose to meet Zaros's eyes. A trace of a faint smile rose onto his lips, helping him convey his thanks. Zaros returned the gesture with a bow as he lowered his head to conceal his expression. He was afraid that the pained look on his face might wound the pride of the former soldier.

Is this how the royalty treats its citizens? wondered Zaros. *They don't even bother with someone who gave his physical integrity for them.*

Amro, on the other hand, found the situation rather amusing. *Silly boy, the fact that he is still alive should be reason enough to consider him fortunate.*

Zaros eventually rose from his bow, leaving the man behind. Each day that went by only gave him more reasons to hate the royalty of his nation. Attacking innocent villages, using their own people as disposable pawns — there was no way their sins could be forgiven. Those were not the actions of rulers. Those were the actions of tyrants.

Sadly, Zaros's small act of kindness had spelled a death sentence for the old man. Without the strength to protect himself, Zaros's gift was the same as plastering a target on his back.

Once Zaros departed, several hoodlums pounced onto the old man. They robbed him of everything he had, leaving him worse off than before.

In addition, this attracted even more gazes from those who had been targeting Zaros. After all, kindness was a rare trait to those of the slums. To them, Zaros's actions were nothing short of a display of weakness.

Even Amro pondered over whether his host's heart would be able to keep up with the ever-growing scenarios he would need to face. His naïve nature needed to be pruned, eliminated.

Ignorant of the consequences his actions held, Zaros decided to look for somewhere to pass the night. Unfortunately, he had no money on him as he had left it all behind. As things were, he was left with no option but to enjoy the warmth of the ground.

Eventually, Zaros managed to find an empty alleyway. It smelled like death, but both the boy and Amro had grown used to this scent. Finding a place inside, Zaros decided to cover himself with an extra layer of clothes before going to sleep.

Once his consciousness faded away, he found himself inside Amro's soul domain. This had been his routine for the past week. Every time he fell asleep, he would find himself surrounded by the same endless black void.

Zaros's mind eventually grew fatigued from not being allowed to take a break. However, Amro insisted that he wouldn't be given time to rest during a battle either. It was evident that Amro was adamant about tempering both the boy's body and mind.

Seeing his host's consciousness arrival, Amro sighed.

Whenever he saw the ambition and innocence in Zaros's eyes, he was reminded of his time as a mortal. It had been millennia since he'd been this close to someone other than a god. Things like struggles, ambitions, and pain had lost their meaning to him long ago.

Being bound to this child, however, had reminded him of his past self. Had he maintained the same desire for self-improvement as Zaros, he might have been able to go beyond his limits. However, it was already too late for regrets.

"Kid, you're still too green behind your ears," said Amro, intent on dispelling his own gloomy thoughts. Far from being a mortal, he had learned to hide his emotions better than most.

Zaros snorted, unable to comprehend why Amro reacted like this whenever they interacted.

"Do you wish to continue training today, or do you want to rest for a while?" offered Amro in a rare display of kindness.

Zaros was taken aback. This was the first time Amro had offered him a chance to rest. 'Only the strong can rest,' was his usual motto.

"Is that okay?" he asked.

Amro's shadowy figure nodded. He had other plans for the night.

"Thanks," said Zaros, no longer hesitating. His figure slowly vanished from Amro's soul domain as he fell into a deeper slumber.

Amro sighed. He knew how much he would have to keep pushing the young boy if they were ever to attain their revenges. At least for tonight, his plans happened to give him the chance to offer the young man some rest.

Following Zaros's descent into darkness, Amro's consciousness surfaced, now in control of their shared body.

Almost immediately, two figures entered the alleyway. It was clear what they had intended to do, seeing how they had appeared shortly after Zaros had fallen asleep.

Amro opened his eyes whilst controlling Zaros's body. He stood up and rotated his shoulders. The body of the child left him feeling slightly stifled every time he took control of it. Getting used to the constrictions of a mortal body was no pleasant feeling.

"Oh, so he was just pretending," said one of the figures who had entered the alley. He was a tall, skinny teenager with pale skin and dirty hair. The shabby clothes on him revealed his place as someone from the slums.

"That's probably right, brother. I just can't help but wonder... where did a rat like this scurry out from?" replied the girl next to him, evidently trying to act rough. "He's probably the bastard child of a noble who's been discarded by his family. No, never mind, scratch that. There is no way a bastard would wear clothes that badly damaged; not even we have to deal with that."

It was clear from the expression on her face that she felt nothing but scorn for an unfamiliar face like Zaros's. Perhaps her own experiences as a child of the slums had made her look down on those outsiders, for she envied not being one of them. Unfortunately for her, Amro was able to see through it all, considering her actions nothing more than child's play.

"It's looks like humanity will never change," said Amro, rising to his feet. "You lot like to look for trouble even when trouble does not come looking for you."

"Oh, it seems like the little noble has yet to experience the streets," replied the tall, skinny fellow.

"It looks like he needs to experience humiliation," said

the girl, taking another step towards Amro. "Consider this our help in making you more humble."

With that said, she cracked her knuckles before running towards her target. Her intent to strip him away from everything he owned was clear from how her eyes momentarily deviated from Amro onto his belongings.

Amro wasn't surprised, however. Even if he understood what they were there for, he had no plans to let them have their way. He simply shook his head as the young girl lunged in his direction. It was clear to him she had planned to tackle him onto the ground.

However, when the girl tried using her weight to throw Amro onto the ground, she felt an immovable wall. Before she could process what was happening, she felt Amro's hand grabbing her shoulder, pushing her aside with ease.

"This is my last warning," said Amro. "Children should listen to their elders."

"Look who's talking," replied the girl's brother, darting towards his target.

Amro frowned. Even if his host was only thirteen years of age, he himself was immeasurably old. Being looked down upon by mere teenagers sparked a slight fire of indignation inside his soul. His feelings caused his next move to be slightly less merciful.

Sidestepping the brother's tackle, Amro kicked the boy's stomach. It effectively made the other kneel onto the ground, puking the bare excuse for a meal he had earlier that day.

This made the teen's sister frown as she tried to stand up from the side. However, her legs gave away before she managed to do so. Slum-dwellers like her lacked training, but they all had very sharp instincts. She could tell the boy before her was far beyond their league.

"Look, kid, we get it. We won't mess with you anymore, just leave this part of town," she said, attempting to negotiate while she got closer to her brother.

"That's right," said the other teenager, barely managing to stand up. It was clear he was still wiping the remaining vomit from his lips. "You better leave before our boss comes and hunts you down."

"Interesting," said Amro, taking both brother and sister by surprise.

He was now smiling at the opportunity that he was presented. Even the boss of a small organization was likely to have enough resources for what he had planned. Their fortune was about to become a catalyst for Zaros's advancement.

I guess it's worth looking into it.

With that in mind, Amro took two steps forward, inching closer to both brother and sister. Before they realized it, Amro's arm was wrapped around their necks in a not-so-friendly embrace. A vicious smile was displayed on his visage, revealing he was up to no good.

"Take me to him," he said, looking at the stupefied teenagers. "I want to meet your boss."

CHAPTER 09

To recruit or to be recruited?

Cold. It was a sensation those of the slums were used to. Both a lack of home and a lack of meals were contributing factors to their familiarity with it. Thus, it was an inseparable part of their daily lives. Unavoidable, just like the sun's departure every night.

However, there was another type of cold those of the slums were used to. This one much darker and gruesome. It was the chill that came from being stared down by a predator. The evolutionary sense of fear ingrained into their instincts.

Two teenagers were now growing familiar to this feeling. Their gut telling them to run away. However, it was now too late. They had a chance to reject his request, to escape on their own, but they had wasted it. They had given in to the cold stare and vicious smile of that boy.

Without any other choice, they guided him to their hideout, reasoning to themselves that a rejection to his request would have been worse. Both brother and sister glanced at each other from time to time, confirming their mind wasn't playing tricks on them. It was unfortunate. Thoughts of running away crossed their minds, but the fear of being chased down made them discard such a notion.

On the other hand, Amro ignored the anxiety contained in his guides' eyes. He wasn't worried by anything they might try to do. Completely relaxed, he stretched as they crossed several alleyways and went through different junctures. Using the opportunity that had so nicely presented itself, Amro took the time to memorize the town's layout with ease.

Many gazes landed on the party of three, judging their every move. Yet once they recognized the brother and sister duo, those eyes quickly looked aside. Hoodlums knew each other, and the two leading Amro had a small reputation of their own.

What caught most of the onlookers' attention, however, was the unfamiliar youth accompanying them. It was clear as crystal that he was not from this side of town.

After walking for some time, they arrived at a rather torn-down brick building. The earthen colors and grime stuck to the edifice made it look like the place had been abandoned for years. The ruckus coming from the inside, however, made it clear that this wasn't the case.

Yet, even if the building looked vandalized, further scrutiny would reveal that it was still structurally sound. A place like this was likely to be a base of operations for those working inside the underworld. Aside from being hidden in plain sight, the sturdy building could probably hold for a while even if it was being besieged by invaders.

The party of three stopped at the door of the building as two burly men extended their hands to block their way. Amro raised an eyebrow at this, but the sister-brother duo him didn't seem to find it unusual.

"Alexander, you do not seem to be carrying tonight's quota. Under what pretense do you expect us to let you enter tonight?" questioned one of the two men guarding the entrance.

Alexander, the tall youth guiding Amro, scratched his head. As a member of the gang, it was expected for him to give a certain amount of tributes every week in exchange for their protection. After all, many of his former victims would come after him for retribution if he didn't.

Unfortunately for him, he was still short of reaching his quota. Even more so when his attempt to rob Zaros had proven unsuccessful. It had placed him in more trouble instead.

"I know, I know. I'll be sure to make it up to you tomorrow," he said, trying to talk his way out of his precarious situation.

The guard frowned, unwilling to buy the teenager's act. He had heard that excuse way too many times already. He was far too numb to the logic employed by this youth.

Sensing his displeasure, Alexander continued. "Hey, come on now, you wouldn't want to ruin our gang's reputation, right? This little brother over here wants to join us. It would be a shame if he missed this chance because of your stubbornness."

Amro's brow rose. When did he tell this youth he was planning to join them? How did this misunderstanding take place?

Hearing Alexander's words, the two men guarding the door looked at Amro. All they could see was a disheveled youth, no better than the two beside him. The two of them exchanged glances for a moment before reaching an agreement.

"He can come in, but whether he comes out will depend on his capabilities. You know the boss hates losing time on people without talent," the second guard said. "It makes me wonder what he saw in you two."

Both guards laughed as they made way for the party of three. Even if the slums were a dark and shady place, occasional scenes of camaraderie like this would sprout from the gloom every now and then. Whether such camaraderie remained during hardships was a different question altogether.

Amro had a calm look on his face as the three of them entered the building. If not for his unfamiliar face, no outsider would have been able to guess that he was a newcomer to the gang. Their steps echoed in the air as they made their way upstairs, occasionally attracting one or two gazes from the people inside.

As Amro and his new acquaintances drew closer to the next floor, Alexander decided to offer some words of advice. Not because he cared for him, but out of worry for himself and his sister. If their boss judged Amro to be unfit for the gang, the consequences might affect them as well.

"The boss is a very scary man, please do your best to show your worth to him. It should be fine as long as you are able to move like you did back there," he said. "In any case, I'm sorry for that. I hope you don't hold a grudge against us."

Amro didn't answer. The kid guiding him still seemed to think he was here to join them. The idea was ludicrous, for Amro had his own plans. A gang of this size was too small to satisfy his needs. Serving his host, however, looked like a reasonable future for them.

When they reached the last floor, they were greeted by a huge room that resembled a clandestine bar. People sat around shabby-looking tables, some drinking their frustrations out while others bragged about their so-called accomplishments.

A small fighting ring made of wood scraps and old clothes was in the center of the room. Inside it, two children were biting and gnawing at each other. Both of them were bleeding profusely as they acted without regard for the other's safety.

Alexander brought Amro to the table closest to the fighting ring. Sitting with a full view of the fight was a man receiving everyone's attention. His hair was a flaxen color tinted with a silver sheen while his skin had the color of freshly harvested wheat. He looked rather approachable if not for the devious smile that was plastered on his face.

The man was too busy with his drinking buddies to take notice of Amro and Alexander's arrival. Under the influence of alcohol and perhaps something else, he kept bragging to the rest of the table about how he had extorted money from the guards that day.

"And then I told them it was their turn to pay me some taxes," he said. "You should have seen their faces. They couldn't even find the courage to reject my request."

Everyone around him laughed in a forceful attempt to please the man's ego. They kept doing so until the man looked to his side and saw the party of three, giving the rest of them a moment to break out of their charade.

"Oh, Alexander, child, what is it this time? Do you need more time to pay this month's quota again?" The amiability in the man's voice was forced enough that even the dumbest of hoodlums would be able to understand the power dynamic between him and Alexander.

The lanky teenager thought of saying something, but his fear got the best of him. The only thing he managed to voice was a small complaint, too quiet to even cause an impression.

Disregarding the words mumbled by the youth, the gang's leader turned back to look at the youth's sister. As he lustfully stared at her body, he noticed some scratch wounds on her arms. He then swept his gaze to Amro, coming to a series of conclusions.

"Sir, I've brought this younger brother. He has expressed his interest in joining us," said Alexander, noticing the unfriendly gaze his boss gave Amro.

"Oh, that is quite the news. You know we welcome anyone willing to join us. Have you explained the rules to him yet?" asked the gang's leader.

Alexander shook his head while his sister smirked at the reminder.

"How come? Did something happen between you three?" asked the man rather mischievously. By taking a quick glance at their faces, he could figure out the story weaved between them, as well as why the two siblings didn't tell the newcomer what joining their gang required.

Alexander's face paled. The friendly tone his boss used was nothing but a facade. One he liked to use in order to play with his subordinates' minds. Since that was the case, his best option was to remain quiet displaying a fake smile.

"Doesn't matter, I'll tell him myself then," said the gang's leader as he turned to look at Amro.

"Look, boy, anyone who wants to join us has to endure the challenges of anyone in the gang openly. Only if you survive every challenger, will you earn the right to join our ranks. Well, if you're brave enough, you can also use this as a chance to advance in our ranks, as you will get the position of anyone you manage to beat. You could even try challenging me if you're feeling lucky."

Amro smiled. This was a convenient system where the strong could quickly earn their rightful place. It just happened to make everything that much easier for him. "I like your conditions; I think they suit the nature of this side of the slums pretty well."

The shady leader smiled ear to ear. It was always an interesting show whenever newcomers took up his challenge. Even if he didn't manage to find a suitable seed worth taking under his wing, he could always let those under him vent their frustrations for a while.

"Good, good," said the flaxen haired man. His vicious smile widened as he stood up and extended his hand towards Amro. "That's the way men are supposed to be. Courageous and daring enough to face all dangers without even thinking it twice. Everyone here knows me as Slyfox, what name should I call you by?"

Amro smiled, extending his hand to meet Slyfox's. "My name is Zaros." For now, he would borrow the name of his sleeping host. After all, it was him who would have to deal with these people in the future.

"Good name! A manly name indeed! Step up onto the ring, child, please give us a good show," instructed Slyfox, the smile on his face growing wider as he softly pushed Amro into the ring.

Alexander and his sister could only shiver when they remembered their own initiations. Back then, they were beaten to a pulp by several of the gang's members. Even their cries for mercy were ignored during the execution of this grim tradition.

Only after a long, torturous beating did both of their suffering come to a stop. In the end, the two of them had been accepted based on their tenacity to take a beating. Given a chance, they would have taken another path. Unfortunately, joining a gang was the only choice they had left back then.

That being said, both Alexander and his sister wished to see the same happen to the young boy they had just met. They considered this their chance to vent the grudges that were formed earlier that night.

Almost like he was capable of reading their thoughts, Amro turned to look at the pair of teenagers, giving them an innocent smile. His nonchalant attitude caused a chill to creep down both of their backs. *How was he able to remain so calm?*

Turning back, Amro continued walking towards the ring. While he did that, the two unconscious and beaten up children from before were being removed from the stage.

With a swift leap, the former God of Death entered the fighting stage. He took a look around, evaluating what his surroundings were like. Despite being made rather crudely, the ring he was standing on could probably withstand the usual power of several unranked fighters. It seemed these hoodlums had paid a great amount of effort to build something like this.

Seeing the smooth moves of this new candidate caused a smile to appear on Slyfox's face. At the very least, the newcomer seemed to have some talent. This was a cause for joy for him because of several reasons.

Those with talent usually had enough pride to match it. Eventually, that pride needed to be beaten out of their bones. That's where this initiation test came to play; over the years, it had proven to be a great way to make even the toughest of criminals submit to other people's superiority.

Slyfox turned to look to his officers. Any one of them would surely be enough to deal with the kid planning to join their ranks. The gap in skill brought by age and experience would guarantee a significant difference in their strength. With an advantage like this, he could start breaking away the boy's spirit, taming him into a loyal subordinate before he grew further.

"Rat! You go in," he instructed.

A burly man with several scars on his arms stood up and stepped into the ring without hesitation. Amongst Slyfox's men, he was a particularly sadistic individual who enjoyed the process of beating recruits into submission. When he looked at Amro, he couldn't help but break into a cruel smile.

Amro waited for 'Rat' to be done examining him with his eyes. Before long, the burly thug started taunting him into making the first move.

"Come on boy, let me have a taste of your courage."

Rat enjoyed seeing the despair on the faces of the new recruits as they realized the difference in their power. Giving them the initiative was just a way to bring that situation to fruition. His taunts grew increasingly humiliating until Amro started walking in his direction.

Alexander and his sister had a bad premonition. This was exactly the same attitude Amro had moments before knocking them down. Each step he took looked full of confidence as if there wasn't a single doubt about his victory.

Amro was happy to entertain these hoodlums. The fight with the mercenaries hadn't been enough for him to get a handle of this body's limitations and he still wanted to try a few other things. He kept approaching Rat calmly even as the man taunted him with his own brand of creative and obscene gestures.

Slyfox frowned. The rookie's nonchalance made it obvious just how arrogant the boy was. He might need to beat him to near-death if he kept the act up. Pride was of no use in an underling. Tilting to his side, he whispered to another one of his subordinates, "Make sure to step in before he dies. You know Rat has a problem stopping himself."

Everyone's gaze had landed on Amro's calm, rhythmic steps as he walked closer to Rat. The way he moved seemed ordinary, yet there was still something unique about it, something everyone found hard to pinpoint. Before they realized it,

Amro was already in front of Rat, holding the wrist of the hand he'd used to taunt him only moments ago.

Crack.

The next thing everyone heard was the sound of bones being fractured. It took a couple of seconds for even Rat's brain to process what had just happened. The moment he did, he screamed in both anger and pain, using his other hand to throw a punch at Amro.

"Die!"

Amro bent his knees, lowering his center of gravity to easily dodge the inbound fist. Before the observers could make sense of the situation, he had already used his momentum to bounce back up, sweeping Rat off his feet. The sudden loss of balance was enough for the hoodlum to fall to the ground. With a light step onto Rat's ankle, another scream soon filled the room.

The crowd stared in silent disbelief. Even if Rat was still an unranked individual, he was considered someone experienced in dogfights. How could a simple child knock him down?

Even Slyfox's eyes shone in surprise. At this time, he knew he had found a rough gem. The desire to make this child his subordinate, one way or another, surfaced in his mind.

Amro, however, had different plans. "That was far too boring. Does anyone else dare to make it more entertaining for me?"

CHAPTER 10

Taking over.

Like a cascade of dominoes falling one after another, groups mouths turned agape at the boy's undisputable win. Not one of the observers wanted to believe a young child had been able to take down one of their gang's leaders. Rat's grunts and screams, however, served a grim reminder that this was their reality.

Amro stood nonchalant and unimpressed. His expressionless face enhanced his aura of arrogance, further evidenced by having his boot over Rat's back. Their current positions looked like a mocking parody of a small stone sitting beside an imposing mountain.

It took Slyfox's thunderous laughter to break the silence permeating the room. "Yes! That is exactly how a man is supposed to be! Facing all challenges with no cowardice, ready to face the world! I like the way you fight, boy."

The opportunity of taking in such a subordinate made him excited about his gang's future. Unfortunately, it seemed like recruiting the boy would be a little harder than expected. None of his subordinates would be able to deal with him, nor did they possess the skill required to break his will. This was a task he had to take himself.

He stood up and signaled a middle-aged man to take Rat away from the ring. There was no use for someone who was turned into a cripple in his gang. That being said, Slyfox approached the ring himself. It was his turn to break some bones.

His decision to take the next fight for himself made surprise appear on everyone's faces. It wasn't very often that they saw their boss take the initiative to fight with someone. They could still remember the macabre results from the last time he did.

Yet, seeing the prideful boy standing atop the ring, Slyfox had no choice but to step in himself. Only by showing this newcomer a true difference in power would the hierarchy of his gang be reinforced.

With a swift move, Slyfox entered the ring. His actions were fluid and calm, calling attention to his physique's nimbleness. He was leisurely enough to flash his subordinates a charming and devious smile as he embraced their attention. Even the flaxen hair on his head displayed an equal amount of grace as it followed his moves. The man had no qualms about behaving just as arrogantly as the child he was about to face.

Amro mentally rolled his eyes. The narcissism of the man before him could rival that of the Goddess of Love. In his opinion, attention should be used as a medium to satisfy one's goals, not vanity.

"I take it you're my next challenger?" said Amro. "This should be easy."

How long had it been since Slyfox faced such disregard? Even as a young boy, people had treated him with respect. Nowadays, even the stuck-up nobles from the eastern side of the town treated him amicably. Only one truth held supreme everywhere in the world: strength.

It took a moment before he resumed his nonchalant expression. He reminded himself not to take the child's words too seriously. After all, the chance to beat some respect into the boy's bones was already his.

Thus, he took a long breath before he answered Amro with renewed control. "Indeed, I'm quite intrigued by your capabilities. Therefore, I've decided to be the next challenger. Of course, I don't intend to bully you. If you're afraid, I'll give you the chance to walk out now."

Amro smiled wryly. He could understand the thought processes of both saints and demons. How could he not see through Slyfox's small scheme?

"Don't worry about me," Amro answered. "However, I seem to recall that I can take the position of whoever I beat in this challenge. Does this mean that if I defeat you, I'll take control over the whole gang?"

Gasps of surprise came about and Slyfox's smile slipped away. Of course, he understood the implications behind Amro's words. The frown on his face could only grow deeper as he realized that even his subordinates had caught the blatant insult.

The hoodlums felt the temperature in the room plummet by several degrees. It was one thing to act arrogantly, but another to act disrespectfully. They felt the boy was taking it too far by challenging their leader's prestige.

Even Slyfox was finding it hard to remain calm now. No matter how much he desired a strong and capable subordinate, he wasn't willing to have someone as treacherous as Amro in his ranks. The cons of having to control such a difficult subordinate had begun to outweigh the pros.

He started forming alternatives as new options crawled through his mind. One in particular shifted his view on the situation. There was a demand for talent. So much, in fact, that buyers from all kinds of markets would be willing to pay generously for it. The slavers' money was as good as anybody else's.

"That is, of course, if you win," replied Slyfox, breaking the frigid silence that had flooded the room. His words seemed to take a load off of everyone's shoulders. After all, a leader's composure influenced the mood of his subordinates. "Still, I don't believe you will be able to."

Amro took a quick glance at Slyfox's body and nodded to himself in understanding. He was aware of his opponent's strength; it represented nothing but a small risk. Slyfox was someone who had tempered his body, stronger than the average man. Much like the man leading the mercenaries he had faced before, Slyfox was someone who had already entered rank one.

"Regardless," said Slyfox, "I don't see a point in prolonging this conversation. Let me see where your confidence stems from."

Slyfox was the first to make a move. Cordiality was nothing but foolishness in a fight, nor was it something in line with the values of the slums' residents. He approached Amro with coordinated steps, a tinge of bloodlust in his eyes.

"I'm different from my subordinates," said Slyfox, throwing punches in a rhythmical, disciplined manner. "I was part of the mercenary guild, you can't compare my moves to theirs."

Despite Slyfox's words, however, Amro dodged all his punches with ease. Slyfox's skills were still far behind that of the captain he had fought in Zaros's village. Despite sharing the same rank, the man's skills were in no way comparable to those of a systematically trained soldier. With nothing to worry, Amro began making use of the fight as an opportunity to perfect his control over Zaros's body.

"Is that all you got?" asked Amro, taunting his opponent. "Quick feet are no way to back such a bold tongue."

Slyfox grew frustrated with every punch that Amro dodged. The anger he felt drove him to increase the intensity of his attacks. He even tried mixing feints into them, throwing kicks while relying on his superior reach to exert pressure.

To the ignorant onlookers, however, the fight appeared to be very one-sided. Many of Slyfox's subordinates breathed sighs of relief as the boy seemed completely unable to attack. None of them were smart enough to look at Amro's nonchalant face and the ease of his movements. The pragmatism behind his moves was considered a lack of skill by those thugs who were used to flashy footwork, violent punches, and overly complicated kicks.

Amro, however, was about to prove them wrong. He channeled a strand of mana into his feet, using them to side-step a kick from Slyfox. Using the opening created by evading Slyfox's move, he closed in, ready to act on this opportunity.

With his leg still extended, Slyfox's eyes grew wide. He tried to recall his limb to move backwards. However, before he was able to do so, Amro circled his left arm around it.

"Got you."

Having Slyfox's leg caught in his arm, Amro used his right elbow to drop all his weight onto the leg's femur. A very brief cracking noise reverberated across the room, weighing on everyone's minds.

"Damn it."

Slyfox quickly twisted his hips, using the force of the rotation to kick Amro with his other leg. Unfortunately for him, the damage was already done. He had evaded the second hit, but there was no way for him to recover use of his leg during the fight.

Amro couldn't help but frown. His last move should have cracked Slyfox's femur. However, instead of displaying his pain, Slyfox had released a slight breath filled with killing intent instead. There was something wrong about the man's current state.

Even though Amro knew he could have employed a more deadly technique, he still decided against it. Not only was it more taxing on Zaros's body, it also carried the risk of garnering him the hate of those around him. Taking control of the gang was his priority, not killing the man before him.

Provided that his host had been just a little stronger, the fight would have been considerably easier to settle. Sadly, that was not the case. Helping him advance through the threshold of rank one was still on his 'to-do' list.

On the other side of the ring, Slyfox stood with a stoic face. The pain he felt in his leg was excruciating, but not enough to stop him for the moment. He had greatly underestimated the child before him. The only reason he was able to hold on right now was because of the recreational drugs he had ingested before the fight.

Something else scared him, though. For just a brief moment, he felt mana fluctuations in his last exchange with the boy. If his earlier guess was right, then he was up for a treat.

Mana was an unbridled force of nature. With great training, those at rank one were able to use it to strengthen themselves. Being from the slums, however, he wasn't able to do anything but occasionally feel it. He lacked the training required to do more.

No, it must be my mind playing tricks on me, he thought, rationalizing his situation. *I shouldn't have mixed elf-weed with alcohol.*

If the boy before him had learned how to use mana instinctively, his value was far from what he could control. Be it as a subordinate or as a slave, the future prospects of someone who managed to use mana without training were not something a rank one like him could deal with.

As the staring contest between Amro and Slyfox continued, those at the sides rubbed their eyes in disbelief. This boy had managed to injure their leader! What circumstances could have given birth to such a monster?

Alexander and his sister were drenched in cold sweat. The amount of regret they felt at trying to rob this monster rose exponentially after each of his actions tonight. Drops of fear trickled down their foreheads as they wondered how they could apologize to the small monster; the possibility of him losing was already gone from their minds.

Eventually, they witnessed as Amro broke the standoff by rushing towards Slyfox. He expertly controlled what little mana he could put into his host's feet to ensure he received no damage from straining his muscles.

Slyfox frowned and took a defensive pose. Provided that he could endure the pain from his leg, he was sure he could find a chance to counter-attack. An opportunity like that was his best chance at victory.

This time, however, Amro smiled deviously. When he was but a small jump away from Slyfox, he shifted into another set of footwork. It suddenly became harder for all the onlookers to predict where he was going to move.

This footwork was the legacy of an age-long warrior who had served him in the past. Even if his current body could not sustain the more complicated moves from this skill, he had no trouble using the basics of the footwork to defeat someone of Slyfox's strength.

Unable to change his stance, Slyfox raised his arms to block Amro's incoming fist. The kid carried strength disproportionate to his frame and age, so taking the blow with his body was not an option.

Yet contrary to Slyfox's expectations, the fist never connected. Amro's complex footwork made it seem like he would be striking him head-on, but he had decided to strike Slyfox's back instead. Underhanded methods were not limited to those of the slums.

"Sleep well."

Amro placed his hand on Slyfox's back and held it there as he emitted mana from within. Successive waves of nature's essence stacked one over another, exponentially increasing the pressure exerted by such an attack.

To others, it only looked like Amro had slapped Slyfox's back, but to Slyfox, it felt like a mace of iron had crushed his spine. He fell to his knees, a mouthful of blood spurting out of his lips before his consciousness vanished into darkness. The waves of mana had stacked until he fainted, causing him to fall into a small pool of his own bodily fluids.

Amro smiled and looked at the room full of shocked people. Everyone gazed at him as if they were staring at a monster. The cute smile of his child-like face morphed into a demonic visage in their eyes. Most of them were frozen in shock, unable to do anything but stare at the surprising victor.

"We pledge our allegiance to the new boss!" Alexander and his sister fell to their knees, bowing their heads to the ground in Amro's direction. Only upon hearing their voice did everyone else wake up from their stupor.

They soon followed the teenagers' lead, kneeling in fear of the monstrous child before them. Strength reigned supreme in the slums. Thus, Amro's display of skill was enough for them to pledge their allegiance without a doubt.

With his strength, they were ready to usher in a new time of dominance and control. Even escaping the suppression of the nobles seemed like a possibility.

Amro smiled as he saw the looks of fear and awe on his new subordinates' faces. It made his goals that much easier to accomplish.

"Who here can help me collect a few materials?" he asked. This had been his intention in coming here ever since the beginning.

Those bandits who had shared a table with Slyfox previously were the first to rush in front of him and kneel as they offered their services. This made Amro smile. It was truly good to have followers at one's command. *How long,* he wondered, *How long would it be before he took back control of his church?*

CHAPTER 11

Pathfinding.

Z aros woke up in an unfamiliar room. His eyes widened when he looked around and found himself unable to recognize where he was. As far as he remembered, he went to sleep inside an empty alleyway. But now, he was somehow lying on a comfortable bed.

His thoughts grew increasingly confusing until Amro's voice clarified the situation.

"Finally awake?" asked the former god, ignoring Zaros's confusion. "Don't worry about your quarters; I did us a favor last night."

Pain flared through Zaros's body as he tried to stand up and retort to Armo's aloof comment. His bones ached and his muscles were sore enough to justify not getting out of bed for an entire day. Just what had Amro done last night?

Unfortunately, he had no way to know what Amro did with his body in his sleep. Not unless Amro told him just what had happened. For a moment, he felt wronged and slightly betrayed.

"I'm pretty sure it was well worth it both times," complained Amro, aware of Zaros's thoughts.

Zaros was about to ask Amro to explain in more detail when he heard a knock on the door to his room, something that was followed by a female voice.

"Boss Zaros, may I come in? I brought the things you requested last night."

Zaros blinked in confusion. Boss? He was no one's boss. Nothing made sense this morning except for one thing: Amro was to blame for everything.

This time, Amro felt wronged by Zaros finger-pointing. Did this kid not understand his efforts to simplify their lives? Feeling a bit petty, he made a mental note to increase the amount of training he had planned for his host in the future.

That being said, there was a more pressing situation for both of them. Amro had to quickly remind Zaros to deal with their visitor. "Don't leave her waiting, child, let her in."

We will have a serious talk later, Zaros thought. After a few seconds where he calmed himself down, he decided to answer the girl waiting outside.

"Please, come in."

A young girl, one who was only a few years older than Zaros, walked inside. She was the teenager who had tried to rob Amro the night before. Of course, Zaros had no way of knowing this.

Her brown hair swayed from side to side as her arms carried the items requested by Amro the night before. Seeing Zaros's gaze land on her, she couldn't help but blush. Zaros was still in bed so she couldn't help but misunderstand the situation.

Zaros continued to stare at the girl. She felt somehow familiar, but he had no idea why. It took a few seconds of staring at the books, maps, and bags on her hands before he finally snapped out of his daze.

"Please leave those on the ground," he said. Realizing he was still inside his bed, he quickly removed his covers and helped her with the baggage.

Afraid to insult her fearsome boss, the girl decided to place the things on the ground like she had been ordered her to. After she was done, she stood there, waiting for a new command. Without an order instructing her to do so, she wouldn't dare leave the room. The scene from the night before was still fresh in her mind.

What does she want now?

Zaros looked at her, clueless as to what was going inside the girl's mind. His face was filled with curiosity and innocence. Yet in the girl's eyes, this seemed like nothing but a ploy devised by a hungry wolf.

Sensing the weird and tense air around them, Amro decided to intervene. He wondered whether he should teach the boy about social cues later on as well.

"Boy, instruct her to leave. For now, we need some time to settle some matters of our own," Amro instructed.

"Thanks, you may leave for now. I'll call you if I need anything else," Zaros said to the girl, following Amro's advice. His voice was filled with gentleness, causing the girl to feel confused by his behavior.

The girl quickly bowed and left. For a brief moment, she felt the boy in front of her was a different person from the one she knew. He had been humble and polite, a big contrast to his arrogant and domineering behavior on the night before. Did her boss have a severe case of split personality disorder, or was he one of those playboys who acted domineering in other men's presence, hiding their subservient side for only women to see?

"What a strange girl," murmured Zaros.

As she closed the door, he sat down and shuffled through all the items on the ground. He could see books, maps, posters, and even some strange ingredients. Needless to say, Zaros was confused about what the purpose behind such items could be.

"Information is power, kid. I'm still not that familiar with this place. Things have changed too much with the passage of time. It's not like a country bumpkin like you could provide me the answers I need," clarified Amro.

Zaros rolled his eyes at Amro's backhanded insult before he took the map and spread it across the floor. His village hadn't had more than a few maps. They were stored in the village elder's home, and he had only seen them before because Alice had invited him over a couple of times.

This map was different from the ones he had seen, however. The details in the mountains and rivers took Zaros's breath away. He had no way to know that a map this detailed was an extremely expensive commodity. Only the wealthy or criminals who stole them had the fortune of possessing maps of this grade.

Through Zaros's eyes, Amro took in the information displayed on the map. They were currently in the border town of Sol. It could be said that this town was divided into five parts. The northern and southern areas hosted the commoners. The west, where they sat, held the slums. And the east had been reserved for the rich. The center of the city was described as an area existing for the sole purpose of trade, and it was managed by commoners, merchants and nobles alike. Given the level of detail pertaining to this city, it could be assumed that this map was drawn by a local.

South of them was the forest of Halt, something Amro had already known. And towards their north were a few towns and villages, all placed in between them and the capital city of Nyx. North of that was a mountain range blocking access to another territory. Unsurprisingly, the level of detail dwindled the further the map covered.

The kingdom seemed less developed to the west where only a few settlements were marked on the map. On the other hand, the east seemed to flourish with several rivers, trade routes, villages and even a couple of towns. The map even included a line marking the start of another kingdom towards the northeast of Nyx.

Zaros stared at the map, impressed by the size of his own kingdom. He understood little of cartography, but that didn't stop him from being shocked at the sheer amount of information contained within.

Amro wasn't sure if the information was accurate, but he currently had no other sources to depend on. At the very least, he was satisfied by Zaros's desire for knowledge. That was a good trait to have in a student.

Following Amro's instructions, Zaros opened several other maps. The information inside them differed slightly from one to another, but none of them contained as much details as the first. After a while, Amro was able to form a mental picture of surrounding areas. At the very least, he was sure they would be able to travel inside the kingdom of Nyx without getting lost.

Amro learned a few details regarding the identity of the groups in charge of the different areas of the kingdom. The power struggles signaled the decline of the kingdom, especially towards the north, where a conflict seemed to be happening. A group of rebel soldiers was backed by the surrounding towns and villages as they fought against the kingdom's royalty.

A few hypotheses slowly took shape in Amro's mind. *Perhaps the order to exterminate the southern villages was done in order to prevent an upheaval from the southern villages. Rather than fight two fronts at the same time, they opted to take preemptive measures. I wouldn't be surprised if this town was next on their purge-list.*

It's either that or the possibility that the forest villages were in the way of exploiting a resource they need. Regardless, the kingdom is currently unstable.

Eventually, Zaros closed the maps and tidied them up. Once he was done with them, he looked at the ingredients brought in by the girl.

"Take them out and smell them," said Amro. He wanted to check each one of the ingredients' quality through Zaros's senses.

"Why?"

"Don't ask, just do it."

The boy carefully took some of the herbs outside their bags, frowning at the scent some of them carried. A few of the ingredients smelled familiar. In particular, the presence of a plant often used by the village's hunters to create poison gave him a bad premonition.

Meanwhile, Amro took a mental note of the ingredients' quality. They were rather lacking, but it should suffice for what he had intended to do with them. While thinking about how he should process them in the best way possible, he decided to explain his current plan to Zaros.

"Kid," he said. "I'll be preparing a concoction to let you advance in rank. After you do so, I'll start training you in the use of both mana and aura." There were benefits to training the child inside his soul's domain, the amount of guidance he could cram per unit of time was just one of them.

"A potion?" asked Zaros. "Did you use to be an alchemist?"

"Not quite," answered Amro, unwilling to touch upon

the subject of his past. "Just know that you need to take this before I teach you how to use mana and aura."

"Why did we not practice them before? Why do we have to wait until after I advance in rank?" questioned Zaros. Amro's previous requests had involved throwing him into painful situations back in the forest. Even if he had witnessed their results, he had grown skeptical about them.

"A mortal's body is weak by nature," explained Amro. "They're unable to handle powers like mana and aura without a unique constitution. Unfortunately for us, your physique is as common as a river rock."

"Moreover," said Amro, "your current body is heavily burdened whenever I decide to use my skills. I need to get that out of my way."

Zaros frowned. He was only a child, but he was already able to hunt forest beasts. This was especially true after he went through Amro's last week of training. He questioned what kind of standards Amro had in mind when he kept calling him weak.

"Nevertheless, you need to grow stronger in order to accomplish your goals. Your heart will never be at peace if I keep doing all the hard work for you," said Amro, a tinge of complaint in his voice.

Zaros finally gave in. It was true; he had requested Amro to help him achieve power. It was only proper for him to believe in Amro's methods now that his mentor offered him a way to solve his plight.

"Okay, what do you need me to do then?" asked Zaros.

"Let me take over, I'll prepare the items first," Amro replied.

❈ ❈ ❈

On the building's lower floors, a girl sat down to eat with her brother. It was Alexander's younger sister, Maria. Sensing her arrival, her older brother turned to look at her, surprised by how quick she had returned.

"I thought you went to the boss's room to give him some food?"

She looked at him with a dejected expression. The tray of food she had prepared was supposed to be a token to ease whatever grudges their boss might still have towards them. She didn't want their future to be destroyed because of a single mistake. Without the gang backing the two, both of them would become victims to the ire of many whom they had offended before.

"Maria," said a feeble voice. "Is there any chance I can eat that?"

The girl turned to look at another child from the gang. His pitiful expression combined with the grime on his face cracked her heart. It wasn't strange to see children starve; even those working under gangs didn't get to eat as much as they should.

"Here you go, Jake," she said, extending the food in his direction. A soft smile blossomed on her face as she saw the boy wolf down the meal. "Don't forget to pay me back later."

Most children inside the gang shared no blood relations. Blood, however, held little meaning to a family of misfits. Noble's children betraying each other under their quest for wealth was enough to evidence the nature of the red covenant.

Alexander took a look at the kid and sighed. He wondered whether the heavens truly had eyes. The gentleness his sister displayed to others, despite the roughness the world had treated her with, was enough for him to believe there was no justice left in the world. He knew that unlike him, she just went along with the whole criminal charade. It was her way to cope with their reality.

"So?" he asked. "What happened when you were delivering our new boss his lunch?"

"It seemed like he was talking to someone," she said. "I didn't want to interrupt because it could end up making things worse for us."

Alexander nodded in approval. A wise choice indeed. Were it not for his sister's hot temperament and her insecurities, she would probably strike it rich with her smarts. Last night's events proved to be a prime example. Maria's plan to mug a young boy had resulted in unforeseen consequences, ones that had led them to their current problem.

Alexander couldn't help but shiver as the boy's devilish smirk drifted back into his mind. He wanted to dispel any misunderstandings between their new boss and them as soon as possible. He wasn't willing to wake up dead because of a small grievance.

"Perhaps you can try again in a few hours?" he asked.

Maria nodded. She agreed with her brother's plan.

Only then did she and Alexander turn to look at their new visitor. He was already done devouring the food, a rare look of extreme satisfaction on his face.

"Sister, you have to treat me to a meal like this again sometime soon," said the innocent child, rubbing his stomach before disappearing. He clearly had no intentions of paying for the meal.

Maria sighed. It seemed like there would be no choice but to buy some more food with what little money she still had left.

"Is there no chance you can chip in?" she asked her older brother.

Alexander sighed, he still hadn't fulfilled this week's quota. As much as he wanted to chip in for this, he didn't have any money to do so.

"I'm sorry. I'll pay you back in the future," he said, uncertain of his own ability to do so. He had no way to know whether the quotas would even remain the same under their new leader.

The duo stood and left the room. They now had to buy and prepare another meal before the sun rose to its fullest. A long day was ahead of them.

CHAPTER 12

Poison is the best medicine.

Inside Zaros's new room, Amro was ready to advance to the next stage of their project. With Zaros's agreement, Amro took over the boy's body. It was necessary for him to be in charge if they were to process the ingredients correctly.

The transition felt strange for Zaros, much like entering a lucid dream. Unlike previous times, he was conscious during the switch. It felt like he was a prisoner within his own body. He could feel, see, and sense everything Amro could, but he had no control over his actions.

"This feels so strange," muttered the boy, now a consciousness floating in an infinite expanse of darkness.

"Tell me about it," complained his partner. Amro was now rotating his shoulders in an attempt to get used to the boy's limited range of motion. Despite taking control of the boy's body many times before, Amro couldn't help but always feel constrained by a mortal's limitations. It was a strange sensation to say the least.

When he was done acclimatizing, the fallen death god went over the ingredients. The first step in the road to power consisted of training the body to a point where it would crave additional sources of energy. Mana and aura usually fulfilled this role.

However, the average human would never temper their body enough to achieve this transition. Only those who experienced unimaginable danger would be able to stimulate their potential to that point.

Artificially inducing this experience was an even harder task. Plans like Amro's required knowledge in the art of alchemy, as well as reagents the average commoner would never be able to afford.

The foul-smelling ingredients were slowly processed by Amro. Some herbs were crushed into paste whilst others were ground into dust. While these plants carried slight imperfections, Amro ensured his own work held none. Every action of his was refined and full of confidence. He held no tolerance towards mistakes.

The concoction slowly took shape. With it, Amro planned to induce the boy into a life-endangering state. One so lethal yet so carefully controlled that it would leave Zaros's body no choice but to rely on mana or aura for survival. Thus, his body's potential would be forcefully awakened.

Of course, none of this information was disclosed to Zaros. Who in their right mind would endure so much pain willingly? Not even Amro could save the boy from this experience. Taking control of Zaros's body while he was advancing could cause the boy's body and soul to fall out of synchrony. It couldn't be helped. Sacrifices were to be made in order to reach their goals.

In that way, Amro continued processing the herbs. He paid no mind to the passage of time, only to the mix before him. The resulting substance carried a tinge of green and mottles of brown. The stench it gave off reminded Amro of the fragrance that accompanied death and decay.

"Boy, cover your body with this," he ordered. "Under no conditions are you to wash it off mid-way. You are to remain covered in this thing until I instruct you otherwise. Understood?"

His voice was strict, yet caring. The risk of Amro's method was that it didn't allow half measures. If Zaros removed the paste before it achieved its purpose, then he would be welcoming death.

"Very well," said Zaros, voicing his understanding.

For the first time in their relationship, he was able to experience how it was for Amro. As a passive observer, he had been bored out of his mind during the past few minutes. He could finally comprehend why the self-proclaimed master of death made conversation with him about every small thing under the sun. Amro must have been both bored and lonely.

"So, I just have to apply the paste evenly across my body?" he asked, confirming the instructions one last time.

"Indeed, make sure to cover your body with as much of it as possible. Don't let a single drop go to waste," Amro answered.

With those instructions out of the way, Amro and Zaros once again swapped control. The boy felt a temporarily dizziness as his senses flooded him with information about the environment. His pupils dilated and his muscles contracted. Enduring the dissonance generated by exchanging one's soul and body was not as easy as Amro made it seem.

After regaining his sense of balance, Zaros stood up and locked his door, making sure no one would stumble upon him. He took off his clothes and started applying the paste all over it. A sensation that felt both burning hot and icy cold battled to claim rights to the skin beneath the paste. The feeling grew increasingly intense over time, slowly becoming painful.

"Remember, not to wash it off."

Amro's words echoed in Zaros's mind. He couldn't quit unless instructed otherwise. He ignored the strange sensation, lathering the paste on heavily all over his body. He was about to place the bowl down when Amro's voice put a stop to his actions.

"The eyes," he said, a hidden trace of mockery in his voice.

"Do I really have to cover my eyes?" asked Zaros, clearly hesitant to follow through.

"Of course, it would be a waste not to."

Feeling nothing but changes in his body's temperature, Zaros followed Amro's instructions one more time. One part skeptical and one part reluctant, he applied the paste into his eyes as well.

"Now, drink the remainder," said Amro, saving the best for last.

With no intent to argue, Zaros drank the remaining bits of the foul-smelling substance and placed down the bowl. He felt the urge to gag but held himself back. No amount of water would be able to wash the taste he had just experienced.

Amro sighed at the innocence of the child before him. He completely lacked the cynicism to think twice about following an order blindly. As a reward, he decided to offer some words for the boy to anchor himself to in the moments that would soon arrive.

"Remember, we're doing this for our revenge, because you need to grow stronger. Endure the pain that is to come and focus on my voice as you do so."

"Of course, I know that," said Zaros, interrupting him. Amro's nagging seemed to grow stronger with every day. He was about to tell the god to be a bit more trusting when a searing wave of pain struck his chest.

Following the lead of the first reaction, the heat of his body continued rising exponentially. The feeling slowly grew overwhelming. A pain akin to glowing red needles piercing his body caused Zaros to fall to his hands and knees.

Zaros grunted in pain, unwilling to succumb to his own weakness. He was so focused on remaining conscious that the notion of removing the paste from his body didn't even cross his mind. As he endured the pain, Zaros felt like cursing Amro. However, he soon found that he was no longer able to speak. He didn't have enough air left in his lungs to do so.

Pain turned into despair. Despair turned into anger. Why did Amro omit telling him about this? Did he consider him that much of a coward? His anger slowly proved to be as good as a bath in cold water. Every curse he sent Amro's way alleviated him from the pain in the same way a drop of rain healed the desert.

Amro felt slightly wronged by Zaros's coping mechanism. Every curse the boy sent his way turned into a new idea to be incorporated into their training schedule. Perhaps reliving this experience inside his soul domain would help his host increase his tolerance to pain.

Sadistic as he was, however, Amro's plans would have to wait. Zaros's body was finally experiencing the desired changes.

The walls that separated humans from the world's energy started to collapse. Every part of Zaros's flesh craved nourishing, something strong enough to grant them salvation from the poison. Even at the cellular level, his body knew it needed something to pass this tribulation. It was exactly the catalyst Amro was waiting for.

I guess I can continue planning tonight's training session after this.

Resigning himself to the task at hand, Amro influenced the mana in the surroundings to approach Zaros. Using his soul as a medium, he wove string after string of mana, guiding them to coil around Zaros's pores like snakes charmed by music. Eventually, they circled every inch of the boy's body without leaving any spot behind.

Instinctively, Zaros's pores opened up to their touch. The strings of mana gladly entered Zaros's skin under Amro's guidance, joining forces with his cells in order to fight off the poison. At the same time, a refreshing sensation emerged from within the boy's body. An inner energy coalesced to fight the poison he'd drank – Aura.

This was Amro's plan. With his homemade concoction, he would both awaken both Zaros's aura and affinity to mana. This painful method ensured the child awakened the best potential his body could offer.

The poison and the two forces inside Zaros's body fought each other. Amro had intended for the poison to leave behind a solid foundation. Thus, the poison would flare until Zaros's body could finally assimilate the mana and aura to their fullest potential.

I'll return this pain to you someday.

Curses and insults went through Zaros's mind as he dealt with Amro's plan. His anger against his partner was what held him awake through the pain until it eventually subsided. Zaros's body had finally adapted to the new sources of strength, giving him the ability to fight off the invading poison.

The changes were now set. However, unlike the youth's expectations, he didn't feel much different. The only thing he noticed was a refreshing feeling caressing his skin. It reminded him of being submerged in a cold river after a day of hunting. His body felt soothed by it as if it now had something else to rely on.

Amro had waited for Zaros's anger to subside. Only until he'd finally run out of complaints did he decide to speak. "These sensations you currently feel are the power systems governing this world: mana and aura. The latter strengthens you from within, allowing your body to accomplish feats impossible to other humans. The former allows you to influence the natural phenomena surrounding you, orchestrating the world and its creatures to follow your will."

Zaros was taken by surprise. He had heard of mana once before from the traveling merchants. It was rumored that those mages from the mainland used it to acquire great power. Through it, they were strong enough to shake mountains and displace rivers, it was a power that could alter the course of nature itself. The thought of controlling such a thing had never crossed his mind before.

However, unlike mana, the concept of aura was new to him. Zaros was trying to understand the concept when Amro continued his explanation.

"You have an advantage now, boy. Most people who reach rank one only open the possibility to enrich themselves with these powers. But in your case, your body has already assimilated them. This will let you accommodate more time for training in other things."

Zaros nodded in a half-hearted manner. He understood only part of what Amro had told him, but the overall message was that the pain he suffered had been worth something. He was just about to dress and continue his conversation with Amro when a knock on the door called for his attention.

"Boss Zaros, I've brought some food. May I come in?" asked a familiar feminine voice from outside the door. It was Maria, the young brown-haired girl who'd brought Amro's parcel earlier that day.

Zaros sighed. He would have to put off his conversation with Amro until later. For the time being, his growling stomach was far more important than his partner.

Zaros pulled the door open just in time to see the girl straighten her back and bow. The slight display of obedience was not something he could easily get accustomed to.

"Please, don't be so polite," he told her.

Once the girl raised her head, Zaros could see a small blush on her face. In his rush to open the door, he hadn't put on anything aside from his underwear.

"Sorry," she mumbled, passing the tray of food into her boss's hands. "Is there any other way I can be of service?"

"Not really," said Zaros, ignorant of the implications behind her earlier question. "Thanks for the food."

Maria smiled slightly, turning her back and leaving her boss to his own devices. As she made her way back to the lower floors, she tried recalling the faint smell from inside the room. It reminded her of the apothecary shop in the central part of town.

Remembering how her boss had requested a series of herbs the day before, she couldn't help but conclude that he was also well-versed in the art of alchemy. Her eyes brightened as that belief gained strength in her heart. There were few things as useful to her right now as learning about her boss.

CHAPTER 13

A treacherous plan.

A resentful Slyfox sat down in a small church on the eastern side of Sol. Even if his businesses ventures belonged to the darker side of town, he'd accrued enough wealth to receive medical attention from the church. Institutions like this would only care about someone's background on the surface; the truth was that wealth reigned supreme for mortals. With enough wealth in your pockets, background could often be overlooked.

Despite his incoming treatment, rage consumed Slyfox's. After last night's defeat, he had chosen to leave the gang's base in a fit of anger. His defeat may not have stung as bad if he hadn't been replaced. His once loyal underlings had bowed down to a child.

What made it worse was that the actions of his subordinates couldn't even be considered a betrayal. Their loyalty was only to one thing: strength. Knowing that made him burn with far more anger, for he could not accept his own weakness.

Over the years, he had grown accustomed to the authority that came from power. His only wish right now was to get revenge on that demonic child in order to recover the organization he had built from the ground up. He could have submitted and become another subordinate to the boy. His pride, however, would never allow for such a thing.

Several plans went through Slyfox's mind. Of course, holding a one-on-one battle was out of the question. Even if Slyfox was prideful, he was not stupid. The child had already proven to be above him in terms of combat ability. Thus, only one option remained: using a hired blade to deal with his opponent.

However, that was easier said than done. Hiring a mercenary was not an option. Rank two mercenaries were both rare and costly, and no rank one mercenary would be willing to take the task. This was also not something he could afford after the church's costly treatment. For some reason unknown to him, many small churches had started raising their fees recently, making the treatment of wounds with holy magic a luxury not many could afford.

So, where could he find someone to deal with the newcomer? Someone who would not involve him, someone who would not require too much of a payment. His mind pondered over it until only one option was left — the nobles.

He would have to convince them that it was in their best interests to stop the child's growth. The best way to do this was to entice them with a mix of potential benefits and dangers.

He could tell them about the child's potential, but he feared that would instead make them greedy to recruit the boy under their own banner. He needed them to believe the child was more of an immediate threat to them. *How should I approach this situation?* he wondered.

Suddenly, an idea then popped into his head. *Would it be possible to make the nobles believe the child was an envoy from the rebel forces, sent to start a new campaign in the south?* It wasn't unheard of to use a child as a long-term infiltration plan inside enemy forces. It was a long shot, but the paranoia currently held by the ruling classes was on his side.

With time, the appeal of the idea started growing on Slyfox. He could let the information flow naturally if he used some of his old contacts. Even if he had his place as the leader of the gang taken away, he still had the power to maintain a healthy network of people that could be of use to him.

The nobles would grow afraid once this rumor spread. Just what had happened to the nobles in the north shortly after the rebellion started? Most of them were hanged, their possessions taken away and redistributed amongst the common folk. The fear of losing their power would scare them into action. They wouldn't hesitate to act. Provided that they did, Slyfox could use the chance to swoop in and recover what was rightfully his.

He wasn't afraid of the gang disbanding or losing members. Slyfox was sure that once he took back control, he could calm the nobles into backing off. In the end, the nobility still required the underworld to accomplish certain tasks for them.

As he sat down, adding more elements to his plan, a priest entered the room. Seeing Slyfox sitting down in such a lethargic state made the priest curious. Just who could have made the leader of the biggest gang in the slums end up requesting help from the church?

"So, what brought you here?" asked the priest.

Slyfox stared at the cleric without answering before he took off his shirt, displaying his back. The shape of a palm the size of a child's was violently marked on it. It looked like he had been slapped really hard by a brute with really small hands.

However, the priest was not foolish enough to think

someone would spend so much money treating a simple slap, much less the man before him.

With two parts curiosity and one part carefulness, the priest approached Slyfox. He placed his hand on the hoodlum's back, carefully touching around the wound. His face soon crumpled up as he sensed a mana different from Slyfox's imprinted on the palm-shaped mark. It felt ancient and deadly, yet restrained and lacking. Much like the dregs of a deadly poison that had failed to meet a lethal-dose.

Unfortunately, it didn't end there. Slyfox's body seemed to have been invaded by this foreign mana. The priest frowned as he pondered whether he should risk offending the owner of this skill just to earn some money. Even more so when he recalled a rumor stating that Slyfox might have been replaced by his gang the night before.

Coming to a compromise with himself, the priest decided to offer a treatment that wouldn't require too much of his intervention. He took a vial filled with water and splashed it over Slyfox's wound, before handing another vial to him. A sizzling sound filled the air as Slyfox felt something akin to boiling water burning his back. His face contorted at the painful sensation, but his anger helped him suppress any displays of weakness.

His calm demeanor changed, however, once he saw the vial and recognized what it was filled with. "Holy water, is that it? Do you seriously think a couple vials of holy water are worth this much?"

"It's more than enough to deal with a wound like yours," the priest answered. "You know the church doesn't like to meddle in the conflicts of exemplary humans."

But you sure like taking my money, don't you? thought Slyfox as he looked at the vial. He was aware the church had recently changed the way they handled their business, but he hadn't thought they would have become so stingy.

Unfortunately for him, he had no option but to take the humiliation in silence. He couldn't afford to make an enemy of the church by raising a complaint. Not at this time, anyway.

The priest frowned as he understood the disappointment behind Slyfox's expression. His church, related to the Goddess of the Harvest, had been experiencing hardships as of late. For some reason, their goddess had stopped answering their prayers, which would have made the entire church collapse if not for the intervention of major churches like the Church of Life.

To offer their usual healing services they had started to rely on the use of consumables, just like the holy water he had presented Slyfox moments ago. Of course, the cost at which they offered these services had increased as well. A much needed move to compensate for the change in their logistics.

Unfortunately for Slyfox, the priest now had two reasons to stay away from this issue. One of them was the mysterious character who had injured Slyfox. The other was the lack of resources his church had as of late. All in all, the old gang leader decided to leave it at that.

After feeling the holy water relieve some of his pain, Slyfox took his shirt and got up. Then, he left the room without saying goodbye to the priest.

The priest sighed in return. It was clear to see that the authority of his church had decreased. Even a hoodlum like Slyfox dared to assume that kind of attitude towards them. Without any other choice, he forced himself to take the payment left behind by Slyfox, putting this issue behind.

Ignorant to the priest's struggles, Slyfox made his way to a tavern in the center of the city. The central area of Sol housed the markets, a place where the rich and the poor were able to mingle. It represented the biggest interest of them all:

money.

As Slyfox took a seat, the bartender approached him and passed him a glass of ale.

"I heard the king lost his throne," said the bartender with a smug smirk. The news had already reached him. No place was better to gather information than one where people willingly spilled it while drunk.

Slyfox struggled to keep his composure. He needed this man's help if he wanted control to recover his authority. Frowning, he took a huge gulp of the ale placed before him. It was part of his plans to make it seem like he was spilling information. Drinking emotionally was a must.

"You must mean usurped," said Slyfox. "That guy has no claim to leading my gang. He's not from around here, and I even suspect he's an envoy from the north."

The bartender's eyes widened with interest. Half of his income came from selling alcohol, but the other half came from selling information. He readied another drink, passing it to Slyfox as he eagerly waited for the man to continue.

"From what I've gathered, he entered yesterday by the western gate," added Slyfox. "Don't you find it strange that the first thing he did was challenge the biggest gang in town?"

Slyfox finished his first drink and took the new one the bartender had prepared. He didn't mind getting a few free drinks while accomplishing his goal. "You know how much work I put into building the gang from the ground up? It was me who unified the entire slums!"

A few gazes turned Slyfox's way as whispers and murmurs started to dance around the tavern. Many recognized his face and were surprised to see his bandaged leg. Who could have done that to the mighty ruler of the slums?

Slyfox suppressed his anger. Taking back his title required taking a few hits to his reputation. The time for revenge would come once this entire ordeal was over.

His eyes move around the tavern, taking a mental note of each men and women whispering his name over their drinks. Very few of those who kept gossiping were even rank one, much less at the boundary between rank one and rank two like him.

The bartender noticed how Slyfox was becoming a bit rowdy, calling too much attention to their conversation. Obviously, he wanted to keep the information Slyfox could share to himself. If the one who defeated the man really turned out to be an envoy from the rebels, he could easily collect a significant bounty by reporting it to the nobles.

He signaled for one of his maids to service Slyfox and calm him down. A girl with an ample bosom approached the flaxen-haired thug and rested her chest on his back. Her intent was to distract him with her charms.

Slyfox momentarily frowned as the pain in his back resurfaced upon contact with the woman's bust. Unable to perceive her intentions, he leaned forward to remove the weight pressing down on him. His annoyed face was enough to tell the woman that she was dismissed.

"Brother Slyfox, how about you follow me to the VIP area? Even if you lose your gang, you're always welcome here," said the bartender in an attempt to recover the situation.

Slyfox nodded, accepting the bartender's offer. He slowly stood up and made his way upstairs to a more private space in the tavern. The bartender followed him, taking along a couple of drinks with the highest alcohol concentration he had available.

Only the maid was left behind, bitter about her services being rejected. Just like the bartender, she had misunderstood Slyfox's action and thought it had a deeper meaning. This bothered her as it would reflect badly on herself. She might even get fired if her boss deemed her responsible for any fallout with Slyfox.

"Tch, stupid eunuch."

Unaware to Slyfox, another rumor aside from the one he was starting would spread from that day onward. One that would make his efforts of chasing women considerably harder in the future.

CHAPTER 14

Refusing the status quo.

Zaros sat at a table with several members of Slyfox's old gang. The past few days had been hectic for him. Not only because Amro insisted on having him spend most of his time training, but also because meetings like this had become a common occurrence.

Even if Amro had displayed convincing fighting prowess while in Zaros's body, many residents of the slums refused to believe Slyfox's defeat. They thought some kind of conspiracy was afoot. This misinterpretation of the events brought Zaros no shortage of troubles.

Smaller gangs had gathered in rebellion to Zaros's new leadership, believing him to be an asset used by the nobles to control them. Because of that, they refused to pay their usual fees to the gang, causing the residents of the slums to worry about an incoming civil war. Reasonably so, given how increasingly challenging their interactions with the nobles were becoming.

Slyfox's old gang had a strong role in the hierarchy of the slums. They had coordinated crime in the city, managed tasks the guilds were unwilling to accept, and even offered protection to those who required it. The absence of their dominion had plunged everything into chaos.

The authority Slyfox once commanded had been built over the years. He had established alliances with the smaller powers in town and even with some circles of nobility; all of this had ensured a semblance of peace and stability to those who were residing in the slums. However, Slyfox's reign was no more.

Zaros had come to understand that his predecessor's methods, cruel as they were, had been the reason for the slums prolonged survival. Through them, the slums had a semblance of order. Had it not been for Slyfox and his gang, this side of the city might have already been demolished, with its past residents sold into slavery by a few of the noble houses.

The way of life in this town was very different from what Zaros had grown accustomed to in his small forest settlement. But that didn't matter. The problem was now on his hands. It was up to him to figure out a way to address it.

"You could just leave," suggested Amro, realizing his partner was still wasting time on this issue. "These slum-dwellers have already outlived their usefulness. What you need now is some real-life experience, not even my soul domain can make up for that."

"Don't you feel bad after taking advantage of them?" questioned Zaros. "They spent so much of their own money buying the herbs and maps we used. We surely can't leave them like this?"

Sure can, thought Amro. *I might just take care of them if you keep insisting.*

Over the course of the last week, Zaros had grown slightly attached to those from the slums. Initially, he had been shocked by Amro's plan. Taking control of a small criminal organization just to take their resources wasn't something in line with his character. Yet somehow, Amro had no qualms about pushing him into situations he wasn't comfortable with.

"Anyway," said Zaros. "Can someone bring me up to date with our situation?"

"Yes, boss," answered a burly man with bronze skin. He and his brother were part of Slyfox's old inner-circle, usually responsible for guarding the entrance of their hideout and handling communication with outsiders. "Our profits have plunged to half their usual amount. Those from the rival gangs have been blocking our avenues of trade with the nobles. If things keep going like this, we won't have enough money to feed ourselves in a few weeks."

The nobles yet again, thought Zaros. Ever since he came to this town, he had come to realize the importance such figures held for society. In the Kingdom of Nyx, nobles held control over the commoners' lives. In one way or another, all business had to go through them, leaving very few avenues for people to move vertically in the pyramid of power.

Nothing seemed able to escape the noble's grasp. It made Amro's theory of the noble's involvement in the King's plan to wipe his settlement that much more reasonably believable, giving rise to a blood-tinged hatred in Zaros's eyes.

"Can someone explain to me why we have to go through them again? Can't we just work with the guilds directly?"

"I'm afraid they wouldn't let that one go, boss," said another hoodlum sitting with them. "The guilds are controlled by the nobles. If we try to go around them, we will be making an enemy of them. Someone tried a few years ago, let's just say it didn't end well."

Despite Zaros's ignorance of how things worked in Sol, nobody dared to shun his authority. Over the past few days, a courageous few had tried. Unfortunately for them, Zaros's instincts had been polished by Amro's personal training, leaving him little room for restrained fighting methods. The luckiest amongst the bunch had ended with a broken arm and a few cracked ribs, granting Zaros a reputation for being ruthless.

Not that he was aware of it.

Zaros sighed, he was unable to come up with an answer to their dilemma. In part, he was to blame for their current situation. His arrival and Amro's meddling had shattered the balance of this town's ecosystem. A situation which was only worsened by his own inexperience.

"Does anyone have an idea?" asked Zaros. He was attempting to solve the issue with his subordinates' help. At the very least, he was willing to listen to others, given how much he had to learn when it came to managing an organization.

However, no one answered. Life in the slums was lived day by day, be it by charity, extortion, or risk. His subordinates still remembered the night he arrived vividly, and what could happen if he felt challenged. They still couldn't relate his amiable side to the ruthless fighter they had witnessed before. The screams from Rat as his bones were broken still echoed in their minds from time to time.

Even after a few seconds went by, Zaros kept staring at the group expectantly. Unfortunately, it didn't seem like the situation would change. Being left with no other option, he held back a sigh and turned to one of the men, pointing at him directly. "You, give me an idea."

The man stuttered, seemingly afraid to answer. "Boss, I really don't know, please ask someone else."

Zaros clamped down on his tongue to keep himself from criticizing the man's lack of spine. The way Amro told him the events from that night, they shouldn't be behaving in such a way. He couldn't help but wonder if Amro had understated the events of that night.

"Boss, can't we just have some more time to think it over?" asked one of the thugs.

"Yes, boss. It's not like we can come up with ideas overnight," said another one.

Zaros realized he might have been a tad too eager. If the hoodlums themselves weren't worried about the nobles taking action, then perhaps he shouldn't be either.

Taking their requests into account, he decided to dismiss them. "Okay. We'll continue this conversation later."

Not long after he voiced his permission, his subordinates ran off, leaving him alone. He felt rather frustrated over their attitudes. Back in his small village, honest work was the norm. Through collective efforts, everyone was taught how to survive by relying on their own abilities. Even someone like him without a family was able to manage, despite the hardships involved.

As to why such a different outlook existed in this 'civilized' town, he had no idea.

It wasn't like he didn't have issues of his own to solve. He still thought of his own revenge every night. That is, the nights when Amro wasn't pulling his consciousness inside his soul domain to train him. Becoming the gang's boss was only a temporary measure. One Amro had created for him to use and discard.

Knowing he couldn't hide forever in the mess hall, Zaros rose from his seat, ready to walk to the door. His internal clock was telling him it was about time for another training session with Amro, the very last thing he wanted to do right now.

"I need a break," Zaros said to himself.

"It doesn't seem like you're getting one anytime soon," said Amro. "Look."

Almost immediately, Alexander entered the room. He appeared disheveled, panting in an attempt to catch his breath, "Boss! The guards are here!"

Zaros returned to his seat, thinking about explaining to Alexander how useless the guards were in the slums. The lanky teenager should have been aware of that kind of information. They were a bunch of good-for-nothings who stole the food from unsuspecting citizens.

It was clear to see that he still held a grudge from his first day in the slums.

"The guards from the noble's district," clarified Alexander, noticing Zaros's increasingly distracted look. "They want to speak with you."

Oh.

Zaros thought about it for a second. He had recently learned the gang had some shady dealings with the nobles. It wasn't out of the ordinary for some of their representatives to come and check on things after a change in leadership.

"I see," said Zaros, realizing Alexander had not been speaking about the rabbit-stealing trash. "Please show them inside."

A minute later, Zaros focused his gaze onto the two men entering the room. One of them was comically tall while the other was as short as a dwarf. Both of them stood clad in metal armor, elaborate and stylish, unlike the uniform worn by the guards placed at the slums.

Zaros noticed their gait carried a hint of arrogance. They acted like the ground below their feet wasn't worthy to be stepped on by their boots. Of course, their apparent disdain was further confirmed by the looks of sheer contempt they sent Zaros's way.

"So, the rumors were true," remarked the willowy

guard. "I didn't expect them to be this accurate."

"Surprisingly so," noted his pint-sized partner. "I didn't expect Slyfox to be defeated by a runt."

Both guards broke into laughter, ignoring the irony behind their joke. Just like the other gangs in the slums, they seemed to believe Slyfox's defeat was a fluke. Their presence was probably intended to intimidate Zaros into lowering his head in obedience.

Of course, they were not planning to do so by making fun of him. They had come under their master's orders bearing serious business.

"Say, kid," added the shortest guard. "When are you planning on paying this month's quota?"

Zaros raised his left eyebrow. *Quota?*

"I take it by your expression that you're ignorant about it," said the tallest guard. He had the devious smile of a merchant, an expression Zaros knew only invited trouble. "You should know, your predecessor had a deal with us. A girl or two and a couple men every month, all in exchange for us looking the other way whenever you cause trouble in this city."

Zaros's expression changed into a frown. Were they speaking of slavery?

With disdain in his voice, the other guard continued, "You know, 'voluntary workers.' You pick them out for us and convince them it's in their best interest to do whatever we instruct them to."

Zaros's frown grew stronger as his suspicious were confirmed. Slyfox's deal probably consisted in offering a few people in exchange for everyone else's safety. Perhaps out of need, perhaps out of greed. He had no way to know. What he could tell, however, was that these guards were set on establishing the same deal with him.

"I want to speak about this deal with your boss," he said, gaining courage from his indignation. "I don't think this deal is convenient for my side. Perhaps, we can reach a new one."

A look of surprise appeared in both guard's eyes.

"The new cub has ambition," said the tallest guard, a smirk full of mockery on his face.

"Indeed, he thinks he's too good to deal with the goons and wants to speak directly to the boss," added the other.

"But, aren't we the ones who are too good to deal with him? Couldn't we just take whatever we wanted to anyway?" said the tallest one as he placed his right hand over his sword.

In Zaros's mind, the image of the guards seemed to overlap with the memory of the mercenaries assaulting his town. Their selfish nature and disregard for others further tarnished the image he had of nobles. He flinched only for a moment before regaining his bearing, his hands subconsciously covered by mana.

Fear slowly turned into hate, and hate turned into bloodlust. For a short moment, his gaze resembled that of a ruthless criminal, evoking a thirst for violence in disregard for his own safety. The missions Amro created inside his soul domain had done more than just allow him to use mana and a few fancy techniques. They had also slowly loosened his morals without his knowledge. As such, death didn't escape from being included in his list of options to deal with these guards should they choose to attack.

After seeing the boy's hands for a brief moment, the short guard placed his hand over his partner's shoulder and shook his head.

"The kid isn't worth it," he said, turning back to look

at Zaros. "We'll let our boss know of your decision. I just hope you'll be able to shoulder the consequences."

Without further discussion, both guards rose to their feet and left as fast as they had come in. Stomping with disdain.

Once outside, the tallest guard expressed his frustration. Displaying disagreement amongst themselves in the enemy's presence was never a wise thing to do. With indignation, he asked, "Why did you stop me, Seth?"

"Mata, that kid knows how to control mana," replied the short, stumpy guard. "It seems like the rumors might be true. We might even earn a bonus once we report this."

"Really?" Mata asked in disbelief.

The answer had taken him by surprise. He might have been a rank one fighter, but every time he managed to use mana was on instinct, not by his will. He found the idea of a child being on the same rank as him hard to believe.

"Yes, the boss will be really interested in this news. If that kid is really an envoy from those bastards up north, then there will soon be blood covering the streets."

"Does it have to be us that let him know about it? You know how the boss gets when he's mad," said Mata, scratching the back of his neck.

The short guard chuckled for a moment, answering only once he delivered a punch to Mata's right knee. "Don't worry, I have a plan to make the news easier for him to swallow."

Mata stared at Seth in an attempt to understand the meaning behind those words. Only after seeing the malicious smile plastered on his partner's face did he realize the plan Seth come up with. Soon, his lips began forming the same grin.

Having reached a tacit understanding, the guards

started patrolling the streets in search of a lucky 'volunteer' for their plan.

CHAPTER 15

A call to arms.

Sunlight shone on Zaros's face, waking the boy up from his sleep. Unfortunately, with the return of his consciousness, something else had surfaced. Pain. Cramps and discomforts that served to remind him that Amro's training wasn't limited to the soul domain.

Of course, that was only the physical side. Zaros couldn't ignore his mental exhaustion either. The constructs in Amro's soul domain had forced him to experience pain ten times worse than the one he lived through in reality. Because of this, Zaros had unconsciously improved beyond his normal learning speed, eager to avoid Amro's torturous lessons. Like that, Zaros had come to learn many techniques that would often be unknown to those of his rank.

According to what Zaros managed to grasp from Amro's explanations, rank one required adapting the user's body to energies like the ambient's mana or the soul's aura. Rank two, on the other hand, required the user to not only accept mana from the environment, but to be able to consciously become a source of it. Humans who achieved this point were usually few and far in between.

Amro had also mentioned something about those beyond the point of rank three, like how they managed to achieve a permanent state of body enhancements. However, Zaros's exhaustion made it a hard task to remember that much information. As far as he was concerned, mana or aura were tools at his disposal, and that's all he needed to know.

Of course, there were also differences amongst those of the same rank. That's why someone like the captain who led the mercenaries to invade Zaros's town and the old leader of the slums, Slyfox, could share the same rank, but still have such a disparity in strength. Not that it mattered to Amro.

Zaros was currently at rank one. He was capable of using the natural mana of the environment to cover some of his body at will, strengthening the effects his actions had over the natural world. However, he still found himself unable to do the same with aura. Fortunately, given Amro's little 'experiment', he could be considered at the threshold of rank two, as his body's inner forces had awakened once before already.

As things were, he needed just a little more time to solidify his foundations and gain full control over his own aura.

That being said, Amro was eager for more improvements. That way, when he decided to intervene and take control of Zaros's body, he would find himself less restricted. Amro needed Zaros to reach higher thresholds — his knowledge and mastery as a former god would become even more useful at that point.

Hopefully today's less exhausting, thought Zaros, rubbing his eyes and straightening his back. He had intended to get some information on the nobles that day. Given how one family of them had already approached him, he knew more would do soon after. The old merchant in his town often argued that calamities came one after the others.

Knock knock

Zaros knew his comfortable lifestyle so far was in part thanks to Amro's decisions. Selfish as he might be, he understood his partner cared about his well-being. That of others, however, he wasn't entirely sure.

Knock knock

Unfortunately, it wasn't time for that. His peaceful moments of introspection had come to an end. *So much for an uneventful day.*

Knock knock

Zaros stood up from his bed, stretching his arms and feet as the persistent knocking still echoed throughout the room. After yawning one last time and enjoying what would probably be the last seconds of peace in his day, he made his way to the door.

Without any rush, Zaros opened the door. He was intent on not having his mood soured by the persistent knocking. However, he came to regret it the moment he did.

Like a stray dog welcomed back to his home, Alexander tumbled through the doorway with haste in his steps. His eyes were red and his chest was heaving, displaying the shortness of his breath. It seemed like it truly wouldn't be a peaceful day.

At that moment, Zaros felt too tired to hide his emotions. His frown evidenced how displeased he was with his subordinate's attitude. What was he doing in his room, anyway? That duty belonged to Maria and her often lacking breakfasts.

"They took her!" Alexander cried, still trying to catch his breath. His words, however, didn't help his cause, which was made evident by the look of confusion on Zaros's face. Only after seeing the perplexed look on him did Alexander realize he had to be more detailed.

"The guards who came yesterday. They took my sister!"

he said, attempting to clarify.

Zaros's mind blanked for a moment, recalling the events from the day before. Amro's soul domain had the cumbersome effect of constantly messing with his sense of time. Eventually, he found himself able to recall the unpleasant folks he had met with, and more importantly, the words they left behind: "Be ready to shoulder the consequences."

Were these the consequences they spoke of?

"Please tell me what happened in more detail," Zaros requested. If it was anything like what he was thinking of, those guards had touched his bottom line.

"Yesterday, my sister and I were walking around during the night. We were collecting some money for our friends when those two guards blocked our way," said Alexander. "We weren't doing anything unlawful, I swear."

Highly unlikely, thought Amro.

Alexander took a long breath, calming himself down before continuing. "They started threatening us, telling us that our presence was making others uncomfortable in town. It was a clear abuse of authority, those bastards! They argued we had to pay a fee as punishment and threatened us into a corner. Since we couldn't pay, they said they would have to take something of an equivalent value from us."

Tears of frustration fell from the teen's reddened eyes. Zaros could already guess what he was going to say next.

"They took my sister," said Alexander, speaking his words with clear frustration. "According to them, selling her into slavery was enough to pay our fines. The gods know I tried to fight them off, but I wasn't able to. I was too weak and got beaten until I finally blacked out."

Zaros sighed, visibly frustrated. The rot of a society appeared not only amongst those of poor backgrounds, like the slums' residents. It also inhabited those who prided them-selves for being of higher birth. It was something he had come to learn during his past week in the slums.

"Do you have an idea where she might be then?" in-quired Zaros. If they truly intended to sell Maria as a slave, he was duty bound to save her. *Where did this sense of duty stem from?* he wondered. Now that he thought about it, alien thoughts were becoming increasingly frequent from time to time.

"When I woke up, I realized they must have taken her," answered Alexander. "My best bet is the slave pens they have under their state. Boss, help me save her! I'll do anything in return."

Alexander knew his request was mildly unreasonable. His boss had no responsibility to save him nor his sister from the consequences of their daily activities. The gang already did enough by shielding them from being directly targeted by other slum-dwellers.

He knew the guards would cause trouble for his boss if he decided to interfere. He even suspected this was somehow related to the discussion they held with his boss the other day. Unfortunately, he had no one else to rely on.

Zaros's fingers tapped the wall in a rhythmic manner as he processed Alexander's request. He knew the frustration one felt when they were unable to save those they care about. Was he really able to help the boy?

"It's a trap," said Amro. "Just in case you were foolish enough not to realize it."

"Clearly," said Zaros to himself. He could instinctively feel that was the case. The warning those guards had given him the day before was enough to make him realize this was related to their disagreement with him. It was unfortunate given how he had never intended to take over the gang. It had all been Amro's plan to begin with.

Even then, it wasn't something he was willing to ignore. He had also received benefits from Amro's plan. Fortunately for him, his finger-tapping served as the perfect cover for delaying his answer.

"I'll go," said Zaros to himself, hoping Amro was listening to his words. "Don't try to dissuade me from doing so."

Surprisingly, Amro didn't try to convince him otherwise. The former god knew conflict and danger could help his host's growth. Strong emotions often shook the body and soul in ways no training could. In fact, gloating him into participating was part of Amro's goals, one he hadn't expected to turn into reality by itself.

Zaros met Alexander's expectant gaze. He could tell from the look in those eyes that Maria meant everything to him. He had to help the brother and sister in some way, lest someone else had to live with a grudge of revenge in their hearts.

"Let's get her back," said Zaros. He would try his best not to let the past repeat itself.

Zaros saw Alexander's shoulders slump down. An enormous weight had been taken off of the teenager's back. In his eyes he saw expectation, and more importantly, hope. Alexander fell to his knees, venting all he had bottled up.

"Thank you, thank you so much!" The words seemed to stick in his throat from time to time. It was the first time someone had shown him so much generosity. Perhaps there were leaders that were worth following. Alexander believed Slyfox would have never agreed to help, not even if it was his own fault. It was then that Alexander discarded all feelings of fear he held towards Zaros.

All that remained was loyalty. Not to his strength, but

his character.

Zaros's felt pained when he saw Alexander's overboard reaction. It reminded him of himself from not too long ago. A man without strength could only endure the unfairness of the world unless he depended on others. Zaros hoped he could one day achieve his revenge with Amro's help, the same way he would help this boy achieve his after recovering his sister.

Zaros reached out his hand, helping Alexander up. The teenager was still crying, making it hard for Zaros to convey his 'first' order. With a slap, he brought Alexander back to his senses. After all, it wasn't the time to cry, it was time to fight.

"Summon everyone; it's time to get your sister back."

CHAPTER 16

Retaliation.

The sound of a marching crowd reverberated across the streets, dozens of men and women were marching in unison towards the same direction. The unexpected noise attracted the attention of those in the central area of Sol. Where had did this many people come from?

Many left their houses. They had been expecting to see an impromptu military parade following behind a visiting noble with great status. Much to their luck, however, they found themselves greeted by the look of what seemed to be a crowd of thugs and beggars.

Shock and surprise painted the faces of the residents in the center of town. None of them had ever seen something like this. Some gazed outside their windows at the growing crowd, eager to figure out their purpose. Even if some of those in the crowd lacked the physiques to make them appear menacing, the sheer number caused an impact of its own.

The crowd only seemed to grow larger as they kept moving east. At the head of the group, a child stood with imposing bravado. His eyes seemed resolute, just like those of a ruler who stood above his subjects. Had it not been for his small stature and the appearance of the unconventional following behind him, he would have looked like an army commander leading his troops.

The men behind the child wore a different kind of look, however. They carried a mix of dejection, fear, and anticipation. First, they anticipated what was to come, for this was the first time the entirety of the slums had gathered under one banner. Second, they feared the child leading them, for they had met his prowess in combat not too long ago. Finally, they were dejected, for they knew it wouldn't be possible for them to grow their authority as long as this child remained alive and in charge of the slums.

If someone had been there to follow them closely from the beginning, they would realize that the crowd was making its way to the eastern side of Sol — the place where the so-called nobles of this town resided.

Zaros had Alexander by his side. Despite being beaten up the day before, the teenager was now filled with courage and valiance. He looked at Zaros with blind faith, reminiscent of a priest looking at his god's imagery. His eyes were overflowing with awe and respect, and his heart was filled with nothing but loyalty.

Zaros used the time marching as a chance to stretch his muscles. In order to gather this much support, he had been forced to use rather 'compelling' methods to 'convince' the smaller gangs to join his entourage. Surprisingly, it had been easier than he imagined. Strength was a language much too familiar to those of the slums.

In the beginning, they had refused to help him. He had tried to argue his intention of protecting his subordinate. Unfortunately for him, his explanation had been taken like a sign of weakness. The strong sense of individuality in the slums made it hard to understand why he would risk offending the nobles for someone else.

Some gangs had taken it further, trying to attack Zaros upon his visit. Visiting them alone with Alexander had painted a target quite too striking on his back. Defeating Zaros was the equivalent of taking over Slyfox's legacy. Unfortunately for those who tried, they were quickly taught the reason behind Slyfox's defeat.

Most of the people watching the crowd started following after them out of curiosity. Some were eager to see what had driven this unruly mob to unite while others wished to be part of whatever fun they may engage in. Only after they neared the eastern side of town did some uninvited spectators leave.

However, this only served to fuel the mob's excitement. When had they ever been able to step inside this part of town with such an imposing manner? The thought was so foreign, they felt like it was a dream.

Some guards and peace-loving commoners thought about stepping up to stop the crowd. None of them felt the mob were there with good intentions. The sheer number of thugs, however, made them think twice about it.

Their hesitation only fueled the arrogance inside the hoodlums. This? This was all because of their new leader. Young as he might be, he had gained their respect with a clear display of power. Some had even started fantasizing about the heights the new head would take them to.

Unable to stop the crowd, the guards had no choice but to go out to report to their respective employers. Most of the wandering patrols belonged to different noble houses after all. Once they delivered their news, their employers became just as surprised as everyone else.

A few merchants and nobles grew weary, making the decision to order their troops to stand by and wait. It wasn't that they were afraid of such a mob. Instead, they knew that those who didn't stand out had the chance to thrive when others went down. As long as they weren't directly targeted, they wouldn't raise their hands. The main reason they remained so cautious was related to some rumors spreading for the past couple of days.

Only one household prepared their troops without thinking it twice. The noble house of Lapas, known for their not-so-secret partnership with the slave markets. The head of the house was currently in turmoil, issuing orders left and right as he organized his private force. A couple of his guards had been able to warn him of the incoming troops and the child leading them, which prompted the arrogant noble into readying himself to meet their march. After all, he knew better than anyone else what had triggered this 'visit.'

Regardless, Baron Lapas was sure of his own victory. His family had always relied on various forces from the underworld to satisfy the demand for slaves in the underground markets. He was used to dealing with force in order to get his point across. There was always an abundance of people with lust equal to their wealth, which had filled his war coffers with enough money to equip a small army of his own.

This would have normally incurred the wrath of authorities like the church or the royalty. However, House of Lapas had managed to remain afloat. They had carefully avoided stepping into other nobles' businesses.

What's more, donating hefty sums of money to the different churches always ensured their cooperation. This had led the noble household to thrive in success, allowing them to grow arrogant towards the populace over the years. In their eyes, common folk were seen as nothing but livestock, even more-so when they had no background. Just like those from the slums.

That being said, the hearts of various merchants and nobles relaxed upon seeing Zaros and his entourage go past their residences without making a fuss. Some of them might live in wealth, but not all of them had enough personal guards to fight off a crowd of this size.

"What is this idiot doing?"

Atop a house's roof, a shady figure stared at the crowd. He had followed after them with as much speed as he could with a partially damaged leg. Strands of flaxen hair covered part of his hidden face as a dark robe covered most of his body. It was Slyfox.

He had heard about the commotion while sleeping at the inn on the town's center. Once he saw the boy leading the mob towards the eastern district, he quickly started going after them. On one hand, he wanted to see how this crowd had come to be. On the other, he wanted to see if the nobles would take action against the boy leading them.

Ironically, he found himself surprised by the kid's prowess. Even he wouldn't have been able to unite the slums in such a manner. He couldn't help but wonder what kind of underhanded methods Zaros had used in order to do so. Uniting them was one thing, but convincing them all to act this arrogantly, without fear of the consequences, was another.

Slyfox frowned at the thought of how the nobles might retaliate against the slums. They might be avoiding the trouble for now, but once they had the time to prepare, they would surely repay this 'visit' on their own terms. This strengthened Slyfox's desire to see Zaros fail. He believed the slums needed a leader as wise as himself.

Did this kid not think about how much his actions could damage the people from the slums?

It took only a while for the crowd to reach their destination. A small army of fifty well-equipped guards was blocking their way to the front of a mansion. Leading them was a fat, bearded man. He was guarded by two familiar figures: Seth and

Mata, the guards who had paid Zaros a visit the day before. The man leading them was Baron Lapas, the head of this family.

The tall and short guards both had a mocking smile on their faces. Just what were these commoners hoping to achieve with such a poor display of strength? They knew each of their guards could handle several of these hoodlums on their own.

Even if most of the guards had not reached rank one, their equipment would still give them a huge advantage. Not to mention their physiques. Just how could the emaciated hoodlums compare to them, people who never had to worry about food? The guards couldn't help but think those in the crowd would probably collapse on their own after a little struggle.

Zaros brought the mob to a stop with a gesture of his hand. Even the more rowdy troublemakers who were about to cause problems were beaten into submission by the leaders of the smaller gangs when they saw Zaros's intent. These leaders considered beating them a favor, lest they incur their new boss's wrath. They had engraved that lesson in their hearts after his personal visit.

Zaros's eyes were filled to the brim with anger. He had already lost his village in the past, so losing a member of his new 'family' was not acceptable. His thoughts were filled with disgust as he looked at the fat man who seemed to be in charge of the small army. It was easy to see that Baron Lapas's sleazy eyes were filled with tangible perversion, as if he was judging everyone around him as nothing but pieces of meat.

"Are you not planning to bow?" asked the fat man with arrogance. The clear disdain in his words served to accentuate his stance. "You're in presence of nobility. Someone like yourself should know your place."

Zaros paid no attention to the man's words. Instead, he

found himself busy looking into his eyes, evaluating his character, weaknesses, and strengths.

The sleazy noble, on the other hand, felt taunted by the boy's disregard for him. Zaros's sharp stare only served to accentuate his rage. Taking a sideway look at his subordinates, he delivered an order, "Mata, Seth, force that child to bow down to me."

"You have one of my people," spoke Zaros, ignoring the fat man's instructions to his subordinates. "Give her back, or pay the consequences."

The noble doubled down on the game of disregarding his adversary's words. Turning sideways, he yelled at his subordinates, "What are you waiting for? Don't make me repeat myself!"

The tall and short guards took a step forward. They couldn't blatantly reject their lord's orders in front of so many people. Despite what little reservations they may have for going against Zaros, they unsheathed their swords. The polished iron gleamed in the sunlight, their blades ready for combat.

An arrogant smile took place on the face of the tallest guard, Mata. Despite his partner's warning the day before, he was still unconvinced about how much strength a child like Zaros could have. Seth, on the other hand, was a bit more cautious. His gaze was carefully tracking all of Zaros's movements.

A couple of burly men stepped forward from the crowd of hoodlums. They were the men who guarded the entrance to Slyfox's old base. Their burly frames and bronze skin made them look as imposing as the strongest battle-hardened warriors in Baron Lapas's camp. Zaros had gotten to know them during the past few days, forming a closer relationship to them.

Both of them were prepared to join the fray and fight against the incoming guards. Unlike Alexander, his sister Maria managed to get along with many of the gang's members. Her quirky temper and her incredible ability for gossip had provided many of them with countless opportunities to profit, gaining her the gang members' appreciation.

However, just as both of them were exiting the crowd, Zaros held up his hand. With it, he stopped both giants from continuing forward. Right now was not the time for pointless chivalry. This situation was to be dealt with at once, in the most efficient way possible. One Zaros knew would fall on him, thanks to Amro's estimation of his opponents' strength.

"I'll deal with them," said Zaros, his gaze turning towards the incoming guards. He planned to make an example out of them, one which would remind the nobles those of the slums were not to be messed with. "Yesterday, you gave a small gift to my subordinate. Please let me repay you today."

CHAPTER 17

Setting an example.

Z aros cracked his knuckles as he approached the two guards. A thin layer of mana covered his hands and feet, rhythmically appearing and disappearing as he walked towards them. It was the same technique Amro had used a few nights before in order to defeat Slyfox. Inside his mental space, Amro smiled smugly with pride. Other than him, who else would be able to teach this young boy such a technique?

Seth's expression turned ugly when he sensed Zaros's use of mana. With this display, he had enough confirmation that the boy was able to use it at will, far beyond what he and his partner were capable of doing. The only remaining source of confidence he had left was their age difference.

How much battle experience could a child have, anyway?

Unfortunately for him, Zaros had a much more eventful life than his. The young man had hunted daily for the last several years. Once that experience was combined with Amro's soul domain, Zaros was like a veteran hunter, one who had seen the sight of blood more than a few times. He was unlike the guards, who only had to deal with a couple drunkards at most every day.

"You know, ever since I arrived to this town, one thing

has been bothering me constantly," said Zaros, walking towards the two guards. "How come there are so many people in need of food, when we have people as useless as your boss, eating to the point his clothes don't fit him?"

"How dare you talk about Baron Lapas that way?" exclaimed Mata, ignoring the cautious look on his partner's eyes. "The citizens of the kingdom live to serve the nobles and the royal family! The resources of the kingdom are theirs to do as they see fit."

Seeing Mata's anger flourish, Zaros took the chance to shorten the distance between the two of them. Before his opponent realized it, he reached out his hand, clasping Mata where the plated armor didn't cover his chest.

Seth's eyes widened in surprise. He could swear the child was still a couple of feet away from his partner just a moment ago.

"Mata, be care—"

"Too late."

Following Zaros's words, Mata fell to his knees. A spear blood shot towards the sky as the injured guard gasped for breath. Before he knew it, his lung had been crushed under Zaros's grip, making it hard for him to breathe.

Watching them from a distance, Slyfox's mouth fell in shock. Was this the same kid that he had fought? His fighting style felt different from the night he went against him. Could his own lie be true? Could the kid really be a representative to an external power like the rebels, hiding his true-self in plain sight?

Beads of sweat dripped from Slyfox's forehead. Deep down, he had blamed his defeat that night on being slightly drunk and careless. But now, he couldn't help but reconsider his own views. Seeing the boy's skills as a spectator had left him with a bitter taste: the realization of his own incompetence.

With his eyes now at the same level as the kneeling Mata, Zaros continued speaking, "And then I realized. The nobles treat the rest of us like we are nothing but livestock. Our lives are nothing to them aside from a means to fulfill their desires.

Royalty, nobility, they are all the same. They're the ones to blame for this kingdom's decay. How can we overcome our own struggles when they intend to force them on us?"

A cry of support erupted from the crowd behind the boy. Not all of them were able to see how he'd brought down the guard, but most could still hear his words. The indignation in their hearts flourished with each of Zaros's arguments. Not even those from the northern and southern side of town could keep themselves from feeling the same way.

Who amongst them hadn't been looked down just because of their status as commoners? Who amongst them lacked the desire to challenge the status quo? They were all the same. Humans who cherished their lives, people with family and friends, feelings and desires. Not one of them could escape their desire for freedom.

As such, they couldn't deny that they hated the nobles' attitudes as much as anyone else.

"It's not that I hate you, or your lifestyle," said Zaros. "I understand that some are destined to be blessed by the heavens while others like myself are not. That I can accept."

"However, allowing you to treat us like livestock? Just what do you think human lives are?" Zaros's voice was filled with displeasure. The feelings he had buried when he departed his town were surfacing little by little.

Seeing Zaros immersed in his speech, Seth started

moving stealthily around him. He was aiming for Zaros's unguarded back while the boy was distracted finishing off his partner. It was a cruel decision, yes, but better than facing the little monster head-on. He had realized the boy was considerably more skillful than he initially estimated.

The spectators were about to scream at Zaros to watch his back. Some hoodlums even started running forward, intent on tackling the guard down and giving him a beating. However, Seth wasn't destined to succeed. Amro was ready to ruin his plan.

"Lean to your left," he said, instructing Zaros in a practiced manner.

Instinctively following his partner's order, Zaros took a step to his left. He was surprised to see the blade that had been aiming for his back, his emotions had blinded him to his surroundings. With no other way to regain his balance, Zaros took Seth's arm, pushing it forwards to regain his body's equilibrium. As a result, Seth's sword pierced through Mata's throat instead of Zaros's back.

Silence and surprise melded into shock. Seth felt his knees tremble and his hands grow weak. It was over, he had taken his partner's life. Even if he managed to kill the kid, his punishment would be no lesser than that of a criminal.

How is this possible? Does he have eyes on his back? No, he is a Demon! He must be!

Seth's mind was flooded with a myriad thoughts as he tried to rationalize the events that had just happened. Confusion had taken the reins of his rationality.

Unlike him, however, most of the slum-dwellers were pleasantly surprised and filled with excitement. This further caused the nobles watching from the distance to grow anxious. It seemed like the rumors might be true — a child had really been sent to infiltrate their town and start a rebellion.

Otherwise, why would someone with so much talent at such a young age lead a group of misfits like the residents of the slums? Why would he choose to make an enemy of the nobles who would gladly recruit him into their ranks because of his talent? In their eyes, he was trying to plant the seeds of discord within them in order to start a new revolution.

Slyfox's lies had borne fruit.

Bystanders aside, Zaros only had one goal in mind. He would retrieve Alexander's sister at all costs, even if he had to stain his hands in blood. The hatred towards the kingdom's royalty and nobility meshed together with the seed of doubt Amro had planted in his heart. *What if the nobles from this town were involved with his village's massacre?*

Unaware to his partner's subtle manipulation, Zaros had already accepted the concept of taking another man's life. He would not allow himself to experience the grief of losing someone again. He wouldn't abandon a follower of his.

Sigh.

Seeing Seth on the ground mumbling to himself, Zaros couldn't help but give the man a look of pity. Whatever his relationship was with the guards, taking their lives was taking a toll on his psyche. Unfortunately for them, his pity wasn't the same as forgiveness.

Without any hesitation, Zaros approached Seth, eager to repeat the same wound he had given the other guard. With his hand enhanced by mana, Zaros clasped his opponent's side, using the pressure of his grip to crush his lung.

Feeling the crumbling sensation of his ribs, Seth was brought back to his senses. Scared, he tried to break away from Zaros's grasp. Try as he might, however, his blade was no longer on his hands, it was now lying in the throat of his old partner.

After a few seconds of struggles, he was able to break Zaros's hold on him. The cost of doing so, however, involved leaving some bits of his flesh behind. His shirt was now torn, revealing five finger-sized holes where Zaros's hand had previously clasped. Blood oozed from the injury, creating trouble he had never expected at the beginning of this fight.

Seth gasped for breath, his eyes once again focused on Zaros. That slight moment of distraction had cost him a heavy price. His comrade had fallen at his own hands, and now, he had been gravely injured. He knew that even if he were to survive this fight, he would still be punished harshly by his master. There was no use for a subordinate who couldn't complete their orders.

Standing in front of the small army, the fat Baron from the house of Lapas stood with a complicated expression on his face. On one hand, two of his best subordinates had been injured to the point he would have to dispose of them even if they survived. On the other, the young boy before him was a precious treasure in his line of business.

Just what kind of price could a boy with such talents fetch in the underground markets? Even if he disregarded Zaros's talent, he was sure he could find a buyer just based on the boy's appearance alone. Plenty of his customers had tastes of questionable morality. Not like he was going to judge them for it.

That being said, Zaros wasn't ready to give up this fight. Using the opportunity created by his opponent stepping back, Zaros took a dagger from Mata's body.

"But then again, men grow spineless with time. Even if your boss is the one giving the orders, it's not like you're refusing to execute them. The same applies to the others. I'm well aware people work from the insides of the slums to supply your so-called cattle," said Zaros. Each of his words were marked with a small step forward in Seth's direction.

In the distance, Slyfox grew silent.

Am I the one in the wrong? he thought. Was he at fault for compromising with the nobles instead of rebelling? It was true that he had chosen the path of least resistance. However, was that really the best for both him and his subordinates, like he had once thought it was?

Just like Slyfox, several people amongst the crowd stared at the ground in shame. They knew they had all betrayed one another at some point to ensure their own survival. Zaros's words, however, revealed the cowardice behind their actions.

Who amongst them didn't have a friend who 'went missing'? Could they justify their choices based on their desire for survival?

Even Amro smiled in approval. The boy had a great talent for influencing the human heart. It was a trait that would become of use as they advanced in their path of revenge. It made him consider something in particular. Was it Zaros's luck to meet him that day, or was it his to have met Zaros?

He knew very well that fate had an interesting way to achieve its goals; so to this question of his, only time would tell.

Far from the audience, Seth was finding it hard to remain focused. He was constantly losing blood from his wound. His eyesight had grown fuzzy and his senses had lost its sharpness. He could hear what seemed like a grim voice buzzing in his ears, mocking him, telling him to accept his destiny already. Strength left his body as an unexplainable weight fell onto his knees. He had to use his sword to support himself in order to remain standing.

That moment was all Zaros needed. Using the opportunity brought upon by Seth's waning strength, he sealed the fate of the guard once and for all. Without care for human life, his dagger slashed across Seth's neck, pushing him to meet his partner on the other side.

Seeing the results of his choices, Zaros could only shake his head. Despite being his first time taking a human life, he felt nothing but apathy. Something inside Zaros made him accept death as part of nature, not something out of the ordinary.

Realizing he was staring at the cold, dead body of Seth, Zaros raised his head. He turned to look at the fat noble and the battalion of guards behind him. They were visibly scared, their morale now as low as their morals.

Ready to make his point, the boy spoke in a voice incompatible with his height, "From this day onwards, nobles, royalty, and everybody else is the same in this town! You won't bind anyone to a fate of slavery or death anymore."

Amro smiled inside his space. He had decided not to intervene unless necessary during this conflict. Only through blood and battle would Zaros temper his character and soul enough to face what the future had reserved for them. Revenge and revolution held one thing in common: death was usually the means to make sure they happened.

Zaros's words were the drop that spilled the glass. Blinded by their emotions and excitement, the unruly mob ran towards the guards ready to vent their grudges with violence.

Seeing the crowd's behavior, the baron's face distorted in anger. Eventually, however, he was forced to order his guards to move in front of him to ensure his safety.

"Protect me! Stop those filthy commoners from entering my state!"

However, he had overlooked something. Zaros's actions had already crushed his guards' morale. The death of

Seth and Mata had made them hesitate. Unfortunately for them, however, hesitation in battle was the same as taking half a step forward into defeat.

Zaros merged with the crowd of people charging forward. His small stature made him impossible to find amongst the chaotic battlefield. As he moved through the crowd, he reaped the lives of a few guards with ease. It was too late to stop. Every one of his moves was now aimed towards his opponents' weak points. An exposed neck, an extended arm, any opportunity available was taken by him to incapacitate his opponents.

Severed necks and pierced hearts were what paved a path to Zaros's true target: the one man whose attitude represented everything he hated.

You're next, he promised silently.

Seeing his personal guards falling one after another, Baron Lapas grew scared. He kept moving backwards as he tried to find a safe place far from the skirmish. As a noble, his place in battles was at the back commanding his troops, not at the front taunting his opponents. It was his own arrogance that had led to his current situation.

Slyfox stood in shock from afar. Was this the start of a civil war? Since when did the people from the slums hold enough courage to do something like this?

However, he knew the answer to his last question. Even he had been momentarily blinded by Zaros's words. Had it not been for the pain still coming from his leg, he might have charged into battle as well. Just what was it that made the boy so compelling? Was it his ideals, or was it perhaps his choice of words? He decided to find out after this was over.

That being said, Slyfox was afraid of the consequences this battle would bring in the future. Could those from the slums actually be victorious? His common sense dictated that it was impossible, but a strange feeling told him that's how it was going to be. Only after watching until the end would he find out for sure.

CHAPTER 18

Vindication.

Baron Lapas ran as fast as his legs allowed him to. If only his wealth could be exchanged for wings, he would be willing to trade it all in this one moment. The scene behind him was terrifying. How could his guards keep falling down lifeless one after the other? His guards' equipment and training should have allowed them to raze the hoodlums down with ease. Why were they being killed like bugs instead then?

The answer was simple: Zaros. After giving his order to charge, Zaros's silhouette had disappeared inside the crowd, leaving his last menacing stare deeply ingrained in the Baron's memory.

The baron recognized that stare. It was the same one slaves gave him before they lunged forward at him, disregarding the punishment they would receive. The difference was that his guards were not able to stop this boy. The speed at which his soldiers kept falling seemed to follow the rhythm of his pulse, increasing little by little.

Had the baron reached rank two or even rank one, he might have been able to see Zaros sprinting from side to side, reaping the lives of his subordinates only to get to him. Unfortunately for him, his life of hedonism would never awaken such potential. Over twenty members from his 'elite' guard had already fallen to Zaros's dull dagger. At some point, Zaros had even opted to change it for a short blade dropped by one of the guards, increasing the efficiency of his deadly harvest.

Body after body paved Zaros's path. He was being baptized in blood; no longer a victim, but a victimizer.

Each of his moves was allowing his feelings to flood outwards. The swings of his blade representing the words in his heart. But even then, a cold sense of rationality kept him in focus. The thrill of battle calmed his nerves in a way he had never experienced before.

Amro kept himself busy as well. Every life Zaros's dagger reaped was quickly refined into the purest essence the fallen god could use. Slowly infusing it into his host's body without him realizing was a task easier said than done. For now, he'd keep this a secret, lest it broke Zaros's attention away from the battlefield.

Eventually, Zaros reached the noble, sealing his only possible path to escape. On one side was the angry mob ready to devour him while on the other was Zaros, a smirk of deviousness displayed on his face. His hair, now bathed in crimson red, had given him the appearance of a demon. One ready to collect on a debt.

"Was it worth it?" he asked, taunting the Baron into making a move. "Was your greed worth paying with your life?"

At first, Baron Lapas didn't answer. Instead, his face twisted in repugnance while his hands clenched into fists. Even at death's door he was unwilling to accept judgment from a commoner.

"How dare you?" he said. "A lowlife like you will never understand the value of a noble's life, nor the power of his wealth. My life is worth a hundred times more than yours. Even if you kill me now, someone else will come to avenge me."

"The value of a man's death depends on the value of his life," replied Zaros. "Since your life has no meaning, neither does your death."

Baron Lapas felt like cursing the boy. Once he tried to speak, however, he discovered only blood flowed out of his mouth. His life had been taken without him even realizing it. Eyes full of despair, he looked at Zaros, only now realizing that the boy held a dagger stained by his blood.

Damn it, he thought. *Seth, Mata, I'll see you in hell.*

Even in death, Baron Lapas refused to accept the consequences of his own actions. He placed all the blame on both of his subordinates, who had decided to instigate this conflict by themselves. The fact that they did so only to please him wasn't enough for him to care.

Zaros felt a huge weight leave his shoulders. A strange, refreshing feeling washed away all the burdens and exhaustion he had accumulated during the battle. For some reason, murder didn't feel alien to him. Instead, it felt strangely melancholic, like it was forever meant to be part of his life.

No, Zaros thought to himself. *I won't let myself become like that.*

He wasn't sure how he should feel about his ability to take away lives with such ease. Even if he ignored Baron Lapas's death, he had taken the lives of many guards as well. If he added the lives of those he had indirectly killed through his subordinates, his kill-count made for a frightening amount. *What did this say about him?*

It says that you make a perfect host, thought Amro, still focused on refining the surrounding souls. The actions of

Zaros were something only he could explain. Inhabiting his body, he could sense the influence his soul had over the boy's.

Zaros subordinates, however, were too busy with their own thoughts to realize the changes happening within their leader. Their elevated morale after this victory was enough to blind them to any future retaliation the nobles might take. With renewed courage, they finished cleaning up the remaining guards. It didn't take long for the few remaining stragglers to get rounded up and stripped away from their weapons.

Zaros broke away from his self-reflection only after he noticed his subordinates' mood. It wasn't time to over-think things. There were more pressing matters he had to take care of right now.

He made his way towards them as he swept his gaze around in search of Alexander. Eventually, he found him in a corner, punching a guard.

"Tell me where my sister is you bastard!"

Question, punch, question, punch. Zaros had a look of pity as he saw Alexander's actions. It was clear to see his overwhelming anger blinded him to the fact that the guard was unconscious, and therefore, unable to provide him with an answer.

"Alexander! Come over here," said Zaros, trying to awaken the teenager from his rage-fueled assault. If he really wanted to save his sister, his actions were proving of no use.

Hearing those words brought the teenager back to reality. The fear of losing his sister had blinded him, making him focus on nothing but the other party's demise. He looked in the direction the voice came, only to find his boss gazing back at him. Tears of pride, relief, and happiness fled his eyes as he ran to kneel in front of his young leader.

Zaros looked at the boy with some understanding in his

eyes. "Come, it's time to find your sister," he said, before turning around to look back at the crowd. "As for the rest of you, divide the loot on the ground equally. Should I find out that you cheated your comrades-in-arms, I'll deal with you later myself."

Zaros's words reverberated in the survivors' hearts. What were the prices of armor and weapons like these? It would be enough to feed them for months to come. Rather than fear the second part of Zaros's statement, they rejoiced upon the first. All of them knew who should be credited for this victory.

If Zaros had demanded to take the lion's share of the loot, none of them would have been able to refute. However, the boy had exceeded their expectations. He had surprisingly decided to leave the loot to them. Sparks of admiration rose in each of the hoodlums' hearts. They felt a new era of prosperity was coming to the slums.

Even the spectators found themselves surprised. They understood the nature of the slum-dwellers very well. Therefore, they knew how people from that side of town usually behaved. It was nothing like Zaros's benevolent actions.

Even some of them felt tempted to go and pretend to be part of the crowd in order to participate in the loot's distribution. The only thing holding them back was the vicious looks of the gang members. None of them had the kindness of their young leader.

A few noble families felt inclined to take this moment to summon their troops and attack Zaros. However, they ultimately chose not to do so. The kid had displayed combat prowess unbefitting for his age, managing to take down Baron Lapas's men without much difficulty.

If they chose to fight him at this moment, they might cause a good amount of casualties, but they themselves would have to pay an equally unthinkable price.

Unaware of the choices being made by in the background, Zaros made his way to the prisoners. A total of 16 men, stripped of their armor and clothes, were tied up as they awaited their judgment. They had a vast amount of bruises on their faces as well as many non-lethal injuries on their bodies. It was clear that they had become a source of 'entertainment' for the hoodlums during the last few minutes.

Seeing him arrive, however, startled the captives. During the battle, these prisoners had occasionally witnessed the small grim reaper harvesting the lives of their comrades. Having him loom over them without any traces of emotion in his eyes was nothing short of mental torture. However, unfortunately for them, their lives were now in his hands. Only Zaros's forgiveness could save them.

Few words could describe the guards' inner-struggle. Some of them were brooding over how they should have taken their chance to escape during the skirmish while others busied their minds considering the scenarios to come as they evaluated whether they still had a chance of survival.

Zaros decided to offer them a chance for salvation only after a few minutes of burdening them with his gaze. "Are any of you aware of whom we're looking for?"

Hearing Zaros's words, the group of prisoners halted their thoughts. Only two of them were able to nod. The rest had no idea what Zaros had meant with his words.

Zaros nodded, satisfied that the latter part of their mission would be easier. Two guards who knew about his missing subordinate should be enough to find her. He couldn't help but smile as he felt some relief course through his veins.

He turned around to Alexander and said, "Untie them, those two will come with us. They can tell us where she is along the way."

Following Zaros's instructions, Alexander quickly untied the two men. He then gave them a moment as they prepared themselves to lead the way to the girl inside Lapas's estate. Meanwhile, the remaining guards stared at Zaros with eyes full of expectation, unaware to what he had in place for them.

Seeing him about to leave, one of them finally gathered the courage to ask what had burdened all of their minds, "My lord, may I ask what will happen to the rest of us?"

Zaros glanced at the guard with a thoughtful face before looking back at his subordinates.

"Release them," he said.

For a moment, hope filled the eyes of the guards who were left behind as their freedom became tangible once again. A few words, however, put a stop to that.

"That being said, cut off one of their arms or legs before you let them leave. You can place the burden of choosing on them if you want."

Zaros could still remember the old veteran he had seen at the entrance of the city. Why should the abusive guards get to live a better life than that poor man? After Baron Lapas's death, it was possible they would be hired by another noble. He needed them to serve as an example. Perhaps sharing the man's fate would serve to deter those threatening the slums.

"Let's go."

Hearing him speak, the two guards guiding Zaros didn't dare to dally. Their reaction caused a grin of satisfaction to surface on Alexander's face. This day, vindication belonged to him.

CHAPTER 19

Jackpot.

The two guards, Alexander, and Zaros all entered the estate of Baron Lapas. Drapes embellished with gold leaf covered every window and exquisite paintings decorated every wall. It was a level of luxury neither of the boys had ever seen before.

The guards led them through several halls in the mansion until they came to the Baron's personal office. Even after the commotion, two maids were on standby by the door. Both were shocked when they saw the two tattered guards being followed by the disheveled children.

Zaros shot them a gentle smile. His face looked innocent, devoid of the cruelty and coldness he had displayed earlier to the guards. After all, as far as he was concerned, the maids had no participation in the hideous acts of their master.

Seeing his expression, both maids were charmed by the boy's gentle look. Despite their orderly appearance, both of the girls grew up in the slums, taken in by the Lapas family in order to be trained as servants. Zaros's disheveled appearance made them feel a sense of sympathy towards him.

Thus, when the guards asked them to step aside, they thought Zaros and Alexander were new recruits sent to their master's slave pens. They couldn't help but pity the boys momentarily. Only a few hours later, would they realize the truth, coming to know how mistaken they had been.

Once inside the dead Baron's personal office, both guards closed the door.

"Please wait for a moment," said one of them.

Ensuring the maids had left, he pulled a lamp on the room's wall. For a few seconds, the noise of gears turning could be heard from under the room. Only after a notorious thud did it stop. The mechanical sound signaled a lock somewhere in the room had been removed.

Once that was done, both guards removed the carpet in the middle of the room, unveiling a trapdoor hidden underneath. They opened it only to reveal a stairway that seemed to lead towards a hidden room in the basement. Zaros perked up as he leaned down to see things closer. The things available to the rich amazed him.

The guards took the two torches on the walls, using them to light their path as they walked down the stairs. Zaros and Alexander followed behind them, eager to find the teenager's sister. Finally, they arrived at the bottom of the stairs and came across a dark corridor in which cries of pain echoed.

When he heard them, Zaros's curious smile faded, quickly replaced by a sour expression. The eerie noises could only mean one thing. No one enjoyed their stay in this place.

"What is this place?" he asked, intent on confirming his suspicions.

Both guards glanced at each other for a second. Neither of them wanting to be the first one to answer.

"Young master, this is where the merch— where the people are kept before they are transported away," he said, correcting himself before using a word that might have sparked either of the boys' anger.

"By that, you mean the place you keep the people before they're sold into slavery?" asked Alexander. He wasn't going to take the softly minced words of the guards at face value.

"If they are only kept here, how come I hear so many of them crying from pain?" asked Zaros. He also felt both guards were still withholding information from him.

The guard who first spoke turned towards his companion, telling him with his eyes that he had already fulfilled his share. This reaction caused the other guard's eyes to go wide in complaint.

You did this intentionally, didn't you? he seemed to say.

Noticing their exchange, Zaros and Alexander grew impatient. Eventually, Zaros had to take his dagger and cough, all in an attempt to rush them.

"Must I repeat my question?" he asked, his voice oozing with killing intent.

Hearing Zaros's question, both guards were brought back to reality. Without hesitating anymore, the second one proceeded to continue his companion's explanation.

"The truth is that before slaves are sold, they are put through some training. After all, no one would want to buy an unruly slave who bites back at every chance. Because of that, master hired some mercenaries to break their minds with all methods available to them. The results are so effective some of them cry and wail even when they're not being tortured."

Zaros and Alexander's faces expressed their distaste at the guard's answer. Young as they were, they understood the implications behind his words. At the same time, such understanding brought Alexander's worries back to the surface. Thus, he shoved the guards forward, desperate to find his sister.

The guards guided Alexander and Zaros through the hallway, walking past several cells. Seeing them, the prisoners inside scurried away with fear. They had seen 'visitors' in the past as well, so they assumed both boys were envoys sent in to procure some merchandise. The fact that both guards seemed to treat them with respect only reaffirmed this idea.

A door covered in locks awaited them at the end of the hallway. Zaros's eyes moved over them as he noticed the multiple key holes, each one of varying sizes. He turned his gaze to the guards, glaring at them in discontent. It was a silent message threatening them to open the door or face the consequences.

One of the guards stepped forward and opened all the locks except one. This last lock had no keyhole and glowed with a black light, leaving him with no apparent way of opening it.

However, before he could say something, the guard carrying the keys felt a cold chill go down his back. A sense of dread filled him as he realized both boys were staring at him. It was obvious that if he didn't open the lock, he wouldn't be able to deal with the consequences.

"Young master, please, hear us out," he said. "This last lock is one we cannot open. It's not that we don't want to, it's just that we truly can't. The lock was designed by an old sage to only work upon detecting our master's life signature. We were afraid you wouldn't believe us, so we had to show it to you ourselves."

Zaros didn't believe them at first. He thought that, perhaps, they were making things hard for him in a foolish attempt to get some revenge. However, he quickly discarded that idea. The guards' pale faces indicated that there were no deceptions in their words.

Seeing them like that, Alexander grew desperate, rage filling his eyes. Had he known there would be no way to open the lock, he would've pushed for these two guards to be dismembered like the rest of their group outside the estate.

It wasn't like Alexander was alone in his regret, however. Zaros was also pondering over the issue. It was then that a kindly reminder presented itself.

"I find it both admirable and insulting that you haven't thought of asking for my help," said Amro.

"Oh," answered Zaros. With everything that happened that morning, he had forgotten about Amro.

Sensing Zaros's thoughts, Amro felt slightly disappointed. He made a note to himself to make the boy regret forgetting about him in future training sessions.

"Come on, I know what that silence means," Zaros said. "Training is hard enough already."

"You don't know hard," Amro retorted.

Knowing he needed Amro's cooperation, Zaros couldn't help but compromise. "I'll put in more effort in the future," he said. "I promise."

After a couple seconds of appeasing Amro, Zaros finally convinced him to help. That being said, Amro's help required him to take over Zaros's body.

For a moment, Zaros's amber eyes seemed to darken as Amro took over. An intense feeling of dread assaulted both guards before Amro withdrew his aura. Even Alexander was snapped out of his anger when he felt something strange emanating from his boss.

Amro's gaze swept over the guards before he scoffed.

Impossible to open? Not even the vaults of heaven are outside my reach.

Arrogant and with disdain, he placed his hands over the lock. 'Life signature' was nothing but a fancy way to describe how a mortal's body reacted to magical energies. After recalling how the Baron's warm blood felt over Zaros's hand, he replicated that pattern with ease.

Clank

After hearing a sound no one expected to hear, both guards felt chills crawling down their spine. They still remembered the man who had crafted the lock — a wandering sage who liked to buy slaves for his heinous experiments. That man was rumored to be on the verge of entering rank four. It was plain senseless for a young man to bypass one of his works with this much ease.

However, they restrained themselves from speaking. They knew there would be no good outcome from voicing their question out loud. All in all, it could be said they lacked the courage to ask the only one who could provide them with an answer.

Unlike the guards' dismayed expressions, Alexander's eyes lit up with glee. Zaros had proven to be a man truly admirable and worthy of his loyalty. Only he could overturn the heavens and the earth to keep his promises. Alexander once again made a vow inside his heart to follow this man's orders for the rest of his days.

Crash!

With a kick, Amro woke up the three men who had fallen victim to their own thoughts. It wasn't time for them to ponder over things, but time to get this over with.

It takes a fool to be impressed by this much, thought Amro. Feeling he had wasted enough time idling around, he entered the room, leaving the dumbfounded men behind. It took the guards a few seconds to regain their senses before they scrambled to light the way with their torches.

The room was filled with weapons, gold, and valuables, showing it had been some kind of vault for the Lapas family. The amount of wealth inside this room could easily rival the value of all the things they had seen while walking through the mansion. Not even the guards had been allowed to enter this room in the past; those of the Lapas family had always entered alone, leaving them behind the door.

However, there was no sight of Maria once they entered the room.

"Where is she?" demanded Alexander.

The guards looked at each other, some doubt showing on their face. "She should be here," they admitted.

Avoiding a senseless confrontation, Amro simply pointed forwards. Following his lead, both guards and Alexander saw a sturdy wooden door. It seemed to hide away something from the rest of the room. Something or someone.

No longer hesitating, Alexander ran towards the door, pushing it open without thinking twice. Inside, he found his sister, sleeping in a simple bed made out of hay. It caused an endless wave of relief to wash over him. He had been worrying to no end ever since that day. Having found her, he stepped into the room, ignoring the worried looks of the guards behind him.

Alexander hugged his sister, crying over her shoulder. She was still sleeping, seemingly sedated out of her senses. He was so emotional, he ignored the fragrant scent of lilacs inside the room.

Catching a whiff of the scent, Amro's expression grew bitter. He shot a judgmental look at the guards who couldn't help but cower in fear. He knew what that scent implied. How could he not when he had several lifetimes' worth of experience in the art of alchemy?

Regardless, it wasn't his place nor his host's to tell Alexander. There were no tangible benefits in doing so. The only thing he was willing to do was shoot a glare in the guards' direction, raising a finger to his lips as a reminder for them to keep silent about it.

Inside the room, Alexander checked frantically his sister for injuries. When he determined she was only unconscious and hadn't been harmed, his muscles relaxed, making him fall to the ground. Tears of joy trickled down his face as he thanked the heavens for keeping her out of danger.

If only that was the case, thought Amro.

The guards felt at ease now that everything was over with. They lit up the torches in the room's walls, giving sufficient time for the young man to embrace his sleeping sister. After Amro's subtle threat, they were convinced of their survival. They had confidence that they would be able to maintain their lives as long as they kept the events that took place in this room quiet.

Once they finished lighting up the torches, both of them stood against the wall, waiting for their new orders. They didn't dare to move at all until the boy told them they were free to go. After all, the memory of their comrades losing their limbs was still vivid in their minds.

"Carry everything outside," ordered Amro. "We're taking it with us."

It would be a shame to let go of all this wealth now that it was without an owner.

CHAPTER 20

An unfortunate coincidence.

The forest of Halt was known as the garden of Nyx. It was the last remaining bastion for wildlife; plants, trees, and feral beasts alike. The rest of the territory had already been harvested for all it could offer. Now, only a former husk of the kingdom remained.

Two men now understood this concept better than before. They were traveling through the lush scenery of the forest, taking in their surroundings with mixed expressions of curiosity and awe. Both of them appeared to be injured, a fact highlighted by the bruises and cuts on their bodies. That, however didn't stop them from traveling at ease. It was like their injuries were naught but an illusion.

It could be seen why trickery and deceit were called their specialty. Even their clothes carried that purpose, carefully resembling those of a forest villager. They were the Weaver brothers, mercenaries with a special talent for manipulating the truth.

They had been hired by the prince of the kingdom in order to achieve a single task: the success of his plans. Their part in this mission was rather simple in fact. They were to spread rumors across the town of Sol, whispering lies to every available listener. Lies that spoke of the rebels' corruption, and how they had murdered every resident of the forest.

In other words, they had to pretend to be survivors of the massacre, using themselves to convince the townsfolk that a tragic event had happened at the hands of the kingdom's enemy. Perhaps some people would be able to see through their lies, but those were far too few to disrupt the course of their plans.

They had been on standby for more than a week, waiting for a messenger from the mercenaries to confirm the operation had succeeded on their side. But that messenger had never arrived, forcing them to take the initiative on their side. As such, they took a detour to merge into the forest, faking their way out of it later on.

They had little choice on the matter. Time was ticking, and they were running out of it.

The kingdom's curfew had already been in place for more than two weeks. By this time, the merchants and mercenaries were already growing restless. If they delayed any further, their plan was sure to fail.

As mercenaries, they understood the value of their mission. Many arrangements had already been done for everything to carry on smoothly. Everything from the establishment of a curfew to the recruitment of lumbermen and mercenaries to purge the forest of beasts.

In other words, any mistake at this stage was way above their pay grade. If they were to delay any longer, they wouldn't be able to hide from the prince's rage.

Unsurprisingly, the Weaver brothers were met with resistance once they arrived to Sol. It was something they had expected given the premise of their lie. However, it all went beyond their wildest expectations.

Once the guards caught sight of them, they immediately took defensive stances. With weapons in hand, the guards threatened them to halt their advance. It was a behavior far too aggressive for the guards of a village where nothing ever happened.

Afraid to blow their covers with unnecessary violence, the Weaver brothers approached the group of guards with their hands held up.

"Noble guards, please help us," said one of them. He hoped his words were enough to ease the tension.

Unfortunately for him, the guards kept their weapons pointed at them. Both he and his brother had no idea how to act. Neither of them were skilled in combat. One wrong move, and they could be looking at death.

An almost imperceptible tear rolled down his face. What kind of sadist god decided to make their journey this hard?

"State your business!" spoke one of the guards. His hands were shaking as though he was desperate to attack but unwilling to harm an already injured man.

"Sir, we are from the villages to the south. We need to inform the town of grave news. We seek an audience with any noble willing to hear us out," said the other Weaver brother.

The guards tensed up when he stated they wanted to see the nobles. One of the guards even pulled back his bow, ready to shoot at the smallest sign of trouble.

Did we say something wrong? thought the Weaver brothers.

"Respectable guards, we mean no trouble. Our villages were raided, massacred, and burnt to the ground. We barely managed to escape and make our way here. Our wounds kept us from covering too much distance every day, so please have mercy."

The guards looked at the Weaver brothers and their wounds. The pitiful look in their faces was enough to make them hesitate.

Perhaps they had grown too tense over the last couple of days. After a certain youth had caused a ruckus in the eastern side of town, they were reprimanded and punished for not upholding their duties as guards. As such, they were demoted to guarding the southern gates for the upcoming month, a task every single one of them loathed.

Rumors said the youth in question might be an envoy from the rebel army. That he was there on a mission to destabilize the southern front of the kingdom. The only reason why the nobles had yet to take action was the unknown origin of those claims.

Now, faced with the arrival of these newcomers, the guards felt a sense of dread. Their appearance further complicated the already delicate situation of their town. The veracity of the claims they heralded could be the final spark needed for a full out civil war.

Away from the two supposed villagers, the guards deliberated over what they should do next.

"Should we report to our higher-ups?" one of them asked.

"I'll be damned if we do. They'll probably use that as an excuse to do away with us if anything else goes wrong in the future," another one said.

"But they have information that might be related to that boy. If we hold this back from the nobles and they find out later, our heads will be displayed on a stake," argued a third.

After some deliberation, the guards decided to tie some rope against the newcomers' hands, only then taking them inside the city. If the two of them were telling the truth, then the situation inside their town was more dangerous than they had originally assumed.

Both of the Weaver brothers felt relieved. It seemed like their explanation was accepted. Even if they felt dissatisfied about the ropes and the roughness they were treated with, it was still a better alternative than telling the prince they had failed to accomplish their mission. If that happened, a tight rope around their hands would be the least of their worries. In fact, the rope might end up going around their necks instead.

Contemplating the results of their failure, both brothers followed the guards. It was an uneventful walk until they arrived at a seemingly wealthy house in the eastern area of the city. To their surprise, the house was crowded with people. Nobles and merchants from all kinds of different backgrounds were engaged in a heated argument.

The conversation was so frenzied, it took some time for the nobles and merchants to notice the arrival of the guards and the two men tied behind their backs.

The first one to approach them was a seductive woman followed by two burly men. Her hair was a dull golden color, reminiscent of the color of wheat, while her eyes were a deep, enchanting green. She was the owner of this house, a 'small' merchant who owned a few stores in the center of the city.

The Weaver brothers were surprised by her appearance. She was a mesmerizing woman with a type of savage allure to herself. The fact that she could command so many to convene in her home was proof of her authority. Both men gulped, unsure of what to say when faced with her domineering, yet seductive eyes.

She stood with her bodyguards behind her, prideful and unmoving. Unlike most of the nobles and merchants here, she had built a fortune of her own through her hard work and decisive — albeit questionable — business tactics. She wasn't one of those who got her worth through inheritances nor political nepotism. This made her all that much scarier. Her methods for dealing with people were unusually crafty, yet effective.

Thankfully for the Weaver brothers, the guards were more familiar with her as they introduced both of them with ease. Seeing the bodyguards were not barring their way, one of the guards stepped forward to say, "My lady, these two come from the small villages in the forest. They bring news that may be of importance."

Silence took control over the room for a moment as many of the nobles and merchants tried to hear the message brought upon by the guards. Noticing their attitude, the woman looked at both brothers with an analytical gaze. Her eyes were just like the prince's. It was unlike the nobles both of the Weaver brothers had met in the past.

"Bring them to my room," she said, turning around to walk away.

Her reaction caused the guards who brought both 'villagers' to feel rather disappointed. A brief "thank you" or a reward of some kind would have been nice given how hard the choice to let them in was to make. Unfortunately for them, they were in no position to make demands.

They weren't the only ones unhappy with the situation, however. Many nobles and merchants threw judgmental looks in the woman's direction. It was clear to them that she was trying to hog the information using her authority as the host of the party. The fact that she left them in the dark was annoying in its own way.

Some things never changed, though. As she walked away, the gazes of many men followed her all the way into her room. Behind her, the two burly bodyguards following her dragged the two so-called villagers with them.

Once she was in the privacy of her room, she took a seat on a lavishly furnished sofa and crossed her shapely legs one over the other. It was all calculated. The action parted her scarlet dress into two tempting strokes of red, causing both of the Weaver brothers to gulp. They were unable to avoid tracing the movement of her legs with their eyes, causing the woman to smile in satisfaction.

She knew she could attribute her success in part to her cunning and talent for business. That, however, didn't diminish the role her looks had played. She knew what she had, and more importantly, she knew how to use it.

Swirling a glass of wine, she said, "Tell me, what is this urgent news the two of you bring?"

The Weaver brothers took a brief moment before they came back to their senses. The allure of the woman before them was so great that they had lost focus of their goal. Sure enough, there were weapons more lethal to men than iron.

"My lady," answered one of them. "Our villages were raided, massacred and burnt to the ground. A troop of men claiming to be the envoys of the rebel forces tried to convince us to join them. However, once we declared our loyalty to the kingdom, they decided to take our families and homes from us. Only we were able to escape. Please, my lady, I beg you. Help us get some justice for our families."

The woman stared at him for a few seconds. Her eyes seemed to convey her interest in his story, for it was much too relevant to her current situation. The arrival of the boy who took control of the slums had placed great pressure on those with power.

She still remembered the benefits she had been able to get from Slyfox and his men. Her shops were guaranteed protection while her competitors' kept suffering accidents every once in a while. But it was different now. It didn't seem like the new leader of the slums was interested in those kinds of services. Word had it that he had taken the task of teaching the combat-capable men and women of the slums how to hunt, just so they could be less reliant on the town's own small economy.

The loss of benefits had bothered her slightly, but it wasn't enough to cause her to lose sleep. It was the information from some rumors that made her worry. Whispers around the streets said that the young boy was actually an envoy from the rebel troops up north.

If that was true, her life as a newly arisen aristocrat was bound to come to an end just like all of those at the frontier. The rebels had no mercy towards people like her, who had sworn loyalty to the crown. It was madness. She refused to have her life torn down by a child who hadn't even finished developing.

She had her doubts about the rumors, but the events from what had happened a few days ago had already influenced her beliefs. As if it wasn't enough to take Baron Lapas's life, the youth had the audacity to raid the deceased noble's belonging. It wasn't even a case of greed. Her subordinates reported he gave them all away to those from the slums, keeping only a small part to himself.

Such daring acts made her and the other nobles worry immensely. What if they became next on his list?

They would have gathered their troops in order to confront him, but the internal conflicts amongst the nobility didn't allow anyone to accept a place in the vanguard. No one wanted to send their troops in first after seeing the boy's thirst for blood. Whoever headed the attack was bound to lose his combat force to the boy's hands. The greed inside the hearts of every noble and merchant here wouldn't allow for such a concession.

And now, the information brought by the two men before her confirmed her worries. It seemed like the rebels had truly chosen to invade the southern border. Their bad situation just kept on getting worse.

There is profit in chaos, however.

A small smile surfaced on the woman's face. She was surprisingly clever. There was always a profit to be made somewhere and her merchant instincts were telling her this was it.

With this information, she could make some wise investments before the other nobles found out. It was her fortune that these men appeared as she called for a meeting in her house. It enabled her to monopolize all the benefits to herself.

With a rough idea in her mind, she took some pen and paper before calling one of her subordinates to her side.

"Quick, go and take this letter to the carrier pigeons. Make sure no one follows you. It must be sent to my friends in the capital."

Like that, she passed on a letter to the burly man. Inside, she had included some careful instructions alongside a portrait of the boy leading the slums. She and the nobles had previously prepared it in order to place bounty posters on him.

"Make sure it's sent tonight, there is no room for error," she said, turning back to look at the two so-called villagers.

"I must thank you for your warning," she added, doing her best to appear amiable. "I'll make sure to inform the proper authorities. I assure you that your families will be avenged."

Both men relaxed. With this, they were sure their mission was a success.

However, the merchant wasn't over with them as much

as they were with her. She put forwards her best smile as she extended a request, "I'd like you to help me with something. Would you be willing to tell the people in the town center about what you went through? I'm afraid they would disregard my words of warning, while yours might be more compelling as survivors from this tragedy."

Both men nodded their heads in an almost instinctual manner. Their mission was to create a story from their lies; they had no reason to refuse.

"Please, do follow my assistant then. He will show you where your lodging lies for the time being. Wash yourselves, I know what you endured must have been exhausting," she said. "Rest well, you are safe now."

"Thank you," they said. "We'll take our leave then."

After expressing their thanks, both men left the room, leaving the shrewd merchant alone on her sofa. She seemed almost melancholic as she swirled the wine in her hand and stared at their backs. Only the smile on her face painted a different reality.

In truth, all she wanted through that gesture was to delay the information from spreading another day. That would be enough time for her to make the right investments and gain a lead over the other merchants. After all, information was power.

CHAPTER 21

Two bishops, one board.

As political warfare raged in the city of Sol, an eerie cooling silence filled the forest of Halt. It had been days since the woods had entered such a state. The cause behind it could be traced back to two particular individuals: a man and a woman.

Both of them were cloaked in black, but that did little to call attention away from their features. The woman was as charming and dangerous as a rose. Neither the attention her crimson lips drew, nor the silver locks of hair flowing from the sides of her hood could do anything to distract people from her seductive gaze. Her two eyes looked like clear sheets of crystal tinged with drops of blood, something that could make even the most disciplined soldier lose his focus.

Whilst she was attractive, the man next to her didn't lose in terms of calling attention to himself. There was a distinct sense of danger to him. His coat did little to cover his underlying muscles while his hood could not distract from his lifeless gaze. The unending vitality exuding from his body and the barren look in his eyes gave him an uncanny and contradictory feeling.

For the past week, they had been scurrying over the

deepest parts of the forest in search of something. Despite their best efforts, however, they met with little success. Only one spot in particular had caught their attention. One where they found the remains of a group of mercenaries next to a beast's decayed bones.

The wolf-like creature attracted their attention because it was covered in a dark miasma. The dark air around it indicated traces of interference with the laws of life and death, a taboo in most lands. However, this didn't disgust them. On the contrary, it filled their eyes with devotion. After all, they were apostles of death.

Several years ago, their church had undergone a massive change. Most of the important clerics and followers had chosen to sacrifice their lives in a massive ritual, leaving only a few of them behind to take care of the church.

Fortunately for them, an old priest had stayed behind to take the role of leading them down their current path. On their own, they would've had little chance of surviving. Now, given the sacrifice made by their peers, there was an abundance of resources left in their vaults, opening a path for them to grow at a speed bound only by their talent and comprehension.

They were currently in the forest for an important mission. Based on the prophecy of a seer, traces of their god's legacy would be found in these lands, allowing their church to once again soar back the place it deserved. Of course, the man and woman felt pride at being entrusted this task. They had been chosen above all their fellow disciples after all.

That being said, the lack of results they had achieved so far did little to please them. The wolf confirmed the legacy was real, for it carried an uncanny energy of death that should not have manifested naturally. However, that only increased their worries. *Just what happened to the legacy they were after?*

After searching the southern parts of the forest to no avail, they started making their way north. Everything was uneventful until they arrived at a village an hour away from where they had found the wolf and the mercenaries. The stench of death in the village still hadn't faded, and the scene of carnage depicted by the blood on the earth was sufficiently vivid for both of them to realize what had happened there.

"Massacre?" asked the cloaked female. Her silver hair did little to hide the excitement in her eyes.

"Must've been," said the man to her side. His eyes were fixed on the village as if he was looking for something.

After dismounting and tying their horses to a tree, both of them made their way inside. The first thing to greet them was a group of bodies lying around, lifeless. Their appearance was similar to the dead men they found together with the un-dead wolf — that of common mercenaries covered in poorly crafted leather armor. The fact that their make-shift armor remained unscathed was particularly strange.

"This is weird," said the burly man. His lifeless eyes gazed at the group of bodies only to realize most of them hadn't even drawn their weapons. "What do you think happened here?"

"I'm guessing they pissed off someone they shouldn't have," said the woman to his side as she removed her hand from a dead body. Her pale fingers were now covered in a black miasma, making it look like she was wearing dark, translucent gloves. "These people died a true death."

Her partner froze for a moment after hearing those words. "A true death?" he asked, his tone filled with skepticism. "The amount of effort required to give someone a true death is no small deal. Are you sure someone did that to a group this big?"

"Yes, they died from damage to their souls," she said.

"There is no puncture damage to their bodies, no signs of poison, no blunt damage, nothing. What's more, there aren't any lingering desires attached to their bodies. Only true death can do something like this."

Normally, after someone died and their soul moved on, their body would be left with vestiges of their experiences during life. Whether they had experienced unrequited love, had an unaccomplished goal, or wanted revenge on someone, all those feelings would coalesce into an essence that would stay behind with their body. The fact that the bodies of those mercenaries had no such thing left on them could only mean one thing: they had ceased to exist.

The man gasped in shock at his partner's words. He walked towards the bodies and carried on the same analysis as the girl before ultimately confirming that his partner was right. How? How on earth was someone able to perform so many true deaths with such ease? He couldn't help but think this had something to do with the legacy they were after.

"Do you believe someone found the legacy before us?" he asked.

The cloaked woman pondered his question for a second before answering. "I would like to think that isn't the case. There are very few seers able to divine a legacy outside the boundaries of their faith," she said. "Moreover, I refuse to believe there is someone able to perform something of this scale without divine intervention. Not in this kingdom, anyway."

The man couldn't help but agree with his partner's words. Despite being a little insane, she was recognized as someone with great potential in their order. Since that was the case, they were better off acting like someone had received their legacy before them.

"Should we keep heading north?" he asked.

After pondering it for a moment, she shook her head in reply. "I'd like to check the rest of the town. What's more, I have some use for these bodies."

"What are you planning to do?"

The girl smirked. "It would be a waste to leave all these ownerless toys lying around, wouldn't it?"

The man's eyes widened at her words. The path of death was broad and thus boasted quite a staggering variety of subjects, ones that could enlighten their followers on its many mysteries. While he had studied the realm of poisons, it was only one out of countless others such as assassination, combat, necromancy, and curses.

He knew his partner was skilled in the last two, so he decided to leave her to her own devices while he scoured the rest of the town. He had better things to do. Seeing her play with the corpses was not as important as gathering more information regarding their mission's objective.

Eventually, the woman started moving the corpses next to each other while whistling tunes and hymns from her faith. The excitement she displayed while doing so was reminiscent of a child playing with dolls. A normal human's aversion to death was nowhere to be found on her. On the contrary, her touch upon the corpses looked more humane than the way most humans treated each other.

Seeing her focused on her own 'games', the man made his way to search for clues around the settlement. He knew finding something useful might take a while. Although the settlement wasn't that big, a proper amount of attention to detail was needed given the importance of their task.

Slowly, he examined every home and building. Aside from the blood covering some trails, the broken doors, and the flattened farmland, everything he could see seemed to be in order. At least, that was the case until he saw what seemed to be a makeshift graveyard.

"Interesting," he said to himself. Using his hands, he brushed away the soil above each grave, only to realize that they had been made quite recently. The soil was still loose, showing the elements of nature hadn't had the time to pound it into place.

These graves were the ones dug by Amro for the villagers. Given the time he had and the physical constraints of his body, most of them had been buried at a shallow depth. Hi actions were more of a token for the dead than a true, proper burial.

Dead mercenaries and buried villagers, thought the man. *Is the one responsible for bringing true death to the mercenaries the same person responsible for burying these villagers?*

It was an oddly compelling thought, one his instincts fully supported.

The man took off the pauldron covering his left shoulder, using it to dig up one of the mounds. The act of desecrating a grave was not beneath him, for he had done it several times already in the past.

After a few minutes of digging, he was able to pull out a body from the grave. It was the remains of a middle-aged woman. Tall boots, a heavy apron, and plenty of cuts on her hands told her a story of her life's work.

"She was probably a butcher."

After taking a look at her, he placed the corpse aside. It was time to get dirty. The man's lifeless eyes seemed to glimmer with a black light as he covered his hand with the same dark miasma his partner had used.

This was the nature of his own aura, something born from the affinity of his soul. Unlike his partner, he wasn't that skilled at using this technique. However, given that she would be playing with her toys for a while, he had no other choice but to examine the body himself.

His hands dug into the butcher's rib cage, a series of different reactions occurring to the miasma in his hand. He felt resentment, sadness, and frustration coming from the woman's body. All of them were traces of the negative emotions that should have overwhelmed her before her death. However, amongst them all, he could also feel something else. Something hidden deep within her.

He focused on the alien feeling as he tried to use his aura to sense and identify it. A few moments later, he finally managed to place what that feeling was. Hope. Something that had no reason to be in her lingering soul. Something that had probably been placed there after the time of her death.

Such a grotesque emotion, he thought to himself. *There are no uses for it. Hope alone can't change someone's fate, only power is capable of such a feat.*

Moving forwards, the burly man decided to keep carrying on his analysis.

"These people were killed by physical methods it seems. They look nothing like the mercenaries from before." Of course, that much was obvious given that the body was covered in cuts and bruises seemed to prove this point.

"Perhaps, the death of this woman and the rest buried over here was under the hands of the mercenaries' weapons. It is then reasonable to think that whoever had dealt with the mercenaries also buried these corpses. Could there be a relationship between them?"

"That must be it," he said, reassuring himself of his own conclusion. Without any further delay, he hauled the butcher's body over his shoulder, ignoring the fluids spreading over his cloak. It was probably better to have his partner look over it.

"Noelle!" he said. "Look at what I found."

The silver-haired woman turned back, an annoyed look on her face. She had been inscribing symbols over the dead bodies of the mercenaries, too busy to worry over her partner's actions.

"What is it?" she asked. It took her a moment before she noticed the body hanging over the man's shoulder. Immediately, she shot up with interest and examined the body, barely letting her partner place it on the ground.

"Oh," she said. Her expression turned into one of curiosity as she placed her delicate hands over the dead butcher's body. After a few moments, her face contorted into many expressions, before it finally settled onto a look of confusion.

"So many feelings," she noted. "I like the taste of her despair the best. It looks like she experienced a lot of it before dying."

A wicked smile painted her face as she continued, "However, I can't help but feel that this corpse was meddled with after her death. It's like someone helped dislodge part of the lingering attachments it had. Had you not brought it to me and with enough time, this soul might have been able to move on its own, eventually entering the cycle of reincarnation."

Finishing her analysis, Noelle stood up and wiped the dust from her knees. "It seems like whoever played with our friends over here also had an interest toward the residents of this little village."

The man nodded his head. As expected from his partner, she quickly arrived at the same conclusion he had.

A glint of mischievousness appeared on Noelle's eyes. Slowly, she extended an offer her partner found hard to refuse. "Bernard, I do have an idea for something quite fun. I'll need your help. Can you tell me whether there are any more bodies from where you took this one?"

"Yes, there were at least another few dozen graves," he answered.

The smile on the woman's face seemed to widen, just like a child discovering that their favorite shop had more than one aisle.

"That's so much better. Bring me all of their bodies, I'll use them to track down the one responsible for all of this. There's a high chance he's carrying our lord's legacy with him."

The man's lifeless gaze seemed to regain all of his vitality for a quick second. Nothing could excite him more than the notion of being useful to his church.

"I'll start digging then," he said. He had already removed his other shoulder pad in order to double his digging speed.

"You do that, I'll finish attaching the strings to my new puppets," Noelle answered. Even before her partner had left, she had already knelt beside the bodies of the mercenaries to continue with her work.

"We'll meet you soon."

CHAPTER 22

Beliefs.

While deep undercurrents were assaulting the forest and the noble's district, celebration reigned through the slums of Sol. The building that belonged to Zaros's gang was filled to the brim with residents of the slums celebrating their victory. Amongst them, only a few had refrained from participating in the festivities. They weren't the kind to reject free food without a good reason.

Nevertheless, a very select group had refused to participate. They were the slums' leaders who had met together with Zaros in order to discuss the events that led to the celebrations. Two figures, however, felt deeply out of place. Alexander and Maria. Many had insisted they had to be present given how the events from that day were so deeply related to them.

"I know I'm in no place to say this, but they won't stay still after all of this," said Alexander. His brows were furrowed while his face was slightly pale.

After rescuing his sister, he began realizing the consequences of his actions. Back when they were in the midst of everything, he was too focused on fighting to think about the backlash that would come their way. Their visit to the eastern district would be taken as a provocation by those arrogant nobles, and they were not the kind of people to let bygones be bygones.

Zaros stood in silence, waiting for the rest of his subordinates to offer their opinions. Amro had already assessed the situation for him, but he wanted to hear his subordinates out before deciding on a course of action. Despite his inexperience as a leader, the boy was eager to do his best for the people under him.

On the other side of the room, Maria mimicked Zaros's silence. She knew the problem was brought upon by her kidnapping. As such, she felt she had no place to take part in the conversation.

Coincidentally, most of the people in the room also remained silent. After today's events, many of them were afraid to say something out of place for fear of inciting Zaros's wrath. Very few had the courage or ignorance to speak freely like Alexander. Even those who did, did so while holding much of their opinions to themselves.

The overall silence filled Zaros with disappointment. One of the most important virtues a person could have was their own courage. A quality all the men before him seemed to lack. To him, they looked more like docile kittens than eager wildcats.

"What we did today had to be done," he said, looking at the group around him. "I don't regret my actions. Someone had to draw a line on the nobles' behavior."

Once again, no one dared to speak their mind, causing Zaros to sigh. It was no surprise then that he felt lucky when the silence of their meeting was interrupted by a knock at the door.

Alexander took off a makeshift dagger from his waist whilst the two burly brothers who used to guard the base's entrance grabbed swords of their own.

"Calm down," said Zaros, signaling everyone to sheath their weapons. "You can come in."

A robed man stepped inside. A few strands of flaxen hair fell from his hood, calling away the attention from his uncoordinated and clumsy gait. It was Slyfox.

Other than Zaros, everyone else felt momentarily astonished when the old overlord of the slums made his way in. They had not expected to see him back so soon. Only after a few seconds did sneers and murmurs regarding his condition start spreading between the smaller gangs' leaders.

Seemingly unaffected, Slyfox stated his opinion on the ongoing conversation. His enhanced senses had alerted him to the topic of their conversation long before being allowed in.

"The solution is rather easy," he said, pointing his finger towards Zaros. "We can offer you to the nobles. I'm sure they would let their grievances go in exchange for your head."

Zaros thought over Slyfox's words before deflecting them with his own assessment of the situation. He had long formed an idea of the way the old leader of the slums viewed him thanks to Amro.

"I won't dig into why you're here of all times after running away. After all, our deal was for you to become my subordinate," Zaros said, causing Slyfox's face to crumble in visible anger. "However, what you just said proves my point. Sacrificing our people to get in the nobles' good graces solves nothing and only delays the problem, weakening our standing for an illusion of peace."

"What do you think the nobles will do after I'm gone? At best, they'll increase their efforts to exploit everyone, weakening the residents of the slums until they can get rid of their threat once and for all. They won't let this go. We've proven we can fight back."

"You dare say **our** people?" replied Slyfox sarcastically. "I'm pretty sure you're not even from around here. Are you?"

"Has that stopped me from taking care of them better than you?" asked Zaros.

Slyfox's brows furrowed as he removed his hood. He was visibly angry, holding himself back only on the realization that he couldn't defeat the kid in a fight. Even more so with his leg still injured.

"You think angering the nobles and placing a target on everyone's back is taking care of them?" asked Slyfox. At this point, his voice was raspy, making it evident that he had consumed a little too much alcohol recently.

"I'm still here for them," Zaros answered. "That's better than you who left them on their own once you had no use for them."

"So, you think that's enough to make up for the damage you've caused?" countered Slyfox. "Nothing but the foolish words of a child. Your shoulders are not broad enough to save others apart from yourself. You're nothing but a naïve, ignorant boy."

This time, Zaros had trouble coming back with an answer. Flashbacks of the villagers' lifeless eyes filled his mind for a second before being dispelled by his own memories of running away. Only the notion of how he had strengthened himself with Amro's help broke him out of his grim thoughts.

Slyfox no longer bothered talking to the child. He scoffed, reassured by the fact that the nobles would probably chose to deal with the boy before attacking the slums as a whole. It gave him a chance to sweep in as a savior, recovering everything that was rightfully his.

The air in the room became tense with each second of

silence that went by. Most of the small gang leaders remained silent, for as much as they had mocked Slyfox moments before, they knew he was still stronger than all of them.

It took the time a few minutes for someone to break the silence. It was Maria, the brown-haired girl who had been serving as Zaros's meal-delivery girl the few days before her kidnapping.

"I think you're wrong," she said. "It hasn't been long since boss took over, but the changes are already visible. There isn't as many people hungry on the streets and our need to be part of crime has lowered. Instead of spending most of our profits on alcohol and drugs, it's being invested in providing food for the others."

"And how long do you think that will last?" interrupted Slyfox, pointing to the rest of the people in the room. "Do you think they will agree with not being able to use their profits as they see fit?"

Those pointed by Slyfox looked sideways, unable to retort the old leader's words. He was far too familiar with their darkest desires. While it was true that they feared and respected Zaros, there was a slight fire of rebellion inside them fueled by the fact that they were being micromanaged.

"How long do you think it will be before they rise against this kid? They might not voice their discontent because of fear, but even if the nobles don't kill him, they will eventually try to do so themselves. The law of the slums has always been the culling of the weak. If we just feed and shelter them, they will grow complacent. How do you think the slums were formed in the first place?"

Zaros frowned. *It's true,* he thought. He had used his strength and everyone's fear of him to enforce his orders. Very few were willing to follow them out otherwise. Initially, he didn't plan to take over the gang, but once Amro had given him control, he had forced his ideals on them. It caused Zaros to feel conflicted. Was he the same as Slyfox?

Maria went silent after Slyfox's reproach. Despite being young, she could understand the meaning behind his words. It was part of human nature. Even she was willing to throw someone under if she or her brothers could benefit from it.

"You're still offering no solution," said Alexander. He stepped up from his place beside Zaros, chin held high. After what had happened recently, he was willing to become Zaros's number one lackey if the boy ever requested it.

"Everything you just argued is something we have to change," he admitted. "If it was a couple of days ago, I might've thought differently. Hell, I might have done so yesterday. If someone had told me that I had to risk my life in order to save someone else, I would have refused without thinking it twice."

Seeing everyone's eyes on him, Alexander gathered his thoughts before continuing. "I have changed, though. When Maria was taken, I had no one to turn to, no way to get anyone's help without compensation. Just who would be selfless enough to help me?"

"Only boss extended his hand. I don't think he is being idealistic; rather, it is us who have forgotten what it means to have compassion. I know I'm in no place to take the moral high ground when I'm to blame for all of this, but I can't agree with you, Slyfox."

The old leader of the slums looked at the young man with curiosity. Never had the teenager been able to look him straight in the eyes before this day, much less challenge him as he had done just now. He smiled, feeling a mix of pride and pity.

"It seems like even my men have been contaminated by your way of thinking," he said, looking at Zaros. "I never thought the day would arrive where not only would I lose my men, but the slums would lose their ideals. You think peace is achievable without sacrifices? Fine, prove it."

"You should listen to him this once, boy. His ideals might be different from your own, but his foresight isn't all that bad; sometimes you will need people like this by your side, willing to make the choices you do not want to," Amro advised.

Zaros's tunnel vision could become his downfall. That's why Amro found it rather convenient to have him clash with people who had a different point of view from his own. With exchanges like this, the boy could grow a much broader perspective. If he didn't, he would have no choice but to learn it the hard way, through more sacrifices of his own.

Zaros disagreed with Amro's words, however. Even if the choice to take over the gang had not been originally his, he had grown fond of them. How then could he forgive some-one who was willing to see his own men as sacrificial pawns? Wouldn't that make him the same as the royal family who or-dered his village's death?

Using his denial as courage, Zaros continued, "You told me I'm a hypocrite for forcing my interests upon my subordin-ates. I won't deny that much."

"However, what does that make you? You are just as guilty of that as I am. All the slums' money had to go through your hands, so don't you dare point your finger at me."

"I won't deny that I took my share," answered Slyfox with a sneer plastered on his face. "But you seem to be wrong about something. I made the slums what they are now. Before me, the nobles did as they pleased with everyone inside. At least under me, they were somehow protected. What is one or two people getting sold as slaves when another fifty get to live because of it? I brought order to chaos."

Hitting his fist on the wall, Slyfox continued. "You haven't even been in the slums for a month, but the nobles have already united to go against you. So what if I kept some profit to myself? At least I was considerate about the consequences my actions had on everyone else."

Slyfox's anger grew as he faced Zaros's criticism. Only he was aware of how much he had to endure, all so he could build his gang from scratch many years ago.

"That's not you being considerate. That's you being a coward," Zaros retorted. "Did you ever fight them? Were you willing to put your life on the line for them? Or, have you convinced yourself that you really did your best?"

Slyfox, however, wasn't willing to leave it at that. "You think it doesn't pain me to lower my head to those nobles? Every person I sacrifice is an admittance of my weakness. I chose wisely, the sacrifice of the few for the wellbeing of the many."

"I think you're losing track of what's important, boy," reprimanded Amro. "I won't comment on your ideals, but don't forget who your true enemy is."

Coming to the same realization as Amro, Maria interrupted their conversation.

"Stop! Don't you see the only ones who benefit from our internal fighting are the nobles? They don't even see us as humans. All they care for is how much profit we are able to provide them." A cold feeling of dread reminded her of something she would prefer to forget.

"Whether it is through sacrifice, or whether it is through fighting, our enemy remains the same. At this point, even that doesn't matter; they will be coming for us regardless of what we do. Their pride wouldn't allow them to behave otherwise."

The silence in the room was broken by everyone's sudden agreement. No one could dispute her words, not even Slyfox nor Zaros. Both of them might disagree on how to do things, but fundamentally, both cared for the wellbeing of their subordinates. It was how they cared about them that varied.

Since the two of them shared this sentiment, it would have been foolish to keep arguing. They could only compromise on what to do next.

"I plan to set up a resistance against them," said Zaros. "I'm convinced we can even get help from the commoners if we convey our intentions to them properly."

"I don't think that will be the case. Not once in my decades here have I seen those spineless commoners involve themselves with our people. Regardless, I'll help you as I deem fit," Slyfox answered. "However, I'll refrain from doing so openly. When your plans fail, I need to be there to pick up your slack."

Zaros smiled, understanding Slyfox's intentions. He planned to help only enough to have a claim to the 'throne' should he fail.

Amro laughed as he watched the mortals squabble over something so trivial. As long as he was here, even if the boy decided to go against the world on his own, Amro was sure he would find a way to win. His restraint from meddling into the boy's business so far was only because he wanted to encourage the boy's personal growth. In the end, while he could guarantee power to the boy, he couldn't guarantee mental fortitude of an equivalent strength. That was something Zaros needed to cultivate on his own.

Thanks to Maria's brief speech, everyone found themselves cooperating to create a united front. They still had much to do before confronting the nobles. Fortunately, after

the recent raid on Baron Lapas's estate, they now had sufficient funding for whatever course of action they wished to
take.

The next few days would be quite busy for every faction.

CHAPTER 23

A cup of tea over a cup of poison.

After last night's party, every hoodlum in town woke up full of energy. The recent influx of wealth in the slums' economy had enlivened all the residents' spirits. For the first time in forever, no one in the slums had to endure a morning of hunger.

That day, the center of the city was unusually filled. Every restaurant and tea shop was filled to the brim with new customers aiming to experience something new. Hoodlums who would have never pictured themselves eating inside an establishment were able to afford the luxury for the first time in their lives.

The shop owners knew where the new customers came from. But given that not even the nobles dared to take action against them, they were not going to stop the new faces from spending their money in their shops. The extraordinarily lively atmosphere in the city center made everyone feel prosperous for the first time in a long time.

This feeling was shared by the commoners to a certain extent. If prosperity came to the western side of the town, the businesses in the rest of Sol would eventually flourish as well. They might even grow into a full-fledged city with enough time.

Such ambiance was enjoyable to the common folk, and as such, even a pair of foreigners were able to enjoy the lively ambiance inside a small tea house.

"I never expected this town to become like this overnight," said a man covered in a gilded white robe. Even though he had a common appearance that would not stand out in a crowd, his playful and lively eyes were charming in their own way. As he waited for his partner's answer, he admired the white hair and grey eyes reflected on the surface of his tea.

"Indeed. Who would have thought that yesterday's commotion would bring today's excitement?" asked the other priest rhetorically. He was too busy combing his obsidian-like hair with his hands to notice his partner's table manners. His expression was a bit more solemn than his partner's, but his opinion about the recent events was all the same.

Both men were envoys sent by the capital's division of the Church of Life to help the Church of Harvest. A couple of years ago, their church had formed an alliance with many smaller deities' churches, taking them in like some form of vassals.

Even if the followers from those churches didn't hold a particularly strong belief in their goddess, they were still able to benefit from the different tithes and offerings collected. As to what reason would have pushed their higher-ups to form such an alliance, both of them could only imagine. Their status in the church wasn't all that significant.

Both of them were rank two priests. Unfortunately for them, in the grand scale of their church, they were nothing special. Being 'ordinary', however, didn't free them from their responsibilities. They still had a duty to manage the vassals their church had taken under its wings.

Their current mission had three sides to it. First, they

were ordered to collect whatever offerings the Church of Harvest may want to deliver to their church. Second, they had to pay attention to the residents of the town in order to find any promising youths who would devote themselves to their faith. Lastly, they were to bless whatever water reservoirs the church kept to themselves.

This was, in their opinion, a waste of their capabilities. Even if they were unable to cast major blessings, they were still able to use minor heals or smite their opponents with their goddess' holy energy. That being said, turning water into its holy variety was still a great underestimation of their capabilities.

Not that they could do much about it.

The desire to delay their mission for a while drove both men to spend a couple of days in the central part of town. Thus, they decided not to report themselves to the Church of Harvest for the time being. At the very least, they felt entitled to one day of rest.

However, not even in their wildest dreams did they expect to see something as unusual as yesterday's events. A group of thugs guided by a young man had decided to assault the troops of a noble. In addition, the mob had actually succeeded and claimed the lives of most of the noble's troops.

Normally, the sight of wanton death would have caused priests of their church to frown in disgust. However, Baron Lapas had a reputation even they knew about. The man was a friend of enslaving people and instigating wicked methods of torture to break their spirits.

Unfortunately, politics and religion often mixed in the worst of ways. Given Baron Lapas's influence over the Kingdom of Nyx, all low-ranking priests had received a directive not to interfere with the man or his business. An order they had been glad to comply with for once.

However, something else bothered them about that day's events. There was an eerie feeling of death within the crowd far too dense to be considered normal. The few dozen kills caused by the mob shouldn't have been enough to condense an energy of death of that level. It was something they would have to investigate before returning.

"So, Lucille, do you think we should report in today?" asked the common-looking priest.

"Probably," answered his partner, taking a sip of his tea. "It's going to be quite troublesome to join so soon after yesterday events, though. They will try to pin their responsibilities onto us. Worst-case scenario, they will request us to heal the survivors from that incident."

Resting his back on his chair, Lucille continued, "Ugh, it's going to be so annoying! Does their church not have any high ranking priests who can use a mass-heal? These backwater towns are such a drag."

"I know, pay it no mind for now. What would you think if—"

As he turned around to look at his partner, the obsidian-haired priest caught a glimpse of something happening on the outside. He didn't even bother finishing his sentence. A big crowd seemed to be gathering, foreboding another bothersome event.

"Can't we enjoy a single day of peace?" he said, placing a golden coin on the table as he got ready to leave. "Let's go check out what's happening, Lucille. More trouble seems to be coming our way."

Lucille stared at his partner with a look of confusion. "Hey, Michael, where are you going?" he asked, watching the raven-haired cleric step outside the store. Seeing he was not going to get any answer, he gulped down the remainder of his tea in one go, standing up and leaving the establishment.

What greeted them both of them as they stepped outside was a crowd gathered around two simple-looking men. It was the Weaver brothers. Both of them looked rather wounded and disheveled as if they had been running through shrubbery for several days and nights. Even their humble clothes had been torn to shreds. Their appearance looked rather dramatic, considering they were in the middle of town.

Next to them stood a beautifully dressed lady with charming features. She was the merchant who had hosted the meeting in the eastern district the day before. Her golden hair rested on her shoulders while her hands rested on her hips, subtly attracting the gazes from those who were not sufficiently enraptured by the commotion.

"Please hear us out, residents of Sol. The rebels are upon us! Please, ready yourselves before you suffer the same fate as we did," said the eldest of the Weaver brothers while looking at the crowd.

The younger brother soon echoed, "Our families were massacred, our friends burned to ashes. Ready yourselves, the rebels are coming!"

As if receiving a cue, the well-dressed blonde accompanying the two of them stepped forward, using her allure to guide all the gazes to herself.

"Do you see, my dear people? The rebels might attack our town very soon. The peace we've worked so hard to build is being threatened. I wouldn't be surprised if they had been working on this for long, eroding the harmony we all had achieved. As a matter of fact, don't you think there is someone in particular who has tried to divide us?"

Down in the crowd, both priests glanced at each other. The questions in their eyes were the same. First, were the rebels really coming? As members of the clergy they were deeply aware of the kingdom's politics. There was no strategic value for their group to attack this town. They were already winning the war up-north without bothering to do such a thing, anyway.

Second, what did she intend to do by sharing this information with the commoners? If anything, she was better off rallying the nobles' personal troops first. Inciting mass panic was counterproductive to the civilians' protection.

"Is that Lady Faraz?" asked the obsidian-haired priest. "I see her reputation precedes her."

"Indeed, those curves and emerald eyes can only belong to her," answered Lucille. Fortunately for him, the church of life didn't frown upon his lascivious thoughts. If anything, they were mildly encouraged. That is, so long as he procreated and eventually formed a family of his own.

This white-haired priest had a not-so-hidden habit of keeping track of the best looking women amongst the nobles. What's more, he held a secret he would never admit. He had joined the Church of Life based on the depiction of their goddess alone, not because of his faith in their creed of the church. If anything, his faith was towards beauty. Something that might explain his slow progress as a priest.

Ignoring the last part of the lecherous statement, Michael turned back to look at the woman speaking to the crowd. He was far too used to his partner's behavior to care anymore.

Passionate and energetic, Lady Faraz kept pushing her agenda. "Don't be fooled, dear people. You can't believe the rumors from the north! The rebels are not as charitable as they are made to seem. Those who refuse to join them are always cut down, just like these two men's family and friends."

"Do you think you will be any different?" she said, subtly compelling the people to take her side. Even if her manipulation had been clear as day, most people were too focused on her eyes and figure to care about it.

"What do you expect us to do?" complained someone from within the crowd. He was one of the very few still sitting on the fence. Hearing him, a few others nodded in agreement. It wasn't like they counted with the same resources as the nobles in order to fight off an armed group of rebels.

Lady Faraz smiled, taking the interruption as an opportunity to further her agenda. "I just want you to refrain from falling to their lies. They will whisper sweet promises into your ears, offering heaven and earth to get you to do their bidding. But they're all lies! I want you to remember that when the traitors hanging amongst us request your help."

Michael frowned as he listened to her arguments. Her voice was compelling, but her words lacked any kind of honesty behind them. To him, her intentions were crystal clear. If there was a threat, she wanted to use the people's emotions and fear of the unknown to take the brunt of the rebels' attack. At the very least, she wanted to make them hesitate from going against the aristocracy of the kingdom.

He was familiar with the nobles' line of thinking. They would rather have thousands of commoners sacrifice themselves on the front-lines than spend a few of their own soldiers and resources to face their enemies.

If only the church didn't forbid us from meddling.

His face became grim as he pondered whether he should break his oath for this issue. After all, such a decision would have ramifications neither he nor his partner could shoulder on their own. The best course of action he could take right now was to send a carrier bird to the capital and let the Church's headquarters make the choice for them.

At that moment, however, a woman pushed herself out of the crowd. She cradled a child in her arms, her expression grave as tears flowed down her face. The face of her child looked no better than hers as black spots had covered most of it. Even the smell of death wafted from his body.

"They poisoned my son!" cried the woman. "Please, my lady, please help him. I found him like this next to the well."

Afraid of coming in contact with the boy, most of the crowd took a step back. They feared it could be contagious. The woman was left at the front with her child, facing Lady Faraz and the two fake villagers.

"It must be those rebels!" she cried. "My family has used that well for decades. It is not by chance that this happened to my son!"

Both priests turned to look at each other, pushing the crowd apart in order to examine the boy. The blonde merchant's eyes widened as she recognized their robes.

Those are members of the Church of Life! she thought with happiness. The past few days had constantly given her a stream of pleasant surprises. Being present when the priests appeared would help her achieve her purpose.

If the priests determined the boy was poisoned, then her argument would gain instant credibility amongst the commoners. Because of that, she cruelly hoped for the boy's death. It would be the catalyst to drive the commoners to her side. Things like the mother's feelings and the son's fate were unimportant — she only cared about her profits.

Michael caressed the boy's face with his smooth hands. His expression turned more solemn the longer he did so. It was clear the boy's condition had something that worried the man greatly. He eventually began chanting a small prayer, emitting a soft white light from his hands. With the use of his healing spell, he had been able to dispel a few of the black spots in the child's face. However, some of them had yet to disappear.

Seeing it had been partially ineffective, Lucille repeated the chant, casting another heal of his own until the boy's face cleared up.

Both men stood up, taking a few steps back in order to give the mother some space to hug her child. They glanced at each other again before the black haired priest mustered the courage to speak.

"Villagers of Sol, as you might have noticed, we are priests from the Order of Life. This boy we just treated was afflicted by a malicious poison. For the time being, we can only advise you to avoid the well this boy visited for the time being. We will immediately investigate this. Please, request the help of the church if you see anyone with similar symptoms."

Having said that, the priests turned to look at the blonde merchant, motioning for her to move closer. "We need you to tell us just what is going on in this city in detail, my lady. Meet us at the Church of Harvest."

After the woman agreed to their proposition, both priests left her to her own devices.

On the other hand, Lady Faraz wasn't going to let this heaven-sent opportunity go to waste. She started going on about her cause, further scaring the crowd about the dangers of allying themselves with the rebels.

As she continued with her charade, both priests discussed the issue at hand. They were currently walking to the church of Harvest but the issue was far too important to leave for later.

"Did you sense the same thing I did from the boy?" asked Michael to his partner. His expression was now considerably grim. It spoke of volumes of how much importance he placed over this issue.

The normally aloof white-haired priest nodded solemnly. "That was the scent of death. That vile poison is something only their kind uses. Do you really think the rebels have allied themselves with that cursed church?"

"I don't know. If they have, our church will have no option but to intervene in the kingdom's war. Our goddess' commands may tell us not to involve ourselves in the conflicts of mortals, but it becomes another issue altogether when those evil foes become involved."

Both men remained solemn as they made their way to the church. Their steps were as heavy as the concerns that had been laid upon their shoulders. Just what would they have to face in the future?

CHAPTER 24

Tainted Alchemy.

"**P**lease, help my husband!"

"Don't let my child die, please! I beg of you, please!"

A crowd of people blocked the entrance to the Church of Harvest endlessly begging for their help. What had started as an orderly line of people waiting their turn, had quickly dissolved into chaos. Faced with the threat of death, very few were able to remain composed.

Eventually, the mob of people started storming their way inside the church, demanding treatment for them and their loved ones. They feared delaying any further would ruin their chance at salvation. Too many had died already.

The reason behind the mob's behavior was simple, however. A deadly poison had spread further than anyone could have expected. After the crying mother had showed up with her son at the plaza, many more cases had arisen around the town of Sol.

The first cluster of cases appeared close to where the first boy was found. Right in the middle of the northern district inhabited by the commoners. Unfortunately for everyone, it wasn't an isolated matter. It soon became common amongst the other districts as well.

Normally, a case of poisoned water would have been dealt with by pouring large amounts of holy water into the contaminated source. However, this case was different and considerably harder to deal with. The Church of Harvest didn't have nearly enough holy water available to purify the threat of a poison made by disciples from the Church of Death.

On the church's ground, a white-haired priest could be seen taking a break. He was Lucille, one of the two priests sent by the Church of Life. His chest was covered in sweat and his robes rose and fell with the rhythm of his agitated breathing. He was completely exhausted. It had been hours since he had last been able to take a break.

As much as he would have liked to return to the job, he needed some rest before he could continue to cast spells and blessings. Never would he have expected the situation would deteriorate into its current state.

As he recovered his strength, the priest couldn't help but recall what led to this moment.

After arriving at the church, he and his partner had reported in with the priest in charge. To their surprise, the head of the church was a rank two priest, just like them. They had heard of the deterioration experienced by the peripheral churches, but they had never expected it to reach such an extent.

Glossing over the obligatory formalities, they urged the church to prepare some holy water to treat cases like the one they had encountered. Their reasoning was simple: events involving the Church of Death never ended with one of two victims. Many preparations were to be made in case more cases started appearing.

Treatment with special resources like this would normally cost a lot of money to those who sought it from the church. However, since the situation was related to the Church of Death, it would have gone against the churches' creed to charge for it. In cases like this, they had to prioritize interfering with whatever plans the apostles of death were orchestrating.

After blessing a couple barrels of holy water in preparation, he and his partner, along with a group of apprentices from the local church, had embarked on a trip to examine the water source from where the first case had originated. But to their surprise and horror, once they reached the northern side of town, they met dozens of people displaying similar symptoms to the boy they had seen at the plaza. Black spots covered their pale faces as the lingering scent of death stuck to their bodies.

Immediately, they proceeded to try to save as many of them as they could.

Seeing the apprentices from the Church of Harvest frozen in fear, Michael couldn't help but start yelling orders at them, "You, newbie, don't just stand there! Treat them with holy water!" After all, those unable to cast healing spells had to make themselves useful in some way.

However, the priests soon realized they didn't have enough holy water to treat so many people.

"What should we do?" asked Lucille. During this crisis, his easy-going behavior was nowhere to be found.

"You should go back to the church and support them from there. I'll examine the well in this side of town first, and then I'll go check those from the other districts. I'll release a signal into the sky if I need any assistance," answered the black-haired priest.

It took some effort to convince the fear-driven people to follow Lucille. Those who resisted were quickly subdued under the duo's forceful insistence. They couldn't afford the luxury of leaving people to their fate. Even those who had no salvation should be treated before dying to a poison tainted by the essence of death. The consequences of not doing so were grave. Incompetence could give rise to a legion of undead.

Once the group led by his partner left the vicinity, Michael made his way to the nearest well. He lowered the bucket next to it and took a sample of the water within. In the beginning, he tried blessing its contents in order to confirm his hypothesis. Unfortunately, he turned out to be right. The white glow that should have occurred from his blessing didn't take place. On the contrary, a black miasma rejected the energy from it.

"Indeed, the contents of the well have been tampered with."

However, despite his earlier conjecture, there were no signs of human meddling on the exterior of the well.

"I doubt anyone had enough time to pour the poison in the middle of the day," he said, talking to himself. "Judging from how many people were affected, this well is rarely left alone. With no doubt, the townsfolk would have noticed anything strange."

Just how did the poison make its way inside then? Michael wondered. There seemed to be no reasonable explanation for it unless someone from the town itself had poured the poison inside the well. However, his instincts told him that was far from being the correct answer.

Crack

Michael suddenly took a defensive stance. For a moment, his instincts had alerted him that he was being watched by someone with unkindly intentions. Decisively, he turned his head around, trying to find whoever was hidden in the shadows.

However, all he could see in his surroundings were a couple of birds and vermin common to the town. He was all by himself. Aside from the dead townsfolk lying around, there was no one else in his vicinity.

Am I being too paranoid?

Confused, Michael turned around. However, that didn't mean he was truly alone. It was his own inexperience that had blocked him from finding the true perpetrator.

Without his knowledge, he had earned the cold stare of a crow perched upon a tree branch. Its pitch-black feathers were stained by a series of red inscriptions, but the creature seemed to care not about them. It just stood motionless, mechanically tracking every move the priest made.

The bird continued staring for a while as if it was imprinting the Michael's appearance onto its eyes. Only after the priest left the well alone did it disappear, flying off into the night's embrace. From then on, its destination would only be known by the creature and its master.

After achieving no results in the northern district, Michael made his way towards the western side of town. The next thing on his to-do list was to check the state of the nobles' side. He originally intended to go to the southern district, but unfortunately, he was now on his own. He no longer held the amount of manpower required to deal with that side of town.

If that was the case, there would be nothing he could do with what little resources he had available at the moment. As such, he decided to go towards the eastern district first, where the nobles would probably provide him with assistance.

However, just as he entered the vicinity of aristocrats' territory, he saw something unexpected. A group of guards were holding back a well-dressed man making a ruckus. Despite his pale complexion, the willowy elder spared no effort to get away from their hands. The energy behind his frantic movements couldn't be underestimated.

"My lord, please, let's visit the church first. Madam needs the treatment," pleaded one of the guards.

"Yes, my lord. Please have some hope, this tribulation shall pass," added another one.

After coming closer, Michael managed to recognize the man the guards were holding. He was a wealthy merchant in charge of a series of businesses across the town. In fact, the insignia sewn onto his clothes was exactly the same as the one hung on the entrance of the tea shop he had visited earlier that day.

Still, the noble in question wasn't having any of it. "I tell you, it must be that accursed boy! Ever since his arrival in town, everything has been turned upside down. I'll murder him myself! If anything happens to my wife, not even the gods will be able to shelter him from my wrath."

It was clear that he was infuriated about something. That being said, the old merchant lacked sufficient strength to escape the hold of his servants. His futile attempts did nothing but make a joke out of himself.

As Michael approached their group, he decided to pretend he hadn't heard the elder's words of blasphemy against the gods.

"Greetings," he said. "I'm a priest sent by the Church of Life, currently staying over at the Church of Harvest. I wonder whether I could have a word with you regarding an important issue."

The noble's eyes lightened once the cleric introduced himself as a member of the Church of Life. Even a novice apprentice from their temple had a standing higher than his. He quickly regained his composure and ordered his guards back.

"Enlightened priest, forgive me for my rudeness, but before you continue any further, I have a request to make of you. My wife has been afflicted by some strange sickness, black marks have spawned across her body. Could you please check her health?"

Michael's eyes wavered upon hearing the noble's request. *I'm too late. It has affected this side of town already*, he said to himself. *I still need his help though. Guess I have no choice but to give him this.*

Carefully, Michael took a small vial from the inside of his robes before passing it to the noble. It was a flask of holy water he had saved for himself, in case of emergency. At this time, he was willing to offer it to the elder in order to fulfill his goal.

"This is holy water blessed by our high priest at the capital. Give it to your wife, it should improve her condition until you make your way to the church," he instructed. "I do, however, request a small favor from you in exchange."

"Anything," answered the old man, carefully taking the vial from Michael's hands before he could regret it. He was willing to offer his own wealth as long as he could save his wife.

"Please have your guards assist me in warning the rest of town to avoid drinking water from the wells. It seems that they might have been poisoned. Also, if you happen to know of anyone else sharing your wife's symptoms, please send them towards the church."

"Of course my lord, as you order," replied the old merchant, turning to look at his guards. "You hear that you useless idiots? Go!"

"Very well," said Michael, uncomfortably scratching the back of his neck. "Thank you for your help. I must leave now, however, time is of the essence."

"Of course, my lord, may the blessing of life be with you."

Michael prepared to leave when he suddenly remembered something.

"By the way, I couldn't help but hear you were blaming someone just a moment ago. May I confirm if that boy you were talking about was the same as the one who caused a revolt yesterday?"

"Indeed, that's the one," answered the old man, the fire of hatred kindling in his gaze. "Ever since he popped up in our town, there has been one calamity after another. Not one person is safe from him!"

It was clear from the merchant's tone of voice that his opinion of Zaros was one he reserved for the worst of criminals. Only after calming himself down did he continue, "I'm sure he's the one behind this damned sickness."

"I see," answered Michael, slightly surprised by the elder's passionate hatred. "Could I bother you by asking if there is anything else worth noting about him?"

The noble was eager to help. Not only did he get something to save his wife, he could also take revenge on the target of his hatred. "Of course," he said. "I've heard from my sources that the little demon is an envoy from the rebels. It seems like he has been stirring those rats from the slums to take arms and rebel against the Kingdom."

"Interesting."

From what the priest had heard earlier that day in the city's center, the boy's relationship with the rebels was widely accepted as a fact. *Have the rebels really formed an alliance with that evil god's church?* he wondered. *Are they really that desperate?*

With a quick farewell, he left the noble and his remaining guards behind. Of course, he reminded them to fulfill his request of reporting the news towards the other nobles. He was short on time, and he still wanted to confirm whether the west and south had been affected by the poison as well.

Now, he had to choose which place to visit first. He was sure that going to the southern district would probably end up being fruitless. It was probably in the same condition as the northern district, with a great number of people affected. More than he could deal with. He just didn't have the man-power, mana, or holy water required to help them on his own.

His best option was to go and confirm whether the western side had its water sources poisoned as well. If the newcomer was really related to the rebels and to the plague like the nobles seemed to think, then perhaps he could get some answers from him.

"Why is my luck so bad?"

He hated having to involve himself in political con-flicts. However, if the boy was related to the church of death in any way, he wouldn't hold himself back. Even if his abilities as a rank two priest were easily disregarded in the capital, they should be more than enough to deal with some kid.

Thus, he made his way to the west.

CHAPTER 25

Broken perspectives.

Earlier that day, as the morning light graced the town of Sol, Zaros sat against a wall in one of the slums' many streets. Try as he might, he couldn't forget Slyfox's words. There was no denying that his decisions had been too rash.

Was I wrong? he asked himself. *Should I have kept Slyfox's system? I don't know how many more people will get dragged into this because of my actions. Perhaps some of them deserve it, but those who don't shouldn't have to pay for my mistakes.*

Zaros couldn't help but recall the way Maria had been dragged off to the slave dungeon of Baron Lapas. Thug or not, no one deserved a fate like that, no matter how short the experience had been. Especially not Maria. Even with a tough mask built from years of living in the slums, she had proven to be someone with a kind side.

Waves of doubt rippled in Zaros's mind. Was he willing to make sacrifices like that every time he wanted to accomplish something? What about his eventual goal of taking down the royalty of this kingdom?

He hadn't thought about it before, but if nobles had their guards, it was likely the royalty had an army defending them too. Would he be willing to take hundreds of lives to avenge a few dozen? Didn't that make him no different from those he so much despised?

Conflicting emotions clashed in his heart. Neither Alexander nor Maria's words had managed to soothe his worries. The seed of doubt was already planted.

After all, wasn't he the same as Slyfox? All the reagents he had used to advance to rank one had been paid by the gang's scarce resources. At first he didn't think much of it, but now he realized how selfish his actions had been.

How could he say he had been guarding the interests of this people? All he did was make choices that would affect them all. Not to mention Maria's kidnapping, something as basic as limiting the sources of their income could completely change their lives.

Under what pretensions had he, an outsider, judged their actions to be wrong?

Crack!

At this moment, Zaros wasn't in the mood to deal with whatever plan the nobles would come up with in retaliation. The small imprint of his fist on a wall made that much obvious. His current guilt and angst gave him too much to think about.

"Times like this make it obvious just how young and naïve you are," said Amro, annoyed by the boy's inability to fight his negative thoughts. "Cut it out already."

"And how old are you supposed to be?" retorted Zaros. "For all you criticize me and my decisions, there is little you have told me about yourself."

Amro sighed in silence, unhappy with being challenged. It took a great amount of self-control not to reveal his identity to the boy in order to make his point. Such rashness would offer him no benefits at this time. Neither would his host's attachment to this town. As far as he was concerned, he just wanted to be over with Zaros's revenge in order to continue with his own.

Of course, some things were off better not said.

"Perhaps it is time you move away from this city, boy. Your attachment to this people is becoming a burden to your mind."

Zaros only thought about it for a moment before giving his answer.

"I'm not weak," said Zaros. "On the contrary, it would be cowardly of me to run away after turning their lives upside-down. I can't just leave them to their own fate now."

Fool, your desire to protect them will be what brings their demise, thought Amro. *I've given you a warning, but it's up to you to deal with the consequences of your choices.*

Ever since the night before, Amro had a premonition. A very small part of his former clergy would try to reach out to him, or at the very least, what they thought was his legacy on earth. After all, the methods he had employed to hide from fate and divinations were far from perfect during the time he crafted his phylactery.

At this moment, however, he had no use for his former clergy. As a matter of fact, getting involved with them could complicate his plans. Being hidden from the pantheon of Gaia was his biggest advantage in his road to revenge.

"Boy, remember my words. Our path is one of death and loneliness. Relying extensively on others will eventually result in a future you're not able to shoulder. Your presence here might be more troublesome to them than your absence. Just think it over and walk away."

Still, that didn't mean he couldn't offer some of his

goodwill to Zaros. If the church tracked him down to this town, the fate of the townsfolk would become complicated. Death always followed behind his followers.

"How can you be sure something bad will happen to them?" mocked Zaros. "No one can see the future, it is in us to forge our own."

"Big words for such a small boy," retorted Amro. It bothered him that his advice was taken so lightly. "Very well, then. Do not complain that I didn't warn you beforehand in the future."

Zaros laughed it off. Bantering with Amro had helped him put aside some of his worries. Truth be told, he knew he would achieve nothing mourning over his past decisions. Right now, he just needed to see them through.

Realizing the sun was already reaching its peak in the sky, he couldn't help but pay attention to his growing hunger. It had been nearly a day since he last had something to eat. It would be a waste not to go and get himself something to splurge on after getting his hands on Baron Lapas's wealth.

Thus, Zaros went to the city's center to find something to eat. What he found was a plaza exuberant with life and joy. People crowded the streets while bards entertained them with music. It was nothing like its usual appearance.

He could see several stores, all of them enjoying an abundance of customers. He could even recognize a few familiar faces amongst them. It seemed like yesterday's loot had made many of his subordinates forget about their economic limitations. All in all, it was a pleasant surprise.

He entered a small shop blessed with the sweet smell of pastries. It was a commodity rarely seen in his village, one he hadn't been able to experience before. He opened the door to the fancy looking establishment, only to see several customers turn to look at him with surprise on their faces. Some of them muttered under their breath while others quickly paid their bills and left the shop.

Ignoring everyone's reaction to his presence, Zaros took a seat. After a few seconds, an attendant stood to his side. Auburn hair with bangs covering her ears gave her a cute but tidy appearance.

"Hello, sir. What can I get you today?" she asked, a deep glint of admiration showing in her eyes. It was easy to guess she was a commoner who sympathized with Zaros.

"Just bring me something sweet," requested Zaros. In the past, the children from his village had often mocked him for ignoring the taste of sweets. Now that he had a chance, he wouldn't hesitate to have some. "And some herbal tea, please."

"Anything in particular, sir?"

"Surprise me."

After waiting some time by the window, a different shop attendant brought him his order. A soothing, golden liquid in a gilded cup, and a piece of strawberry cake were placed before him. His mouth watered as he experienced the smell of desserts for the first time.

He couldn't help but mutter his praises unconsciously after having a bite, "Delicious."

The flavor of the strawberries perfectly complemented the spongy texture of the cake. His experience was only enriched by the gold-colored tea he had ordered. If he could enjoy something like this every day, then he might consider a new road in life.

Childish, thought Amro. Did such a simple dessert merit such praise? What kind of delicacies had he not tasted in this world? If only his host truly understood the importance of power, then the boy would realize that with it, he could eat whatever he wanted.

Even the attendants thought Zaros's reaction was a bit overboard. To them, it was just a piece of cake, nothing special. Wasn't he supposed to be the new lord of the slums? What was it with his behavior?

Nonetheless, Zaros kept enjoying his cake, ignoring the reactions of all of those around him. This was a new experience for him. Ever since he was a child, most of his diet had consisted on the leftovers the villagers gave him out of pity or the meat from those wild animals he managed to hunt. Enjoying the delicacies before him was worth ignoring his surroundings.

That being said, Amro was determined to not let the kid enjoy his snack. After all, the surroundings his host was so set on ignoring were quite important right now. "Boy, don't you think you should see what that's about?"

"What?" asked the dumbfounded Zaros. The call of his cake was far too strong for him to ignore. So strong, in fact, that he failed to notice the commotion that had been currently occurring outside the shop.

"Look out the window to your right," replied the annoyed death god. At times like this, he couldn't help but question whether fate had done the right thing by tying together their paths.

Reluctant to stop eating, Zaros looked out the window. Once he did, he found what Amro was going on about. A crowd seemed to be gathering around two men and a woman. The men were dressed like the people from his village used to, and the woman wore an eye-catching dress unfit for any manual labor.

"I think you better check what's going on around there," advised Amro.

Unwilling to leave the first dessert of his life unfinished, Zaros gobbled it up in a matter of seconds. It was unrefined, but effective. After placing a gold coin on the table, he opened the window, using the ledges in the building to climb towards the roof. From that vantage point, he could hear and see everything going on with more clarity.

"Please hear us out, residents of Sol. The rebels are upon us! Please, ready yourselves before you suffer the same fate as we did," said one of the two men standing at the center of the crowd.

Zaros's eyes twitched as he listened to the man's words. He claimed to be from the southern villages, a survivor of some kind. It was a situation he was skeptical about. When he and Amro investigated, they found no survivors left.

Not giving him time to think things through, the other 'villager' echoed. "Our families were massacred, our friends burned to ashes. Ready yourselves, the rebels are coming!"

And they are just showing up now? pondered Zaros. *The events they speak of happened nearly a month ago.* More than anyone, he was aware of the events that had transpired down south. The fact that he had seen other villages affected, meant village had been the last on the mercenaries' list. For these two men to have appeared now, he couldn't help but feel that something sketchy was going on.

"Do you see, my dear people? The rebels might attack our town very soon. The peace we've worked so hard to build is being threatened. I wouldn't be surprised if they had been working on this for long, eroding the harmony we all had achieved. As a matter of fact, don't you think there is someone in particular who has tried to divide us?" said the woman next to them.

It was clear she was using her appearance to hide the deception behind her words.

Anger erupted from within Zaros's heart. Was this the plan of the kingdom's royalty? Did they really intend to use the tragedy of his people as a political tool?

He couldn't continue listening to the words coming out of her mouths. Instead, he ingrained their faces into his memory. Zaros was now convinced those two 'villagers' were somehow involved with what had happened to his village.

Amro, however, noticed something else. "Boy, keep watching."

Zaros suppressed his emotions, focusing once again on the crowd. A woman carrying a child in her arms made her way through the rows of people, pushing everyone aside without a second thought.

"They poisoned my son!" cried the woman. "Please, my lady, please help him. I found him like this next to the well."

"How did you know that was going to happen?" asked Zaros. He felt Amro's foresight was incredibly uncanny at times.

"I sensed a putrid aura coming from that boy," answered Amro. "Someone used a bastardized version of the power from death's laws on him."

Zaros's eyes grew wide. The only other time he had heard Amro mention the so-called 'laws of death' was when he was instructing him inside his soul domain. It was still something far from what he could comprehend, but he knew it carried some serious implications.

"Boy, you might want to go back to your subordinates," instructed the fallen death god. "It's too late to leave town. Whatever targeted that boy will be coming for the town next."

Hearing Amro's serious tone, Zaros ran back to his base, jumping from roof to roof until he reached the slums. On his way there, he noticed more people lying around on the streets than normal. They seemed strangely fragile, almost like they were struck by disease.

A feeling of dread filled him, causing him to approach a man lying down on the ground. He turned the man over, only to see his skin covered with decaying black spots.

"What in the heavens?" gasped the boy. It was his first time seeing something like this up close.

"Shade of death," explained Amro. "A failed product created by mixing nightshade, cores of Goz beasts, and a few other ingredients. It's the result of combining beginner necromantic and alchemical arts."

"Can you cure it?" asked the boy, ignoring the words he wasn't familiar with. He didn't want to see people affected by something he sensed was related to him.

"It would be best if we just left town," argued the fallen death god. "This is related to your presence here."

"No, I feel that there is something you're not telling me," retorted Zaros.

With an annoyed grunt, Amro decided to answer the boy. "I warned you about it earlier, but you took it as a joke. Last night, I felt someone use a tracking spell on us. They should be the ones responsible for this."

"They?" asked Zaros. He felt Amro knew more than he let on.

"Apostles of death, or at least cheap imitations of the real kind. This poorly crafted poison is probably their work," Amro explained.

"Apostles of death?" asked Zaros. "No, never mind. Can you save them then? If this is our fault, it's the least we can do for them."

Sensing a headache would assault his incorporeal soul if he refused, Amro reluctantly agreed. "I can, but I feel it is more trouble than it's worth. If anything, I'll do it because letting them die to this failure of a poison would be an insult to my craft."

Not understanding the comment, Zaros decided to push his luck a little further. "Great, what do I have to do to save them?"

"Just give me control. It will be easier that way," said Amro.

Not long after he finished saying those words, Amro felt Zaros's consciousness leave for his soul realm. It seemed like the boy truly cared about saving the people from the slums.

How annoying, thought Amro. *I'll have to punish whatever fool is leading my church for interfering with my plans.*

All he could hope for was that the poison hadn't affected too many people. Amro hated bothersome tasks.

CHAPTER 26

Hope.

A series of makeshift beds had been set up in the slums' streets. Dozens of people lied down on the torn sheets and bundles of clothing, either gasping for breath or coughing out phlegms of dark color. They were the victims of the poison spreading inside the town of Sol.

While those afflicted by the poison had no choice on the matter, those who were still healthy had two paths available to them. The first choice was obvious: they could flee the city, prioritizing their own safety above everything else. The second, on the other hand, was less attractive and chosen only by a few. That was, of course, to stay.

It had been hours since the situation had developed into this state, but the hearts of the afflicted remained strong unlike their northern or southern counterparts. The reason for their strength stemmed from a single source — Zaros.

While he looked naïve and childish at times, at moments like this, he was proved them he was very reliable. Of course, no one amongst them knew that they were dealing not with Zaros, but Amro.

Amro offered them an opportunity for salvation. As such, he was free to give orders left and right, driving all the efforts necessary to achieve this purpose. Most of his subordinates were tasked with collecting reagents, trading for them when possible and looting when necessary. The rest, on the other hand, were tasked with gathering everyone affected by the poison in a single place, facilitating their accessibility to treatment. Finally, a small strike team led by Slyfox had been charged with sneaking into the Church of Harvest and 'retrieving' as much holy water as they could.

Amro made use of his time to prepare what little reagents were brought to him over time. With his skills, he was able to concoct something capable of neutralizing the poison afflicting the townsfolk. As the true lord of death, how could an imitation like this stump him?

Of course, the amount of antidote he could provide was limited. Because of that, the slums needed Slyfox's side of the plan to be successful in order to save the rest. Once that was done, dealing with the culprit would be the only task left.

As for the consequences that may occur from robbing the church, neither Amro nor Slyfox cared. They didn't get along with the clergy anyway.

All in due time, Amro thought to himself. Calming Zaros's consciousness had already become second nature to his actions during the past hour.

Despite being disconnected from humanity and their emotions for millennia, Amro's soul-link to Zaros had made him remember one fatal weakness of mortals — empathy. Because of this, he had no choice but to make an active effort. His link had made him realize how much his relationship with Zaros would deteriorate should he choose not to take action. In the end, if he helped and the results were still not favorable, he could at least wash his hands of the matter.

Alas, fate was a cruel mistress, and roadblocks were meant to be placed before every goal. While he was working on finding a solution, someone else had made their way to interfere with his plans. From the distance, a black-haired man covered in the white tunic of a cleric could be seen staring daggers at him. It was clear that his intentions were not good.

Noticing his presence, Amro sighed at the advent of another bothersome event. By his robes alone, he knew the bothersome fellow was a disciple from the Church of Life.

The cleric glared at him, not hiding his murderous intent at all. He had noticed the substance Amro was currently crafting, leading him to make all kinds of unkindly associations.

What is it with mortals and their inability to see beyond their horizons? thought Amro. This wasn't the first time since he had reincarnated into Zaros's body that a mortal thought they could take him on. It was increasingly frustrating to have to hold back his punches towards this kind of impulsive, ignorant human.

Sure enough, the priest made his way to Amro, ignoring all the people from the slums barring his path. His gaze was set on the boy and the alchemical solutions he had in his hands. It was clear beyond doubt that he had misunderstood the situation.

"You!" he said, his finger pointing towards Amro's face. "It was you who caused all of this. You dare to create such a thing out in the open? It must have been you who unleashed this calamity upon this town. Surrender now to the church for further questioning!"

Amro's eye twitched as he suppressed his anger. *It seems humanity has grown increasingly arrogant,* he thought.

In his first interaction after reincarnation, mortals had tried to intimidate him. The second time, they thought they could walk over him and make him the victim of robbery. And now, a mere mortal thought he could order him around?

He might have taken it from Zaros as listening to the naïve boy's requests was useful to him. But to take it from a random priest from the Church of Life? No way.

He dropped everything before him, grabbing the priest's finger with a swift motion of his hand. Once he saw Amro's movement, Michael tried to retract his hand. Unfortunately, once he did, he came to realize he couldn't move. His finger was already held within the boy's grasp.

How? thought the priest to himself. He could sense the boy was no more than a rank one. At best, he might be bordering rank two. Even then, that shouldn't have been able to match him in terms of hand-speed. Could a boy so young be knowledgeable enough to know how to hide his real rank?

"If you want to blame someone, blame yourself, priest. To not even realize you've been aiding them shows your own incompetence," said Amro. His grip over the priest's hand remained strong. Still, he had managed to control his ire just enough to avoid harming him.

Stopping him had been his priority. He knew how stupidly fast things would have escalated if he had left the priest to continue rambling.

Michael tried to use some mana to break away from Amro's grasp. To his surprise, however, he found that the mana in the environment wasn't being responsive. He had no way to know Amro had already suppressed it along with his chances to fight back.

Without it to enhance his strength, Michael knew he had little ways of getting away. Only then did he bother processing Amro's words. *My fault? What is he talking about?*

Fortunately for him, Amro soon answered his question. Not with words, but with actions.

Taking one of the stones he had been using to crush the herbs, Amro spoke up again. "See for yourself."

With a swift motion of his arm, Amro shot the stone into the sky. Surprisingly, instead of vanishing into nothingness, it suddenly came to a stop.

Thud!

Michael and the rest of the onlookers soon found out why. A crow missing a wing fell to the ground. Its feathers were as black as the night sky, making it nearly undetectable during its flight. Even after crashing into the ground, the creature struggled, apparently trying to get away.

Michael's eyes widened as he looked at the fallen bird. He quickly realized what the boy meant with his words. Even if they were slightly different from the ones he knew, the inscriptions covering the creature's plumage were something he recognized. They were the work of a necromancer; a forbidden class of mage who specialized in controlling dead bodies as their puppets.

"How — how did you know?" asked the astonished priest.

"Things are easier to see when you actually care to look for them," answered Amro. "With that out of the way, priest. Do you care about saving lives, or are you just here to toot your own horn?"

The priest remained quiet, unable to understand the boy's underhanded insults.

"I'm a busy person. Right now, I'm trying to neutralize the poison affecting these folks. Are you at least skilled enough to bless some holy water?"

Hearing his words, the priest finally broke out of his stupor.

"Of course I am!" he said. "I'm a rank two priest, someone trained in the capital!"

A snort was all Michael received from Amro regarding his so-called-training. For all the fallen god cared, the priest was a glorified water filter.

Michael was still confused. Thus, he tried to make sense of things by continuing with a barrage of questions. "How are you able to neutralize the poison of death? Are you not an envoy from the rebels? Are they truly working with the church of death?"

"Maybe, maybe not," answered Amro, going back to his work. "As for how I am able to deal with this so-called-poison, you're still too young to understand it."

Amro didn't even bother to look at the priest anymore. All his focus returned to grinding the herbs on his table and finishing the concoction he had started before the interruption.

"Why don't you take these people to the church? Are you even sure you'll be able to cure them? We can use the holy water stored in the church to wash away the poison once we're there."

Amro continued to crush the herbs without pause. It took a few minutes before he finally offered an answer to the priest. "Am I supposed to believe the church will actually treat them? Think about it yourself, priest. If these hoodlums were to appear at the same time as the nobles and the commoners, who do you think would receive treatment first? What's more, does that small church even have the capacity to treat a pandemic of this size?"

Amro's word struck Michael with sudden realization and guilt. He was right. The rich and powerful would always receive priority when it came to healing. Their faith was the same to the gods, but without the nobles' support, the church wouldn't be able to hold as much influence as it did. It was a matter of politics.

That made Michael realize that not everyone would survive this night with the church's help alone, much less the residents of the slums.

He turned to look around and saw the few healthy residents of the slums working in tune to the boy's instructions. It was much different from the chaotic north or the selfish east. Was this boy really trying to cause trouble like what the rumors said?

"That doesn't explain how you'll be able to counteract the poison. You might be talented for your age, but you're only a kid. How do you expect me to believe you have that kind of knowledge?" he questioned.

"Think about it yourself, priest. I'm under no obligation to answer," rebuked Amro.

"Stop calling me 'priest.' My name is Michael. Rank two cleric from the Church of Life, envoy to the south and temporary supervisor to the Church of Harvest's operations in this town."

"Then think about it, priest," repeated Amro, disregarding all the titles the priest had used to name himself. "What do you call someone with knowledge limited to the gods, yet disproportionate to their age and background?"

Upon hearing that, a sudden realization dawned upon Michael.

"Are you perhaps, a 'Chosen'?" asked Michael with equal parts worry and fear.

This revelation shocked him. The Chosen were existences considered as the paragons of a church. They were people chosen by the gods to enact their will in the mortal world. Blessed by the private guidance from their deity, they were individuals with extreme maturity and knowledge disproportional to their age.

What is a Chosen be doing alone so far away from the main-land? Was he perhaps sent by his god to stop this attack from the Church of Death?

"You can think of it that way," said Amro. "Anyway, are you planning on standing there or are you going to get me some holy water? People are dying as we speak."

With the wake-up call, Michael rushed to bless some basins of water placed next to Amro. The fallen God of Death could only smile wryly at his ability to fool humans. Give them a few clues, and they would fill the blanks on their own. It was too easy. After all, who could understand the mind of a zealot better than a fallen god who used to have thousands of them under him?

Meanwhile, as he blessed the basins of water, Michael watched from the side. He could see the boy focused on his task without regards for his surroundings. The small hands worked rapidly as he crafted the medicine with a speed befitting only the best alchemists in the capital.

However, the time it took for each cycle of potion to brew and the rhythm at which they were being consumed soon made him realize something. There weren't enough re-agents to save all the afflicted here. Even if he was to intervene and try to heal the rest, there were simply too many people. They would never be able to save them all.

Is he really not aware of it?

Michael was about to ask, or at the very least, inform Amro about the situation. However, even before he could do so, Amro shot him a glare. The meaning behind his gaze was clear: 'keep quiet.'

Why? he thought. *Why don't you tell them?*

While he pondered about it, Maria ran towards their

group. Behind her, a group of young children from the slums carried several pouches in their hands. Even as exhaustion threatened to overtake her, a smile filled her face as she handed a pouch of herbs to Amro.

So that was the reason... hope.

CHAPTER 27

A puppet master's performance.

E ven dreamers had to face reality. The situation on the west side of town, while better than what anyone could have expected, was not looking too good. Less than a third of the people affected had been treated, yet the resources needed to keep aiding them were pretty much gone. Even the black-haired priest from the church of life had to admit that what had been accomplished so far was already pushing their luck.

However, not everyone understood the situation. Those with family and friends who still had not been treated couldn't help but keep pleading for assistance. Unfortunately, as much as they cried, there was little anyone could do.

Eventually, someone voiced what was inside everyone's mind. It was Maria, the teenager whom Zaros had rescued not too long ago.

"We won't be able to save everyone, right?"

"No," said Amro. His voice left no room for doubts.

"Is there anything else we can do?" she asked, trying to garner whatever hope there was left.

Michael shook his head. "I don't think so. I would suggest going to the church, but I'm sure that at this moment, they're flooded with everyone from the northern, southern and eastern district. Doing so would probably turn out to be nothing but a waste of energy."

"We already have someone taking that approach. I just don't know if he will be able to accomplish our goal," said Alexander, butting into the conversation. He was currently distributing wine and ale to those who had been helping. People had grown thirsty because of the exhaustion, but the wells of water in the city were currently unusable.

"Slyfox will find a way," said Amro. "He is a sly old man, the kind to get things done regardless of the price."

His words surprised those subordinates who knew of his relationship with their old leader. No one expected him to speak in Slyfox's favor.

Eventually, the antidotes ran out, leaving nothing else to do but wait. With that, the mood darkened, driving everyone into silence. Only the occasional cries from those who still had affected friends and family could be heard.

This isn't right, thought Amro to himself. *I'm the God of Death, not the God of Massacre. The laws of death shouldn't be used in such ways. Have those idiotic priests gone stray without my guidance?*

During his time, his church had indeed plotted some massacres, but they always had a purpose. Be it overthrowing a tyrant, eliminating a village to stop a disease from spreading, or sieging cults to the demons, his orders to the church of death always had a reason behind them. Things like poisoning the common folk were beneath both him and his worshippers of old.

The situation forced him to think about the state of his church. It was worse than he had initially thought. During his battle with the other gods, he had ordered his followers to sacrifice everything they had available to him. It was a choice made out of desperation. One that intended to help him regain his strength during the first siege led by a group consisting of many middle and lesser gods.

Given the situation and his need for some free time to think, he decided to pass the baton onto Zaros, not before giving him some words of advice.

"Okay, boy, I did what could be done," said Amro. "Whatever choices you take next are up to you. However, if I was you, I'd leave this place along with anyone you cared about."

"Why?" asked Zaros, feeling rather confused.

"I have a feeling that whoever did this didn't intend to finish it with the poison alone. Something worse is coming, and my instincts tell me it's aiming for you."

* * *

The sound of maniacal laughter broke the silent atmosphere in the desolate woods bordering Sol.

"I knew it! I knew it! Leave it to those bastards from the church to snoop and find what we were looking for." A young woman with silver hair and scarlet eyes was sitting on the ground as she held a red crystal in her hands. It was Noelle, the apostle sent by the Church of Death.

Next to her stood a tall man with muscles straining his robes and a pair of desolate eyes. He was looking towards the direction of the town. It was Bernard, the man tasked to accompany her during this mission.

"You found him?" he asked.

"Of course, you oaf. Can't you see how happy I am?"

That was insulting, thought Bernard. At times like this, he opted to ignore his partner's behavior. She grew too excited when it came to matters related to their god. "Did you see it? The legacy we're looking for?"

"No, I wasn't able to see anything reminiscent of a legacy on him. However, I could tell it was him. He found my cute flying toy without any help. It is impossible for a child to do that without divine assistance."

"A child?"

"Yes, a boy no older than 15," she answered. "He has cute, pale skin, black hair, and amber-colored eyes. He's our target."

Bernard nodded. An eerie smile appeared on his lips as he started stretching both of his arms. "Does this mean we can finally move in?"

"Indeed," she said, turning to look back towards the forest giant as she did so.

Behind them, an army of disheveled and dirt-covered men and women stood in wait. The only defining characteristic they shared were the markings scribbled across their bodies along with the rotten stench they gave away. Noelle's gaze softened as she looked at them, her eyes filled with as much warmth as a mother looking at her children.

On the other hand, Bernard kept looking forward, ignoring the disgusting army following behind them. He only spoke up after he realized his partner had become too distracted with her 'toys.' "If your crow successfully delivered my packages, the poison should have weakened them sufficiently by now."

Shaken out of her distracted state by Bernard's words, Noelle smiled. It was finally time for her to release her hounds of war. "Go on, it's time for everyone to play," she said. A glint of insanity shining in her doe-like eyes.

As if her words were a key that unlocked a set of invisible chains, most of the undead began running forward wildly. There was no order to their movements, making them look much like a swarm of wild beasts. It even seemed like they were competing against each other to be the first to reach the town. That was their instinct, telling them there was food for them inside.

The horde encompassed not dozens, but at least a hundred 'people' running in unison. Many of them had remained hidden within the forest's foliage, unseen until the order to attack had been given. Amongst their ranks, even a mix of the forest's most common beasts could be seen. Their target was clear: the city of Sol and their inhabitants.

It didn't take long for the beasts to overtake the running speed of their human counterparts. They became the first group to clash against the few men standing guard at each gate of the city.

"What is this smell?" exclaimed a guard at the southern front. Unlike his counterparts from the northern and western sides of town, his armor had a shiny luster that drew one's attention to its embellished insignias. He was one of those unfortunate guards serving a noble that had received the task of guarding the southern gate as punishment.

"I have no idea, but it smells like rotten meat," complained one of his partners.

"Hey," said another one of them. "Do you all see that, in the distance?"

"Just what is that?" asked the first guard.

"We're damned, we're majorly screwed."

"Is that..."

"By Alexandra's shiny tits..." exclaimed a guard, dumbfounded at the scene.

They were finally able to see the inbound horde of beasts, men, and women making their way towards them. From their ravenous movements, it was easy to conclude that their intentions were in no way friendly.

Clank

The sound of metal hitting the cold hard stone was like a bell, waking everyone up from their stupor. One of the guards had dropped his gear in order to increase his mobility, taking a head start in escaping with all the speed he could muster.

The scene, however, wasn't limited to their side. It didn't take long for a similar display to be seen at each outpost on the western and eastern entrances. Realizing the futility of their efforts, some guards had decided to escape, leaving their comrades behind in order to gain time for themselves. Just like that, the town's defenses soon fell to the first wave of the invasion.

The townsfolk would have probably noticed the commotion if most of them had not been busy trying to save their lives from something else: the black-death. A name they had given to the poison that reaped the lives of so many.

The situation had caused the many townsfolk to split up three-ways. The first group was composed by those who had gone to try their luck at the Church of Harvest. The second by those who had escaped from the town, afraid of the condition being contagious. Lastly, there were those whom had found salvation in an unexpected place. More specifically, Amro's side.

Unfortunately, this meant that everyone was too busy to realize what was happening on the outskirts of town. As such, by the time the guards were overwhelmed by Noelle's frenzied army, everyone else had yet to realize the attack that was coming for them.

How could the people at the church know something that was happening at the borders? Not even the sound of screams could reach them given the commotion they were currently dealing with. Despite the church's repeated announcements that they had no holy water left and that their priests' mana reserves were nearly spent, the populace kept on pushing for help. No one wanted to give up on their loved ones' lives, much less their own.

All of this presented the perfect opportunity for the savage, fiend-like army to creep onto the crowd. A group of people all gathered in one place with little room to move? It was the perfect target.

It didn't take long for heart-wrenching screams to merge with the sound of people requesting help for their families.

Perhaps the first group of people who realized the change in this situation were the guards following after the nobles. With both soft and hard approaches, they had convinced the clergy to treat their lords and comrades before the commoners. Since that was the case, they refused to lower their guards in case the common folk revolted against them.

"Jonathan," one of them said. "What are those commoners doing over there?"

The man turned to look where his partner was pointing, only to find a group of people taking bites off of someone else.

"It looks like they're eating each other. Are these disgusting fools really that starved?"

Both of the armor-clad men laughed for a second. Having fun at the expense of the commoners was almost second nature to them. However, a third guard noticed something they didn't.

"Hey, guys... isn't the same thing happening there?"

"Holy Kovas, you're right. Wait, it's happening all around the perimeter!"

"Those fools have really gone crazy. Call the clerics, tell them it's an emergency!" Jonathan instructed a squire behind them.

The squire soon returned, followed by a white-haired priest in a white robe. He was Michael's partner, Lucille.

"Here he is, sir. His name is Lucille, he's an envoy from the church of life," spoke the squire while presenting the priest at his side.

"Why did you call me? We have our hands full. We can't be bothered to deal with insignificant matters," said the priest in a rather stern manner.

"Hey, priest, look at those people over there. Is our master healed already? We need to get out of here."

"What?" exclaimed the shocked priest, taking a quick look towards where the man was pointing. He quickly saw a group of men and women with strange scribbles covering their bodies. Eyes opening wide, he screamed, "Defensive formations, now! Those are ghouls, undead vessels of hatred and death. Kill them at all costs and give them a well-deserved trip to the other life!"

The guards recoiled when they heard his words. Ghouls? Those were monsters they had only heard of as scary bedtime stories when they were children. They didn't even think they were real. Yet now they were being attacked by such creatures? Just what had happened to their peaceful town, for it to become so hectic the past couple of days?

"Move you fools, now!"

There was no time to dally. Hearing the priest's commands, most guards took battle formations, readying their weapons after fastening the straps of their armors. Fortunately for them, the crowd of civilians had slowed the undead from reaching them too quickly.

They were ready to advance, allowing some frantic civilians to take cover behind them. However, a separate group of men carrying the same marks as the ones the priest had called ghouls made their way forward. They were dressed like mercenaries, the air around them completely different from the wild and ravenous ghouls that were eating the civilians.

Their movements were orderly, and they even their eyes seemed to carry a hint of intelligence. If not for the marks covering their bodies, they were just like a normal human. A black-haired woman was in front of the group of mercenaries. Her crimson eyes drew the attention from some dim-witted men amongst the guards. Only a thundering shout from the priest was able to bring them back to their senses.

"You cursed woman! What is an apostle of death like you doing on this side of the continent? Your kind is not welcomed here!" screamed Lucille.

Ignoring the priest's tone, Noelle only smiled. She adjusted her robes before answering him in a teasing tone. "Oh dear, shouldn't I be asking the same? What is an envoy of that flat-chested goddess doing here? I thought your division of the church was too busy trying to conduct peace negotiations at the northern border to worry about a small town like this."

Lucille's eyes twitched at the backhanded insult towards his goddess. He was a man who respected all beauty. Having the biggest star in his firmament insulted in such a manner snapped something inside of him.

"You dare insult the Goddess of Life? I will have you whipped to death for your crimes!" he said. "I can sense it was you who unleashed this accursed situation onto these people. State your motives, you necrophiliac whore!"

The woman's eyes seemed to glow with an eerie red before she spoke again.

"I'm just searching for a lost toy of ours. But do not worry, my partner is already on his way to pick it up. As for me, I came over here to have some fun. After all, my children over here were feeling quite hungry," she said, pointing towards the ghouls.

The priest's expression turned grave. Defeating a necromancer was a difficult matter. Their methods were always underhanded and engaging them in a battle of attrition was never a smart thing to do. Fortunately for him, the Church of Harvest was just behind him, which meant he would have the assistance of several low-ranked priests in order to deal with this woman.

A group of brown-robed clerics soon came out of the church. They had been quickly informed by the same squire from before about the transpiring events. Most of them went pale in fear, realizing the situation was way beyond their capabilities. Only a handful of them, including the rank two priest in charge of the church kept their calm as they quickly came to stand by Lucille's side.

"Unholy wench, by the authority given to me by the Goddess of Harvest, I command you to leave this place," said the leader of the local church. "Unless you're prepared to declare war to our holy mother, leave at once."

Noelle could only laugh at the priest's manner of speech.

"Haven't we already been at war for the last couple of centuries? What makes you think I'm afraid of murdering a few more priests?" she said, taking a step forward. "I mean, I'm not even afraid of killing a couple of scumbags either." With that, she used half a step to turn around and grab someone by their neck with her right hand. Her left hand, instead, was now blocking a dagger aimed to her chest.

It was Slyfox. He had been lying in the shadows, waiting for an opening to steal some holy water for both himself and his people. Unfortunately for him, he had been delayed by the amount of troops surrounding the building. Whilst waiting, he had seen people attacking others at the perimeter, and soon realized that something strange was going on. After hearing the screams of the white-robed priest and listening in on his conversation with the scarlet-eyed woman, he quickly realized the gist of the situation.

The black-haired woman was the one responsible for this incident. The situation was clearly caused by her will. As such, using the discussion between the priest and the woman as a distraction, he had approached the necromancer, ready to stab her from behind.

However, she had not failed to notice his intentions.

"Oh, sweetheart," she said, smiling coyly. "You know nothing about the undead, right? A master and her servants share everything. Whatever they see, I see as well. Sneaking up on me like that was a nice try though, I'll give you a star for the effort."

Her hand tightened around Slyfox's neck, the sound of bones grinding away along with the man's consciousness. The strength on Noelle's hand was something not even Slyfox was able to handle.

"I really wish you better luck in your next life," she said, letting Slyfox's limp body fall to the ground. "Now then, where were we at, Mr. Priest?"

Lucille and the rest of the priests' expression darkened upon seeing her easily break Slyfox's neck. Just how much strength was required for such a thing? It was clear to them now that this woman was rank three if not higher. She was an opponent they couldn't afford to go easy on.

"Charge!" yelled one of the guards behind them.

"No, don't be foolish!" warned Lucille to no avail.

His voice was dampened by the cries of war given by the guards. Right now, they had eyes for one thing only — fighting to break out of the encirclement they were slowly being driven into.

CHAPTER 28

Target.

The orders came too late. Dozens of men armored in leather armor had stepped forward to battle the creatures. Their blades skillfully sunk in the fleshly bodies of the ravenous ghouls, releasing the smell of pungent rot into the air. The monsters, however, didn't react to their moves. After all, they were devoid of any self-awareness and could not feel pain.

Yet one thing was for sure. Attacking the beasts had moved their attention from feasting on the commoners to retaliating against the guards. Not something the guards had intended out of the good of their hearts. To them, it had been a grave mistake. Their feeble mental resilience, still shaken by the wanton savagery going on in their surroundings, was not prepared to handle such retaliation from the human-shaped monsters.

The ghouls sank their mouths and fingers into whatever flesh they could grab, quickly bringing several guards to the ground. This only worsened the situation with the remaining guards, for it shattered whatever hope they had of survival.

That was, at least, until a green light covered them all.

"Bark armor!" shouted the priest leading the Church of Harvest. Seeing the armored fools walk into a fight with an opponent they knew nothing off did little to ease his nerves. He had to do his best to tip the balance to their favor. The priests from the church of harvest were not battle-oriented, so the most he could do was improve their chances of survival.

The guards quickly collected themselves. They had forgotten they were not alone. Who could be better suited to fight the undead menaces than the faithful servants of the church? They soon gained some distance and started using the advantage of their weaponry against the undead.

"Ora, it's not nice for the grown-ups to involve themselves in their children's games," said the crimson-eyed beauty. "What do you say? You big boys and I can play something else. Mind leaving the children to their own?"

Hearing her words, the priests began making their own preparations. The weakest clerics started moving the few surviving and rational commoners inside the church while those with some battle experience made their way to support the few guards with what little they could do. Only the white-haired priest, Lucille, and the head-priest for the Church of Harvest remained to face off against the black-haired beauty.

"My name is Noelle, by the way. I'll be keeping you two company for tonight so I hope both of you are ready. Please do your best to last as long as you can, it's no fun otherwise," she said, taking a moment to bring a finger to her lips. As she did so, she seductively whispered her next words, "Mind Flay."

After uttering her spell, a world of darkness enveloped both priests. Their eyes were filled with nothing but an expansive void, one which extended across their entire horizon.

"What is this?" spoke the head-priest for the Church of Harvest, dumbfounded. His church wasn't wealthy by any means, the amount of knowledge he had access to was pretty limited.

Unlike his temporary partner, however, Lucille knew what this place was. It was a soul domain. A space limited to those who had reached a certain level of attunement with their own soul. What's more, it was a foreign soul domain, one they had been brought to against their will. As expected of a necromancer, they were most skilled when it came to the matters of the soul.

Alas, Noelle never intended to give them much time to adapt to their new surroundings. "He he he, do you like how I decorated of our battlefield?" she asked.

Turning around, both men soon saw a familiar figure. With the same long, black yet silver tinged hair and crimson-eyes, she stood in front of them with a smile. Unlike the rest of this grim world, her appearance still retained colors. Her eyes, especially, seemed to contain way more liveliness than they had before.

"Welcome to my mind," she said. "I'll take it you silly boys know what this place is and thus know how I can do whatever I want in here. I hope the two of you can entertain me properly."

As she finished her words, chains shot from the floor and the sky, quickly binding both priests against their will.

Lucille knew there was still some hope left. Bringing a foreigner into your soul had its own set of risks. For starters, if she was not strong enough to overwhelm their spirit, they could easily wreak havoc from within; such was the risk of letting an outsider into the innermost part of your being. Additionally, any physical advantages would be abandoned inside this domain, which meant only the strength of one's mind and spirit mattered.

"I wonder how much of this someone can take," said Noelle, extending her hand.

A pike rose from the ground, appearing before her. With a skip in her step, she took it and made her way towards the priest from the Church of Harvest. Once she was in front of him, she tapped the pike against his stomach before, carefully testing its flaccidity before driving it inside.

This is not real, this pain is nothing but a lie, the priest thought to himself. He wasn't willing to give his opponent the pleasure of seeing him in pain.

"Oh, no screams?" asked the apostle of death. "I bet I can change that."

Finishing her words, she drove a second pike inside the priest's body. "And here I thought you priests were more lively than that."

Endure it, the priest repeated to himself. *She can't have the strength to keep this spell going on forever.*

"Are you perhaps thinking about enduring?" Noelle asked with a giggle. "Are you not aware that pain hurts, whether you call it an illusion or recognize it as reality? Stop being so stubborn. Embracing it is your only choice."

A third, fourth, and fifth pike were then inserted into the priest's body. "How long can you last, I wonder?"

Outside, barely a few seconds had passed before the head-priest for the church of harvest fell to his knees. The unfocused look in his eyes was evidence enough that he had passed on towards his goddess's embrace. Despite sharing the same rank as Lucille, his mental endurance was not up to par. He had been too weak to resist the gory games carried on by the crimson-eyed beauty.

His collapse brought a surprise to those who saw it. Not a minute ago, he had still been ordering around the rest of the church's staff. Why then was he falling to his knees? Had that woman done something?

Of course, none of them knew the answer. They were not experiencing the hell both priests were inside Noelle's soul domain.

Back inside, Noelle giggled to her heart's content. "How surprising!" she said. "You're the first one to resist more than a hundred. It seems like the rumor is true. You members from the Church of Life are indeed the only ones worthy of being our adversaries."

A repertoire of tools, weapons and many other things were scattered around her feet. Taking a pensive pose, she suddenly had an idea, "Let's try a different approach, shall we?"

Lucille's blank gaze rose to meet Noelle's. With a grim smile on his face, he used all his strength to mutter some words, "Try your best, bitch."

Noelle's smile widened as shivers racked her entire body. This was a pleasure she had never experienced before. It was the first time one of her targets had managed to rebel after enduring this much. Bringing them pain was pleasurable, but breaking their spirit was an ecstasy nothing else could compare to.

"Rest assured dear, I will."

* * *

Zaros's subordinates kept trying to do what little they could to ease the pain from those still afflicted by poison. Their bleak expressions, however, could not be hidden. There was a limit to how much their minds could endure.

Not even Michael's efforts were enough. The priest had tried blessing countless basins of water, exhausting all his energy and mana. It would be some time before he could return to action.

Seeing so many people still lying on the ground pained Zaros's heart. Unfortunately, he had more pressing matters to deal with. It was something that required his full attention.

"Is that the direction they're coming from?" Zaros asked.

"Indeed," answered Amro. "I can feel them coming near."

Following those words, screams and wails echoed in the distance. A man running with all he could was now approaching the boy, no hint of dignity left on his face. It was someone Zaros recognized. Someone he still had a vague memory of. It was none other than the barrel-chested guard who had been guarding the western gate the day he entered the slums. The fool who thought stealing from him was a commendable action.

"Help me!" he cried. Snot was coming out of his nose, swinging wildly from side to side. "Please, help me!"

"What the..."

It was an image that took Zaros by surprise. Never in his wildest dreams did he imagine seeing the same arrogant guard from his memories coming to him for help. It was a display that made him feel disgusted with the man's lack of dignity.

Should I help him? thought Zaros. Truth be told, he was feeling somewhat petty over the issue. It was an idle thought that stemmed from within his soul against his better judgment. A feeling that felt foreign yet natural.

"Do some—"

Unfortunately for the guard that slight moment of hesitation was all it took to seal his fate in stone. Before he could cry for help a second time, the silhouette of a fox-like creature appeared from an alleyway. Immediately, it pounced unto him, tearing a piece of flesh out of his neck.

The undead beast seemed to enjoy the piece of the guard, gnawing away as it ignored the man's frantic attempt to knock it off his back. Each time the guard came close to succeeding, the fox-like creature simply anchored itself with its bite. With time, a group of reinforcements came to its aid. Several other undead animals appeared from the same alley, pouncing onto the guard without a shred of reluctance to share their meal. The guard was enough to feed them all.

Before Zaros realized it, Michael was standing to his side, staring at the scene with a ghastly expression. Unlike the boy, he recognized the symbols covering the beasts in the distance. It was the omen of a greater threat to their lives.

"Everyone! Take whoever you care about and run," instructed Michael, looking towards the people standing behind him and Zaros. "These are not normal beasts, just run!"

"What are they?" asked Zaros in a small voice.

"Undead," answered Michael, looking at Zaros with a confused look. "It seems like you haven't been a Chosen for long."

Chosen? thought Zaros, still unfamiliar with the term.

"Nevermind that," said Michael. "If they are here, it means something even more dangerous is coming our way. We should use this chance to run away."

"Oh, how perceptive of you," noted a voice coming from within the alleyway. "I didn't expect anything less from a member of your church."

The owner of the voice soon revealed himself. It was a man, tall and burly with black robes covering most of his body. His eyes looked particularly interesting, for they were completely devoid of life.

"Oh, where are my manners? My name is Bern-"

Swift

A throwing knife slid past the Bernard's cheek, interrupting his words. Despite his best efforts to dodge it, he found a hissing mark burning away the skin of his cheek. It was evidence that he had not been fast enough.

Michael stood with his hand extended, staring at Bernard's face with incomparable hatred. His earlier attack had been ineffective but he was still preparing another set of knives. It was evident he didn't take his opponent lightly.

"And here I thought I was being rude," said Bernard. "Chucking blessed steel away like that is not a nice thing to do to someone you just met. Is a regional church like yours really able to throw that much money away?"

"What is an envoy of death doing here?" asked Michael, his voice seething with disgust. "The Church of Death has no place outside the mainland."

"And why exactly should I tell you?" retorted Bernard, taking a small vial from underneath his robes and pouring it onto the wound in his cheek. "It isn't like you have any authority over me."

A hissing sound came from the liquid Bernard poured on his face, causing the wound left by Michael's knife to fade away. Blessed steel had special properties against the undead, ones that could make the mana that kept them stable grow erratic. Fortunately for Michael, his guess had been right: Bernard wasn't entirely human.

Seeing them fight with their words, Zaros took a chance to have a talk with Amro. He was having trouble fully grasping the situation.

"Is this is the threat you warned me about?"

"No," answered Amro. "That brute is far from being a necromancer. Not that he is any less threatening to someone with your strength."

"Necromancer?" asked Zaros. As a child from the forest, he was ignorant about the different paths those of faith and magic could take.

"Nevermind that, boy. You just got to know that it's in your best interests to deal with him as soon as possible."

Even at a time like this, Amro wanted Zaros to deal with the situation. The way he saw it, it would drive the boy into a situation that would further stimulate his growth. On the other hand, Amro wanted to remain in the shadows. That way, he would be able to find out what the apostles of death were trying to do.

At this moment, Michael disturbed Zaros's conversation with Amro to request his help. "Hey, kid, you're a Chosen right? Help me deal with this guy. Otherwise, things are going to get ugly."

Zaros nodded before he turned back to look at the people from the slums. "Maria, Alexander, take everyone who's capable of fighting and protect the injured from those beasts. If things turn sour, don't hesitate to flee."

"Yes, boss!" came the answer from the two siblings. They could tell it was a fight they had no place in from the look in Michael and Zaros's eyes. Thus, they immediately moved everyone towards safety.

"Ok, priest, what's your plan?" asked Zaros.

"We hold him down and pray for Vita to guide our way," said Michael.

Like she cares, thought Amro. At this time, the Goddess of Life was probably too busy focusing on her own plans to worry about the life and death of a few mortals.

"Are you done?" asked Bernard, his lifeless eyes lingering on Zaros. "If it isn't too much trouble, I'd like that young man to come with me. You said he was a Chosen, right? I'd like to have some words with him about that."

CHAPTER 29

Break.

A blast caused by alchemical fire knocked away a group of survivors who were trying to flee. Fortunately for Zaros, neither Maria nor Alexander were in that group, as they were still helping others evacuate. The one responsible for this was none other than Bernard.

His hands still held a few orange vials in them, much like the one that had just been thrown. The vicious explosion caused by them had been not something to scoff at. Not that Bernard agreed with that sentiment. It was evident by his cheeky smile that he wasn't afraid of using the remaining ones should Zaros and Michael refuse to listen to his instructions.

"Well then. Are you willing to come with me, boy?" asked Bernard once again.

Michael's eyes pleaded for Zaros not to step forward. God knows what the church of death would do if they got their hands on a Chosen. *Though, what god is he a Chosen for?* thought Michael, realizing he hadn't asked all this time.

"I won't," answered Zaros.

His answer took Michael by surprise. The boy had not given him the impression that he would reject the proposal so quickly. From their previous interactions, he seemed like the kind of person who would have stalled for time in order to come up with a strategy. Perhaps even Amro would have shared his astonishment had he not shared a connection to the boy.

"I don't think you are someone who would keep his word," said Zaros, explaining the reasoning behind his choice. "If you want me to believe you, you could start by getting rid of those beasts, at the very least."

Bernard's felt his interest in Zaros increasing after receiving such an answer. He originally expected a simple rejection, not a counter with such a rational request from the young man. He found it amusing, truly deserving of someone with the courage to steal his god's legacy.

Breaking into laughter, Bernard pretended to clutch his sides, giving plenty of opening to his two opponents. He was luring them in to take action. One could tell from his body that he focused on close-combat.

"Oh, naïve boy," said Bernard. "You think these beasts are the only undead on our side? Let me show you something else."

With a clap of his hands, a file of people exited the alleyways and filled the streets. It was a small mob, covered in the same glyphs as the beasts from before.

Zaros's eyes went wide when he saw the group of newcomers. A spark of hatred and rage erupted within his heart and soul. Even Amro was temporarily stifled by the vivid feedback he received from their connection. Both of them knew the identity of those walking corpses.

A woman with a leather apron and brown hair, a man with a quiver tied to his back, even a child with a series of scars on his arms. All of them had familiar faces. They were the villagers who had once lived with Zaros. The same men and women Amro had given a proper burial despite their circumstances. Yet here they were, defiled and tainted. Their humanity besmirched, now vessels of hatred, hunger, and disdain for the living.

"Oh, that's a nice reaction," taunted Bernard. His lifeless eyes seemed to gain a spark from the sadistic revelation. "So, you wanted me to kill these fiends, right?

Zaros refused to answer. His instincts told him that no matter what he replied, he still wouldn't like the results. He had to do something. The anger in his heart would never settle if he didn't erase this man's existence.

Amro was secretly jubilant. This was it, the catalyst he had been waiting for so long. The reason he had tried to leave the boy to face his own troubles as much as he could. After experiencing this anger, Zaros's body was finally about to awaken.

If advancing to rank one was akin to making his body compatible to external powers, the advancement to rank two required his body to become the origin of that power. Now, the strong emotions the boy felt, combined with the instinctive need to draw blood from his opponent, caused his body to no longer be satisfied by the mana in the atmosphere. No, it now needed something else. Something it could only provide itself.

The currents in Zaros's soul soon fed that power to the boy. Aura. Not a shallow awakening, but the kindling of a torrential amount of power under his control.

Clank

Zaros's dagger was blocked by the steel armguard in Bernard's hand. The quick slash from his dagger had barely been visible, carrying speed and strength incomparable to what the boy had displayed in previous occasions.

Even Michael's eyes went wide as he realized what had happened. The boy had achieved a breakthrough.

The sound of metal clashing against metal soon echoed through the slums as Zaros continued a barrage of attacks against Bernard. The techniques he displayed were not something usually seen in someone who had just achieved a breakthrough. They were the results of someone who had trained under the best teachers for many years.

However, Zaros wasn't just 'someone'. He had been trained under Amro's tutelage for the last couple weeks, achieving a mastery over his body not befitting of his rank. Now, with the acquisition of a new power, the boy could fully display the prowess he had acquired from within Amro's soul domain.

Even Michael was surprised. Was this what they meant when they said the Chosen were aberrants? Could someone really display this much combat prowess just seconds after a breakthrough?

Clank

Sensing a familiar feeling coming from Zaros, Bernard's eyes held a mix of confusion, glee, and fear.

"So it truly was you, our guess wasn't wrong. You truly obtained our lord's legacy," he said. He wasn't afraid of his secret being revealed to the onlookers. His voice was hidden from outsiders by the repeated clashing of his armor against Zaros's dagger.

The boy, on the other hand, refused to speak as he kept attacking in a practiced manner. The only thing on his mind right now was how he needed to use his abilities to stop Bernard once and for all.

"You can't hide it from me! That's the scent of our lord. Those are even the same knife technique he passed down unto us. A simplified version, perhaps, but the same technique altogether."

Clank

"Come with me boy. You can join our order, worship our god and be bathed in his glory. You can help us usher in a new age of glory and power for our church. Stop this foolish beha—"

Slash

Finally, one of Zaros's hits successfully broke through Bernard's defenses. It sliced through skin and bone, robbing him from one of his hands. Black blood oozed from it, evidencing the fact that the man had long been dead.

So that was it, thought Amro. *They opened the vault.*

During his reign as a god, he had left behind a depository only for his most loyal, ordained priests to access. It contained secrets of many kinds like forgotten arts, spells, and scriptures. Bernard's black, oozing blood was the effect of a particular scripture he had left behind. One that taught a method for unnatural life through death.

As the God of Death, Amro was opposed to having his followers use such a method. However, he understood the value of immortality in the mortal world, and had left it behind as a legacy in case it was ever needed for his church's survival. It seemed like after his fall, someone had decided to open the vault, making this method accessible to others.

Through this technique, people would be able to sever their soul from their mortal coil. It was much like the technique practiced by necromancers in order to produce a phylactery. But unlike necromancy, it wasn't a part of the soul that was severed, but the entirety of it. Once done, they would be able to bind it to whatever person they could overpower, killing the body's original soul whilst retaining control of it.

Amro could see some flaws still present in Bernard's use of the technique. For his body to be dying like that meant he wasn't fully able to adapt his soul to the vessel he had chosen. It was very likely he needed to frequently change bodies, which would further erode his soul. If Amro had to guess, he would estimate that without the help of an outsider, Bernard's soul wouldn't last more than a couple more transfers before dying a true death.

The erosion of his soul was even more visible when he compared Zaros's battle prowess to the undead man's. There was a visible gap in their physical ability despite sharing the same rank. Amro could tell it wasn't a matter of skill, but a matter of control over their own body. Being a foreigner to the flesh he controlled, Bernard could not fight to the full extent of his capabilities.

Slash

A second attack succeeded. This time, Zaros had managed to use his short stature to sneak an attack on Bernard's right leg.

"How?" asked Bernard, falling under his own weight. He couldn't believe the pipsqueak before him had been able to best him in battle. In order to achieve success, he had drunk several elixirs before it had even started.

Slash

Zaros stood by his decision to not speak another word to Bernard. With a final strike, he separated the apostle's head from his body, quenching some of the anger on his heart with the man's death.

It was finally over. The coagulated dark blood staining his dagger dripped to the ground, falling at the same rhythm as the drops of sweat on his forehead.

And while Zaros dealt the finishing blow, Amro made

sure to seal their victim's fate. Simple manipulation of the environment's mana made it easy to ensure Bernard's weakened soul was scattered, therefore preventing it from taking one of the undead beasts in the vicinity as a new body.

Zaros turned to look at Michael, a slight look of melancholy in his eyes. "You do it," he requested.

"Huh?" said Michael. "Do what?"

"You're a priest, right? Please give them the peace they deserve," Zaros said, pointing towards the undead villagers assaulting the remaining slum dwellers.

Michael complied, although not without asking, "Are they related to you?"

However, Zaros didn't answer. He instead moved towards the priest's throwing dagger. The same one he had thrown at Bernard moments earlier. Without requesting any permission, he took it for himself, tying it to his belt.

For a moment, Michael felt like asking for it back. The cost of producing blessed steel wasn't something his meager salary could pay for. Unfortunately for him, his contributions in the last fight hadn't been enough to grant his words any authority. He couldn't complain. The dagger had found a more capable owner. Instead, he chose to continue eliminating the undead, breaking away the power of the sigils inscribed on their bodies. Every time he did, the bodies crumbled away into the wind.

With this, Zaros hoped his former villagers would finally be able to rest in peace, no longer tormented by the greed and selfishness of the living. This didn't lessen the pain in his heart, but it did offer him some solace.

Clap, clap

Unfortunately, the battle wasn't over just yet. Slow, deliberate claps drew Zaros's attention to the one responsible for raising the bodies of the villagers.

A beautiful, black-haired, crimson-eyed woman walked up to him. Her eyes carried certain playfulness to them, while her demeanor made it obvious that she didn't mind the grim atmosphere created by the carnage around them.

"I wouldn't have expected you to take Bernard on and win," she admitted. "I told the fool he should have gone to play with me at the town's center for a while. He should have known better."

Michael looked at her, his eyes filling with realization. The smile that had appeared on his face after Zaros's victory had now entirely vanished. He knew who this woman was, and more importantly, the danger she represented.

"Young, crimson eyes, and black hair with silver strokes. Wanted for the massacre of dozens of towns in the northern parts of the mainland. Hated for her perverted desecration of public figures' dead bodies. The 'unholy banshee', Noelle," he said.

"Oh, you've heard of me?" asked Noelle, hints of playfulness coming from her voice. "Good things, I hope."

Michael's face looked tense, a clear indication of his disagreement.

"By the way, that cute white robe of yours reminds me of someone I just met," said Noelle. "I must say, he was quite a persistent fellow. We really had a blast playing together. Perhaps, after all of this is over, I'll take his body back home with me."

Michael's eyes widened as a spark of anger appeared in them. His appearance now resembled Zaros's from a few minutes ago. It was clear that her words had struck a chord within him.

"You filthy whore! Tell me what you did to Lucille!"

"Come on, there's no need to get angry. We only played for a while, you know. If you're that desperate to see him, you can become my toy as well. That way we can play together."

"Damn it!" cried the priest. The loss of his friend and partner had dealt him a severe psychological blow.

"For the time being," said Noelle, "I brought someone else for you to play with. He's a new toy of mine."

After saying those words, a tall and well-built figure with flaxen hair and red glyphs around his body walked forward. It was Slyfox. No, Slyfox's undead remains.

CHAPTER 30

Revelations.

"**D**o you have no respect for the dead?" protested Zaros. Slyfox's appearance had reignited the foul mood he had when he saw his fellow villagers in such a state.

Noelle tilted her head to the side. *'In what way am I disrespecting the dead?'* her face seemed to ask. As far as she was concerned, the undead under her command were nothing but playthings created in order to appease her need for entertainment.

Even Amro was disappointed at such a shorthanded understanding of what it meant to use the laws of death. While some degree of freedom was allowed when it came to every person's understanding of a law, Noelle's complete disregard for the dead irked him quite a lot. Whoever was in charge of educating the priests for his church would be in a great deal of trouble when he got to meet them face to face.

"Do you really fail to see them as anything other than playthings?" Zaros asked. "They were once living humans like us. Their lives, goals, and regrets don't simply cease to exist because they die!"

That's right, thought Amro. *The correct way to raise the undead is by getting their consent in life. Undeath is an extension the law of death grants in order for people to give meaning to their lives. Her short-sighted views on the matter is what forces her to use those glyphs to bind her will onto those bodies. Pseudo-undead like hers will never be true incarnations of the law of death.*

"You know you're no fun, right? I make these toys, it's only fair their everything belongs to me. So what if they used to have great desires while they were alive? They no longer are, they're dead," answered Noelle, turning her irked expression towards Slyfox's undead-self. "Go after him, boy, teach him to respect his elders."

At her command, the undead Slyfox shot after Zaros, using beast-like movements to try to tackle the boy. His ferociousness rivaled what it had been in life, but that was all there was to his moves. His tackle lacked skill and was nothing more than an instinctive and feral answer to Noelle's earlier command.

The undead Slyfox didn't have a chance from the start.

His body was promptly thrown against the ground. With a swift cut behind the knees, Zaros had lacerated his tendons, taking away his ability to run. Despite the impressive pain tolerance the undead could have, they weren't able to move without the proper tissues needed to support their movements.

"That's no fun," said Noelle. "You're supposed to run and cry for help when someone comes after you."

Zaros ignored her as he carried Slyfox's flailing corpse before throwing him towards Michael.

"Bind him," he ordered.

"Shouldn't I just purify him instead?" asked the priest.

"Just bind him," said Zaros. "I'll deal with her somehow."

"Are you ignoring me, boy?" complained Noelle. "I thought you were a cute child, but it's now clear to me that you're just an ill-mannered brat. You might have dealt with that particular toy, but how will you deal with the rest?"

Another group of undead came into sight. Unlike the previous ones, however, these were covered in armor common to mercenary groups. The markings on them also seemed different. While they had the same reddish hue as those of the other undead, the composition and structure of the glyphs were comprised of an entirely different pattern.

It took a moment before Zaros recognized the undead beings before him. To a certain extent, part of him had even expected their appearance after seeing his desecrated villagers.

They were the group of mercenaries who had once attacked him and his village. They still had the same weapons, the same armor, and the same faces as before. All etched deep into his memory, making them impossible to forget. Only one face was missing amongst them, but he soon found out why.

It was a headless undead with his missing head cradled under his left arm. It was wearing an armor more elaborate than that of his companions, and even the eyes on the detached face seemed to carry a hint of intelligence. He was the man who had once been the leader of the mercenary group. The one who had revealed his identity as the king's vassal in an attempt to sway Amro to his side. It was none other than the dead captain of the army's 22nd Division.

"These are my masterpieces, boy. Without souls to resist my control, I was able to craft the most beautiful and obedient toys. I was even able to make a Dullahan! They won't rebel against me, nor will they move without my orders. They are my perfect creations!" boasted Noelle. "And I have you to thank for them. It's thanks to your usage of our legacy that I was able to get my hands on bodies in such perfect conditions. To not even leave a trace of their souls, just how did you do it? No, nevermind. Just hand over the legacy and I'll be able to do it myself."

That's fundamentally wrong, thought Amro. *They aren't perfect creations, they are just dumbed-down adaptations. For an undead to truly achieve perfection, they should still have a will, a consciousness, and a soul. Achieving a compromise with that soul is the true perfection of this craft.*

"Legacy?" asked Zaros. *Is she talking about Amro? Is he related to them?*

All he knew about his partner was that he was some kind of spirit with unknown origins. Amro was knowledgeable about all sorts of things, but he was extremely secretive about his past.

"If you won't give it up, it just means I'll have to take it by force," said Noelle, as she turned around to look at the undead mercenaries. "Now, children, go and rip him to shreds!"

Seconds passed by, but nothing happened. The undead stood in place without making a move. They refused to listen to her commands. This took Noelle by surprise as these undead were supposed to be her ultimate creations. Their obedience was a given.

"Attack him! Now!" she ordered again, thinking her command might have been a bit too complex for the undead to understand. To her chagrin, however, they still didn't move.

"That was bound to happen," Amro told Zaros. "I banished their souls myself, so my imprint is still in their bodies. Under no circumstances will they raise their blades against us, for their bodies still fear me instinctively."

However, Noelle wasn't as happy as Zaros was with the

situation. "You! What did you do to them? They are my toys! Mine!" Her playful behavior nowhere to be found, replaced only by the insanity of someone who had their favorite thing in the whole world ruined.

"I did nothing," said Zaros shrugging along with a coy smile. Amro's words had given him the confidence to face the woman before him.

Seeing the curve of Zaros's lips caused Noelle to grow flustered. She was convinced the boy had done something to her new toys. In fact, she believed he must have used the legacy of their church to steal her control over them.

It doesn't matter, she thought. *As long as I take his life, I'll be able to look for the legacy with plenty of time.*

Reaching a compromise with herself, Noelle started to laugh. "You sure think of yourself as a strong-minded boy, don't you? Facing me and my toys and still managing to hold your ground. I have to admit that's certainly impressing in some ways. As a matter of fact, it makes me want to test your spirit myself."

Zaros's instincts warned him to stop Noelle before she could make her next move. Thus, he took out the blessed-steel dagger, preemptively running forward in an attempt to strike her throat. However, before he could, Noelle had already made her move.

Extending her hand towards Zaros, Noelle voiced her command, "Mind Flay."

Zaros felt lightheaded and found himself unable to control his body anymore. He momentarily lost the ability to see, and by the time he regained his vision, he found himself standing alone in a black void. An expanse of infinite darkness extended across the horizon. The scenery he found himself in was simultaneously familiar yet unknown.

"Is this your doing?" asked Zaros inwardly, attempting to get an answer from Amro. He felt confused as to why his partner would pull him back at a moment like this.

Unfortunately for him, it wasn't Amro who answered back.

"Welcome to my domain, boy," whispered Noelle from behind Zaros. "You must be surprised. This is my realm, somewhere where I reign supreme; not that I expect you to understand. None of your petty tricks will be able to save you here."

A crimson-tipped spear appeared from the void, falling gently onto Noelle's pale and delicate hand. At the same time, chains of darkness coiled around Zaros's arms, robbing him of his ability to move. Her intentions were clear.

"I will take my time to savor your screams, your pain, and your agony. I will have you tell me where you placed our legacy and how you knew where to find it," she said. "Once I'm done with you, I'll just start over again, enjoying myself until all that is left of you is a husk of your former self. You will beg me for mercy, but all you will receive in return will be despair. I will enjoy this game until your soul can no longer stand it."

"Sounds like a fun game," said a voice from the endless expanse of darkness.

"What?" Shock laced Noelle's voice. She spun around in an attempt to locate the source of that comment. Aside from her, no one should be able to speak so freely in her soul domain. It couldn't be the boy before her, for he was currently bound by her will, unable to escape. There was no way someone as young as him could have the mental fortitude to resist her soul's pressure over his.

She looked around warily until a rift opened up in the endless void. A boy, identical to the one trapped by her chains, strutted out from the darkness.

"Were you looking for me?" he asked.

These two boys are not the same person, Noelle realized. His gaze, his stride, and even the inflections in his voice were all completely different. She was in front of something else – an apex predator.

"Who are you? How were you able to sneak in here?" she asked. Her rational side told her she was still in control, but her instincts were screaming at her to end the connection with the boy's soul.

"Me? You should already know me," answered Amro. "You claim to belong to my church, to know my teachings. Yet here you are, unable to recognize me."

As he said those words, Amro shifted into a black-robed entity, a farmer, a reaper, a warrior, and many other forms, before he finally settled back into Zaros's appearance.

Noelle was taken aback. Her knees shook as she realized the situation she was in was something far exceeding her expectations.

Impossible. This should have been impossible.

Many would have taken those transformations to be a useless display, nameless characters with no meaning behind their image. Noelle, however, was different. She had seen them before in the innermost parts of the main temple of her church. She had been allowed inside only once in her life, but the characters represented by each of the statues were still fresh in her mind. How could she ever forget the images her god had once taken?

Now here she was, facing someone who claimed to be him. And how could she deny it? Both his aura and appearance had coincided with those of the statues in the chambers of her church perfectly. A place reserved only for the head-priest and his personal disciples.

"Kneel," ordered Amro.

Noelle instinctively followed his command. Her legs lost all their strength as she felt an unimaginable pressure fall onto her shoulders. The crimson-tipped spear slipped from her hands as she was forced to bow to the god in front of her. Her mind grew muddled and her body heavy. Without permission to move or speak, she wouldn't be able to do either. She had lost control over her own soul realm.

Amro approached Zaros. The latter was still bound by the chains that had melded into the darkness. With a simple wave of his hands, all the bindings trapping his host vanished into nothingness.

Zaros fell to the ground, still incapable of moving because of the foreign suppression binding his soul. Slowly, his gaze rose to meet Amro's, confusion reflected inside.

Without bothering to explain, Amro simply tapped his forehead as he had done many times before. Immediately, the boy vanished from the soul realm.

He must be it, thought Noelle. Inside this realm, no one aside from her should have been able to control anything. Despite that, the man before her had created and destroyed on a whim. His authority over her soul even bigger than her own.

"Now, tell me, who's in charge of my church at this time?" commanded Amro. His words left no room for deception nor hesitation. They demanded only one thing: complete obedience.

"My lord, after that accursed day, the one who took command of your church was master Argent," she answered.

"Argent, was it?" The name didn't register inside Amro's memories, meaning the man who had taken control of the church wasn't one of his inner circle. Those foolish followers of his probably took his request too seriously that day, sacrificing even themselves in order to provide power for his fight against the other gods.

"My lord, come back with me to the church," requested Noelle. "Everyone will sing praises for your descent. We will be able to face that damned Church of Life and once again and spread your authority amongst all the kingdoms and nations. Everyone has been waiting for your return ever since the prophecy was divined."

"A prophecy?" asked Amro. Common mortals shouldn't have the ability to peer into the divine. Even if this fragment of his former self was no longer a god, no seer should have been able to predict his reappearance.

"Yes, my lord. One of our seers gave his life to foretell the following, 'In the southern forest of a war-broken kingdom, our Lord's last gift will appear. With it, the world will undergo the winds of change one last time.' In his final moments, the seer also told us that it was fundamental for us to take control of this gift. To see it was not a gift, but you yourself who came down, I can't help but rejoice."

"I see, so that was it," said Amro, realizing the meaning behind the prophecy. "Thanks for the information."

With a wave of his hand, chains of darkness formed from the void, coiling around Noelle's neck, hands, and feet.

"Now, I remember something about you wanting to play a game. I can't help but disagree with your methods, but they'll be very useful for correcting your misunderstandings on what it means to follow my path. I'll ingrain these teachings into your very soul, so you can serve me better in your next life."

Misunderstandings? thought Noelle. *How come? I've learned everything perfectly from my teacher!*

She wanted to say it wasn't her fault. That she had

learned everything from someone else. However, once she tried, she found herself unable to speak.

Unable to even plead for mercy.

* * *

Only a few seconds had passed in the outside world, but many things had happened during them. The first one to notice them was Michael. Slyfox had grown still, no longer flailing around in resistance. After that, the undead mercenaries collapsed. Their bodies turned into a goo composed of rotten flesh and coagulated blood.

Not long after that, Zaros's body fell to his knees, ready to hit the floor. Fortunately, Michael was able to catch him. He wasn't sure what had transpired, but the words 'Mind Flay' that came from Noelle's mouth gave him a pretty good idea. That spell was known as a forbidden art even amongst necromancers, for its risks were too great. Confrontation of souls, where the mental resilience of an individual was faced against the caster, had incredible risks, even for the one using the spell.

Against all odds, Zaros seemed to have come out as the victor. It didn't take long for him to open his eyes as he realized everything was over. In his mind, he still had a vague memory of what had happened inside Noelle's soul domain. Yet unlike his times inside Amro's domain, he wasn't able to recollect anything that happened in detail. The only vivid part of it was Amro releasing him from that realm as he took control of the situation.

He glanced at Michael, releasing himself from the priest's arms. "It's over," he said.

Michael stared at him with a myriad of questions in his eyes. *'Just how did you achieve it,'* his gaze seemed to ask. He didn't want to admit it, but a young boy having stronger mental resilience than his old partner was a fact he didn't want to accept.

Zaros approached Slyfox's rotting body before cradling the former gang boss in his arms. To Michael's surprise, Slyfox opened his eyes as well, a small amount of vitality still left in them.

"Huh, you somehow did it, boy," he said. "I saw everything."

Zaros didn't answer and only nodded; he seemed to have realized that Slyfox didn't have more than a few seconds left. Now that he no longer had anyone supplying the mana his undead-self needed to function, his body would start collapsing before eventually releasing whatever was left of his soul.

"I have a small request," Slyfox said in a volume too low for anyone else to hear. "Please leave. Being bound to that bitch made me realize some things about you. Your presence here will only bring my men more damnation."

Zaros understood the underlying meaning behind his words. While Slyfox wasn't blaming him directly, he was reminding him of his involvement with this invasion. It was his presence that had brought this calamity onto this town. Even Amro had tried to have him leave.

"I will," Zaros promised. After all that had happened, he knew they would be better off without him.

Just like that, without knowing whether his words had been able to reach Slyfox, Zaros saw him breathe his last. Zaros could only close the man's hollow eyes after placing him back to the ground.

"I'm leaving," said Zaros to Michael.

The priest was momentarily surprised. Why was he leaving now? There were many things he still wanted to ask.

Like the boy's origins, or why Bernard and Noelle seemed to be so interested in him.

"I'd like you to come to the capital with me," admitted Michael. He needed to request at least this much for his church. "There are many things about this attack I need to discuss with you."

"I can't help but refuse," answered Zaros. "I do, however, have a request of my own. Give him and everyone from the slums a proper funeral. There should be sufficient gold to pay for it inside that building."

"I know being a Chosen must be hard," offered Michael. "But I'll have to report your existence to my church."

"Do what you must, just accomplish that request of mine," said Zaros as he turned away. He didn't understand the implications of the title Michael and Amro had given him, nor the trouble this would bring him in the future.

With his biggest regret being handled by Michael, he disappeared from everyone's sight. The priest couldn't afford to chase after him. Not only was he unable to catch him, there were still many who needed his assistance.

He reminds me of that self-righteous brat, he thought, recalling the silhouette of another Chosen.

* * *

Zaros sat on top of the roof of the church of Harvest, shrouded by a black cloak. The memories he made during his stay at this town would forever remain with him. In the last month, he had experienced many struggles with just as many opportunities to grow.

His choices had paved his own path, bringing him closer to his goal. However, he couldn't stay here forever. Regardless of his intentions, his choices had caused far too much damage to those of this town. It was a burden he wasn't yet ready to carry.

He realized his subordinates would live just as well as they were doing now without him. Thinking otherwise was nothing but arrogance, he now realized that. He couldn't help but have some lingering worries, but he knew time and experience would take care of those.

From atop the church, he saw Alexander and Maria carefully treating the injured, helping those who were still alive.

Farewell, he thought. *I hope to meet you all again in the future.*

Zaros departed from the town, shrouded by the night. The only words he left behind for his subordinates were written in a small envelope he left back at their base.

He felt a lingering attachment to this place, to his newfound friends. However, it was time to continue his journey, for there were still many things he felt chained to. The tragic fate that had been forced onto his villagers even after their deaths had reminded him of his one true goal – revenge.

EPILOGUE

Wanted.

What a bothersome task, a man thought to himself. His long, black jacket was covered in insignias that denoted the man's ranking in the Kingdom's army, as well as his familiarity with bureaucracy. However, the elegance his uniform could convey was betrayed by his disheveled appearance. His brown eyes had bags under them and his black and short messy hair made his annoyance towards this task evidently clear.

After the 22nd Division's captain went MIA, he was assigned a mission to find him. His mission details didn't provide much information as to why his fellow captain was so far away from the capital, but the rumors unofficially spoke of the man in question receiving an extermination mission that had to be carried out in secret. As luck would have it, these same rumors stated that he had decided to become a deserter because of the mission's gruesome contents.

Much to his annoyance, an additional task had been piled on his shoulders. There was a report from the local nobles that there was rebel activity in the south. They swore the rebels sent a child as an envoy to convince the local citizens to revolt against the regional powers.

How moronic, he though.

He would have wanted to overlook such remarks. Unfortunately for him, the royal family had caught notice of them. The stance they took was surprising, to say the least. It seemed like the war in the northern border made those reclusive royals feel afraid of any additional uprisings. Much to his annoyance, Kleiber was forced to take the mission.

That's why he was now on his way to the south. Tasked with finding a missing captain and deal with a troublesome child.

I really need a vacation, he thought to himself. *At times like this, I can't blame the deserters.*

The man in question was the proud captain of the Kingdom's 10th Division. The fact that this was the best use of manpower the kingdom could find for him made the situation rather depressing. If anything, it was a sign of the kingdom's decline.

Years ago, he became a general blessed by Altea, the Goddess of Wisdom. How was it that now, his skills were used as nothing more than an information gathering tool? This was a task best suited to someone like that annoying woman hidden away in the 7th Division, the one he so despised.

However, it was too late for complaints. Their destination was already visible on the horizon. If there was something he couldn't wait for, it was getting down from his carriage. The long periods of shaking had left Kleiber's legs feeling numb. If he got wind of which logistics officer had been responsible for assigning him such an annoying means of transportation, he would make sure they got an equally annoying earful.

Knock knock

"Sir, we have arrived," spoke a voice from outside the

carriage.

Finally, he thought to himself. *Another minute and I would have flipped my shit.*

As he got out of his torture chamber, Kleiber was finally able to see the rotting southern part of the kingdom. The joke of a town that was supposed to responsible for developing the kingdom in the royalty's name. It was sufficient to say that before such a goal had been accomplished, the civil war to the north had made all development stop.

All in all, the town now felt desolate and barren. Yet somehow, Kleiber believed the atmosphere was a little too much even for this town. That left the captain with a couple questions of his own.

"Hey, squire. Just what happened here?" he asked. As a captain, he was used to delegating annoying tasks like information gathering to his subordinates.

"Sir, we're currently asking the locals about it. From what we can gather, the water wells were poisoned shortly before an attack by a group of feral undead."

"Undead? In this part of the kingdom? There's no way that's true. Those imbeciles from the Church of Death don't have the manpower to waste in such a small town."

"Sir, we tried calling over some surviving nobles and staff from the church in order to confirm this information. However, it seems like they're currently too busy handling the aftermath to come."

"Fine, we can just go to the church and meet them there if they're so busy," Kleiber said, rubbing his shoulders. The faster he was done with this, the faster he could go back to his main task. After all, his mission was to search for the kid and the missing captain, not to deal with some stuck-up nobles and the equally irritating clergymen.

It didn't take long for him to arrive at the local church. The temple to the Goddess of Harvest was fitting to their deity's image. Just like the poor crop yield in recent years, the place left much to be desired.

"I need whoever is in charge of this place to step forward!" he commanded after entering the church.

A black-haired priest with bags under his eyes was the one to answer his call. From how his robes looked, he was not a follower of the Goddess of the Harvest.

"Don't mess with me," said Kleiber. "What is a priest of life doing so far away from the capital? I thought your kind only worked where the money's at."

"Captain Kleiber, I presume. We were told you might come sometime soon."

"Cut to the chase, cleric. What happened in this town?" Kleiber asked.

"Please, call me Michael," said the priest in a relatively calm fashion. "It's a long story, so would you mind having a seat?"

Realizing his rashness would take him nowhere, Kleiber had no choice but to sit with Michael and discuss his mission over a cup of tea. Despite his exhaustion, the priest did his best effort to play the role of a proper host.

"So, you want me to believe a thirteen-year-old Chosen appeared in a backwater town?" asked Kleiber. "And this kid is the same one from the portrait I showed you?"

"Indeed, that's the case," answered the priest.

"And you let this kid go because…"

"I had no way to hold him back. I'm afraid I was outclassed," said Michael.

"Your kind doesn't travel solo. What happened to your

traveling companion?"

The priest's expression grew sour. "He's dead. Killed off by that woman I told you about."

"And yet the kid was able to defeat her?"

"Like I said, he outclassed us."

"So, were you able to confirm the boy's relationship to the rebels?"

"No. But neither was I able to find any evidence pointing toward the contrary. When my partner and I arrived at the city, we heard the boy had been creating quite the storm. He even executed a small-time noble in public daylight."

"The slave-trader, right?"

Michael only nodded. His throat had grown dry from answering the endless barrage of questions. Despite the nature of these questions, he had been able to grasp some information for himself. For example, the captain before him seemed to be believe there was a relationship between the appearance of the boy, the apostles of death, and the disappearance of an army's captain.

Organizing the information in his mind, the priest took a sip of his tea before continuing the conversation. "Would that be all then, captain?"

"I guess so, cleric," answered Kleiber. He wasn't fond of the Church of Life nor their priests. The way he saw it, the clergy from that church always behaved as if they were above the rest — his Church of Wisdom included. Since they sported that behavior, rivalry was bound to happen. Even amongst fellow believers.

"I wish you good tidings then," said Michael as he stood from his seat. He had enough things on his plate to bother with the captain any further.

After sending some pigeons to report the situation to his church, Michael had been thoroughly reprimanded for not gathering enough information about the Chosen. As punishment, he was tasked with aiding this small town, relieved of all his other duties until further notice.

"Captain, where to next?" asked the squire.

"Contact the capital. I want posters placed in every city, town, village and even inside the smallest settlements. That kid is our top priority. It seems like the rebels got themselves a good weapon in the making."

"And what about the issue with the Church of Death, captain?"

"That's a matter for the churches to deal with. Given that our target actually killed a couple of apostles, I don't think he has a good relationship with them."

"Understood, captain," replied the squire. He was writing Kleiber's words on a piece of parchment in preparation to inform the capital of his orders. "Any information on the missing captain?"

"No, we're going south for that. Tell HQ we'll be updating them later regarding that issue."

"Roger that, sir."

How bothersome, thought Kleiber. It seemed like the northern campaign was about to get even more lively.

SIDE STORY

The dusk of the gods.

Sitting in a hall of gold, a group of worshipers were singing praises to their god. Their ceremonial robes were immaculate, further enhancing their aura of battle-hardened veterans. Scenes like this could be found every day in the temple of the God of Battle, Kovas. Even if he wasn't as great as the God of War, the minor deity still had a sizeable following of his own. One that incited the envy of many others.

The spoils of battle accrued by his followers amounted to many small mountains of gold, silver, and gems. However, the favorite type of tribute that the God of Battle sought was in the shape of weapons. Be it an enchanted spear, a sword used to kill a famous general, or the first weapon of a so-called hero. Each and every offering would reap many rewards in return.

Every sunset, a battle would be carried in front of the temple. Two volunteers would be selected from the guilds, towns or cities to be placed into a ferocious one-on-one fight. Only one of them would exit alive.

The victor would always be rewarded by a blessing from Kovas. Skills, strength, and potential, all were within his domain. As such, victors were usually offered a position in the armies of famous commanders. The blessing of the God of Battle was seen as a sign of luck to any battalion who rode into war.

Two fighters stood against each other. One of them was a young man wearing farmer's clothes. He had given it his all in an attempt to overcome his fate. However, he was now covered in wounds. Mangled flesh hung from each of his sides.

The other was a young man wearing a military uniform. The lack of insignias revealed he was a rookie. But even that little amount of training had made a world of difference. All he had was a small wound on his arm, evidence of a desperate bite taken by his opponent.

Priests sang hymns to their god as both of them punched and kicked each other. Feints and trickery were not above them, as both sought nothing but victory. Even at the cost of the other's life.

Finally, the young farmer revealed a gap in his moves, caused by the loss of blood. His senses had grown dull, presenting an opportunity to his opponent. No matter how much he desired for victory, his ability fell short of his wishes.

Seeing the farmer stumble back, the recruit used his elbow to knock the air out of him. Things like mercy and fairness were nothing short of delusions in a life or death duel. Once the unfortunate peasant was on the ground, the trainee's knee fell onto his throat.

With time, the recruit kept punching the farmer's head, turning it into a bloody mess. Displays of insanity and bloodthirst were usually well received by the priests. Their creed told them that such qualities were useful for battle.

Because of that, everyone watched in delight until the recruit rose to his feet. The young farmer was now dead. Only the victor remained.

"Come."

Upon confirming the farmer's death, a priest approached the recruit, covering him with a crimson robe embroidered in golden patterns. He then proceeded to guide him victor into the inner temple. Since there was no longer a show for them to watch, the crowd around the fighters started to disperse.

The ceremony was something only the priests and the victor were allowed to attend. As a procession of robed men chanted hymns to their god, the recruit and the priest leading him entered the temple, making their way into the ceremonial hall.

The newcomer was in awe. Each of the decorations in the room used to receive him was enough to feed him and his family for the rest of their lives. The greed in his eyes was only contained by the fear he held towards Kovas and his church. Anyone caught stealing was better off dead. At least that way, their soul wouldn't have to endure a millennium of punishment.

Amazed by the decor, he followed the priest until they reached a gigantic statue. It depicted a tall man who carried a broadsword in his right hand and a shield in his left. On his back was a simple but sturdy bow and on his waist and thighs were daggers of all kinds. The recruit fell to his knees, completely in awe of the statue. It seemed to exert a heavenly pressure over him, making him feel like a worm in front of a mountain.

The priests smiled at young boy's submission. They had witnessed this scene hundreds of times before, but they never grew tired of it. They had yet to see a mortal who could stand against the imposing presence of their god.

Pride rose in their hearts as the priest next to the boy also knelt. As both of them worshipped the statue, the rest of the priests started singing once again.

Usually, their hymn would be followed by displays of grace from their god. However, this time, something different happened. They were interrupted before they could reach the final stage of their ceremony.

"Move out of my way!"

A priest covered in an elaborate robe ran into the room, frantic and agitated. The rest of the priests would've murdered such a man if he hadn't been the leader of the temple.

The recruit on his knees was surprised when he saw the temple's leader. The presence of such an important person was not commonly seen by someone of his status. It was rumored that Kovas's pope only exited his chambers a few times every year. To be able to see him was his fortune.

The leader of the priests ignored everyone as he moved towards the statue of his god. Nothing could enter his eyes except the glory of his one true master. With a hand over his heart and bloodshot eyes, tears began to fall down his cheeks.

"My lord, please use me to fuel your strength, please use us," he pleaded, kneeling at the statue's feet. He kissed the ground and bowed his head in reverence, but nothing happened.

The rest of the priests were dumbfounded. Could it be that their leader had another divine revelation? Hearts filled with doubt, they shortened the distance towards him, trying to hear what he would say next.

"You must not want us to sacrifice ourselves for you, my lord. How noble of you, your kindness knows no bounds. But don't worry, we are nothing more than extensions of your will. We will present you with sacrifices to help you replenish your strength."

The head-priest stood up, a look of madness in his bloodshot eyes. Immediately, he pointed at the recruit and yelled, "Sacrifice him! Sacrifice him to our lord!"

However, he knew that wouldn't be enough, so he continued, "Sacrifice everyone! Burn the towns, bring their heads, kill everyone you can find. Offer all of their lives to our lord!"

The priests didn't dare to dally. If this was a command from their god, they wouldn't be able to escape divine punishment should they relinquish their duties. They soon ran to the walls, grabbing the weapons that were hanging on them.

The priests from the church of battle had all been baptized in blood. They didn't lack the experience nor the mental fortitude needed for what was to come. They quickly made their way to the villages, prepared to gather sacrifices for their god. The few who remained took the recruit by his arms, leaving him unable to move.

The newcomer trembled, a look of fear in his eyes. He had clearly heard the order given by the head of the temple. Escape was the only way for him to keep his life. However, he was already weak from the previous fight. He no longer had the strength to shake off the battle-maniac priests.

Resigned to his fate, the recruit was soon taken to be sacrificed by a group of priests. Only one man remained in the hall with Kovas's statue. The head of the church was too busy to take care of something as insignificant as leading the priests to battle. The tears of blood falling from his eyes revealed his current dilemma.

"We must hurry, our lord needs more sacrifices," he murmured.

Several scenes similar to this were happening simultaneously across the world of Gaia. Many small churches had become erratic. Yet none of them could compare to the chaos that was going on around the Church of Death.

In a mountain range, far from civilization, a group of

robed men were offering sacrifices without a break. After running out of tributes, they had even begun to sacrifice their own kin and brothers-in-faith. They were the followers of the God of Death, Amro.

A few hours ago, their pope had given what seemed to be his final command before offering his own soul to his god. They were to sacrifice everyone available in the mountain as the ultimate display of faith. One in which they would join their god's side forever. Many would have considered the old man senile if they hadn't shared the same view as him.

One thing differentiated the church of a greater god to one from a minor deity, however — the prowess of their god. Deities like Amro were strong enough to simultaneously deliver a revelation to all of their followers. Relying on word of mouth to pass their messages was something below them.

Flames of life extinguished one after another. Some even decided to go further and extinguish their souls in sacrifice, welcoming true death. Those who became devotees to a church would often lose all sense of self, regarding themselves as nothing but pawns for their gods to use. The priests of Amro's church were no different.

That being said, every rule had an exception. Such was the case inside Amro's church of death, where some initiates were hiding. They were afraid of joining the ranks of those sacrificed to their lord. Since they had just started their indoctrination, their faith was still nowhere close to those who had lived decades inside the church. Soon after the revelation, they had come to hide in the most inconspicuous place they could find.

Ensuring their safety was a priest. He was unlike the other members of the church, for he had not joined until he was of old age. Before that, he had lived as a wandering mage, collecting knowledge about the occult across the lands.

The reason he accompanied the newbies was no other than his own selfishness and greed. He hoped to find a way to achieve immortality. Something rumors spoke was hidden deep within the vaults of the Church of Death.

The fact that such a chance had just presented itself was nothing short of a blessing. He never thought such a massacre would happen before he had managed to accomplish his goals.

Rather than being discouraged by this event, a glimmer of shrewdness in the priest hinted how he had already moved onto a new plan. If all these fanatics sacrificed themselves to their god, who would be left to command the church's resources?

Like this, he remained hidden along with the novices. However, they weren't the only ones who did so. Many pockets of disciples hid throughout the mountain in a similar fashion.

As faithful as some members might have been, humans were rarely loyal to anyone but themselves. It was only through the manipulation of their ambitions and desires that one could truly ensure their allegiance. This weakness in human nature was something the church understood.

This day would later be remembered as the Dusk of the gods. A day that marked an age where gods and their churches were no more. The reasons for it would remain hidden to the annals of history, but the consequences of such an event was obvious to all of humanity.

End of Book 1

Printed in Great Britain
by Amazon